The Second Time Around

MARY BEESLEY

Published by Montlake, Seattle

www.apub.com

ISBN-13: 9781662516412 (paperback)
ISBN-13: 9781662516429 (digital)

Cover design by Ploy Siripant
Cover image: © Geraint Rowland Photography / Getty; © Galina Chet / Shutterstock; © Karlygash / Shutterstock

Printed in the United States of America

To my mom, Bonnie Jean, for believing in me

Chapter 1
CLAIRE

The cotton canvas lay before her like a white sky, blinding in its blankness. It was only two feet by three feet, but she thought it would swallow her whole. She'd disappear into that vast emptiness. Who would notice? Her daughters? They had left. Moved on.

Claire Kehoe set her half-drunk tea on a paint-splattered table in her garage and picked up a brush. She rummaged through her watercolors, her stack of textured papers, and the basket of fabric scraps and broken seashells. No fertile energy rose from her soul. No seeds of creation sprouted. She peeled back her lips and hissed at the emptiness, trying to fill it. The sound echoed through her ribs and, finding nothing to cling to, dissipated into the heavy silence.

Maybe she shouldn't have taken down the love notes from her late husband that she'd pinned to the wall. At the beginning of their relationship, twenty-two years ago, Stevie had written her lines of love like a romantic poet. They'd stopped coming after the first six months, before the baby was even born.

She'd ripped them down one particularly bad night seven years ago. He'd stumbled into the house, drunk as the bourbon bottle he set on the kitchen counter. Claire dropped it, empty, into the bin before following him to the room they shared.

She caught him pissing on the bathroom counter.

"Stevie! That's the sink, not the toilet." She kept her voice quiet so the girls wouldn't wake. They'd been asleep for hours.

He turned at the sound of her unhappy voice and sprayed urine over the hand towel and wall. Glassy eyed, he looked over the mess as the last of it dribbled onto the floor. He giggled. He laughed so hard he couldn't get his pants up.

She bit her tongue, holding back from demanding he fix it. Fix it all. Confrontation would only make him mean. She knew from experience. She'd tried all the tactics. Giving in and steering clear worked best. Maybe he'd feel guilty in the morning and try to make amends. Clean up the bathroom at least.

She didn't plan on it.

Instead, she'd escaped to the garage, torn up the notes, the lies, and painted until she couldn't keep her eyes open. She'd taken her daughters back-to-school shopping with the earnings she'd made from that epic piece of artwork. Salmon salads for lunch in Newport and the stupid-expensive donut place for dessert. They'd stopped on the way home and gotten Indi her second set of ear piercings. From a night of pain, Claire had made a day of sparkles.

Now, glancing over at the racks along the wall of her garage turned art studio, she could almost still see the papers clipped there and their hastily scratched messages.

> I just wanted to thank you for being so good to me . . . you make me so happy . . . I've loved you since I first saw you waltz into our sophomore chemistry class . . . I am amazed by how big of a heart you have . . . I will protect you from harm . . . I will always treasure you. Love, Stevie

She ran her fingers through the silky paintbrush hairs, trying to remember what she'd felt back when Stevie's words crystallized into a double-edged sword, cutting her up inside and fueling her art. Reminding her of the fireworks she'd felt at the beginning of their high school romance and the pain she'd felt when their love had burned out, leaving only ashes and faded dreams.

She closed her eyes, looking inside herself for that creative flicker of heat and life and passion, but her internal fire was cold, same as yesterday, and the day before that, and the day before that.

She set down her brush, picked up her lukewarm tea, and walked back inside her clean, quiet house.

She circled her bedroom—bed made up, dresser dusted, laundry folded. In the bathroom, the mirror sparkled, and her makeup was assembled in neat rows in the drawer. Stevie's sink was bare, except for the rattlesnake plant that lived where his soap used to be. No beard hairs on the counter or pee on the toilet seat.

It was ten thirty in the morning, and she'd already done all the chores she could think of and a Pilates session. She floated down the hall. Her daughters' rooms were dark and lonely. No girls to mess up the vacuum lines with their dancing and their scattered accessories. Mona and Indi hadn't lived at home for years, but her baby, Edith, had left for college a mere month ago, a month when time seemed to have warped into a meaningless hole.

Claire was officially an empty nester. She hadn't realized how much she'd clung to her role as mother to give her a sense of purpose until Edith had cut her loose. Claire was a ship without anchor.

"A melodramatic ship," she whispered. She tried to lighten her mood with a chuckle, but it fell flat.

Her kitchen was small but open to the main room and had a window facing the greenery dividing her from the neighbors. She'd already cleaned the teapot. She could bake banana-walnut muffins. That would take an hour. Who would eat them all? Her freezer was full of baked goods, and her friends must be sick of getting her treats. She'd felt pathetic last week when she'd dropped off bread, the third time she'd made her neighbors food this month—since Edith had moved to college. Claire checked the counter. No bananas.

She didn't have an appetite anyway.

The phone in her pocket buzzed, and she nearly dropped her mug in her rush to answer it. She lit up when she saw her youngest daughter's face on the screen.

"Hi, Edith, honey. How are you?"

"Good, Mom." Her peppy, young voice brightened up Claire's kitchen.

Claire didn't burden her daughter with how much she missed her; the ache pinched sharply in her chest. "How's your morning going?"

"Fine. I'm just trying to use my debit, and I forgot my PIN."

Claire was caught between exasperation and pleasure. Her daughter still needed her, if only because she wasn't responsible enough to remember four digits. Edith was smart enough to make her mom memorize them for her. Resourceful in her own way. And spoiled. Another day, Claire might have been annoyed. This morning she wanted to be the keeper of Edith's PIN forever. "Four three eight oh."

"Thank you. You're the best. I've got to run. Love you."

"Love you." The line went dead on the last word.

Claire sighed. She dumped the cold dredges of tea down the drain and hand-washed the mug. As part of a family of five, with three daughters and a husband, she used to run the dishwasher at least once a day. Now, she ran it when it started to get musty and needy.

She plopped on her couch and took out her phone. She checked her texts. Nothing new. She opened the thread with Indi, her middle daughter, who lived up in Boise. They'd last texted yesterday when Claire had sent a funny meme of a hippo dancing. Indi had laughed at it but hadn't continued the conversation. Claire couldn't think of anything to say this morning except I love you.

Indi didn't respond. Hopefully she was in class, but there was a good chance she was still asleep.

Claire snapped off her phone and leaned her head back. She should be painting, but she couldn't go back into the garage and face the empty well of her creativity. She didn't think she had the strength to get off this couch. It seemed to suck her in, leech away the passion that used to fuel her through frantic late-night art sessions.

She couldn't stay like this, static and hollow. And not making any money.

It was time to move on, enter a new phase of life not defined by motherhood or past grief. But she had no idea how to step out of fear and into adventure. Even thinking about it sent a pang of worry down her spine. She felt stagnant, but there was comfort in the safety of her quiet life.

Besides, what job could she get? She was forty years old, with no college degree and no work experience. Her skills lay in somewhat successfully raising daughters (the verdict was still out), being patient with grumpy husbands (which she refused to do again), and cooking (in her home kitchen only). She couldn't put art as a skill because she didn't have that anymore. Her talent with the brush had eroded over the years since Stevie's death, crumbling in correlation with her increasing apathy. She might be bored now, but she'd choose that over being in pain. Convictions aside, she still needed a job.

At lunch yesterday, her friend Raven Char had mentioned a nannying gig. Claire had dismissed it, determined to get back into the swing of her art. And also, kids were exhausting, and she'd just finished raising three of them. Her oldest daughter, Mona, needed help with her baby. Claire didn't have more to give to a stranger's child. And to be honest, she didn't generally love other people's children all that much.

Her phone rang again. Lucky day. She hesitated when she saw it was Roger Char, Raven's husband. She assumed he'd be calling to talk to her about the nannying job, stepping up to the plate after Raven had struck out.

"Hello, Mr. Roger." She felt clever coming up with that name wordplay.

"Clara! How's my favorite granny?"

His deep, cheerful voice sent an instant grin flaring over her face. Only Roger could get away with calling her Clara or granny. "Always the funny guy."

"I hope so." He hesitated. The moment when he should say why he'd called stretched into silence. She didn't bail him out with small talk.

Finally he cleared his throat. "Raven said you're interested in spending time with the most adorable five-year-old on the planet."

Claire laughed. It blasted through her quiet living room.

"Please reconsider. Banks is a good man, and he's struggling to take care of his son while drowning in the grief of his wife's passing."

Claire felt sorry for the stranger, even if she couldn't relate to the same intense heartbreak. More pain before her spouse died, less pain after.

"He's generous and has a beautiful house. He's honest and hardworking, and his son really is a great kid. You'll like them both."

As she enjoyed his round, happy voice, she thought about how much she liked Roger. Wished she had more of him in her life. More male friends. More masculine energy. With Roger she never had to worry about romance. He was happily married to her best friend. He was safe. Newly widowed men were far from safe. "I don't think so. I've never been a good babysitter."

"Don't think of it like that. It won't be a hard job. It's one well-behaved child who needs someone to pal around with after school."

That did put a different spin on it. She reminded herself she'd spent the morning wishing she had her daughters back, people who needed her.

"Consider how much fun you could be having with a new young friend." His voice had turned pleading.

She could use a new friend, not that she wanted to admit that. "Why are you pushing for this? Has he had trouble with other nannies?"

"He hasn't tried for one yet. His wife, Helen, died end of May, and his sister helped him over the summer. And now I think he doesn't know where to even look. He's overwhelmed, but he's also protective and doesn't want to risk a stranger."

"I'm a stranger."

"Not to me. I know you, and Banks trusts me. I told him I would and have many times wholeheartedly trusted you with my child."

"I love Jimmy and did not get enough game nights with him before he grew up on me."

"See! You aren't done with babies."

She snorted in disagreement, but her heart swelled at his statement. She silenced whatever that was about and focused on feeling flattered by his praise. She insisted on not caring that Stevie hadn't appreciated her, but it felt deeply pleasurable to be recommended. She had been the best mom she knew how to be. She had healthy relationships with her daughters.

"Banks is a good friend. I've known him for over twenty-five years. I want to help him, and I think now that your girls are moved out, you might enjoy it."

She did want—need—out of her house right now. She certainly needed money.

"Will you please at least meet him?"

She wouldn't deny her friend such a simple favor. A flutter in her belly betrayed her curiosity.

"You don't have to agree to anything more than one meeting with Banks and Tommy."

Tommy. A little boy. She'd never had one of those. She imagined sticky fingers and baseball caps. Her heart contracted painfully. She welcomed the sensation. "Okay, fine. One meeting."

Chapter 2
BANKS

Golf was Banks Sexton's *manly* form of grief counseling. He traipsed across the green and loomed over his ball. *Go in the hole, you stubborn rock.* He exhaled, aware of Roger lounging in the golf cart, watching a crow strut across the path. The birds were more interesting than Banks's golf game. He swung back and tapped the ball. Too hard. It overshot the hole. After fourteen weeks of playing a half round with Roger every Thursday morning, how was he not better at this? Few things managed to evade succumbing to Banks's will for so long.

He stalked past the mocking four-inch hole. The hot September sun licked his neck, leaving sticky wetness dripping down his back. He should be avoiding his feelings while sitting on the beach with a cold one. The summer tourists had taken their children back to their landlocked homes for school, and the Pacific Ocean was warmish. It was Laguna Beach perfection. But instead of enjoying the sand and surf, Banks was fighting with a defiant ball no bigger than his testicles. He tapped the puckered thing with his putter. It rolled, sinking into the hole with a satisfying rattle. Banks scooped up the defeated sphere and joined Roger in the golf cart.

Roger put his foot on the gas pedal. "You're never one to give up."

And there it was. After nine holes, the first words of encouragement. And most likely the last heavy thought of the day too. There'd be another morsel of motivation when they'd meet again next Thursday morning. Or maybe not. Companionable silence was their proven prescription.

Banks used to grumble about the outing. He didn't love golf or the gray cloud of the recently widowed that he inevitably brought with him everywhere. He should be at the office, and Roger Char ran a busy chiropractic practice. But over the months since Helen's funeral, Banks had come to realize how much he needed these mornings with Roger.

"Let's get a drink before we head out," Roger said.

Banks frowned. That was out of their routine. Roger's life motto—get in, get the job done, get out—usually applied to their weekly nine holes of golf. One of the reasons Banks liked Roger. No fluffy bullshit. "I can't today. I've got to get back." His inbox had run away from him. Not the way he usually operated.

"Let me rephrase. We're getting a drink." Roger might be the only person still alive who could get away with speaking to Banks like that.

Roger parked at the cart return, and a young man approached to take their clubs out to their cars. Banks passed the kid a twenty before he followed Roger into the air-conditioned entry of Viceroy Bay Golf Links. He wiped the sweat off the back of his neck with a monogrammed handkerchief as he braced himself for an intervention—he was not in the mood for a *talk*.

Roger ordered two from the tap while Banks settled onto the leather barstool and turned his attention to the sports channel on the big screen. In silence, they watched highlight reels from last Sunday's football games.

"So, Ivy went back to Vegas?" Roger asked.

Banks gave the bartender a genuine smile when the cold beer appeared. He took a long pull. Ivy, his older sister, had stayed with him all summer, mothering Banks's youngest son, Tommy, and playing nursemaid to her pathetic widowed younger brother. But she'd finally had to return to Las Vegas for her son's high school to start. Ivy was a saint, but she hadn't been able to completely conceal how relieved she was to be going home. Banks knew he'd been a heavy burden on his sister. It had been a rough summer for everyone. "Yeah. She left. It's been a long eleven days."

"But who's counting?" Roger grinned as he took off his golf hat and ran a hand over his bronze bald head—a sore spot since Banks still had a full head of hair and they were both fifty years old. Banks had kept himself in better shape too. It helped he'd lost those pesky twelve pounds when his wife died. Look at him looking on the bright side.

"What am I going to do? Tommy is in kindergarten now. They said it was all day, but the bus drops him off at two twenty-five Monday through Thursday and at one twenty-five on Wednesdays. Since when is that *all day*?" Banks puffed out annoyance.

His thirty-year-old son, Smith, who lived five miles north in Corona del Mar, had been a big help, but Smith wasn't a long-term solution. Banks had already leaned on him too much.

"I've got a girl for you," Roger said.

Banks groaned. Even if he ached for a woman's body every night when he crawled into his cold bed, he could not add a girlfriend to the massive pile of crap he was carrying around right now.

Roger waved a big hand. "No. No. I mean a hired helper."

"Like a maid?"

"Like a nursemaid. But don't use either of those labels."

"Why?" Helen had been a stay-at-home mother / homemaker, whatever it was called, and she'd loved it. And now Banks had a hefty appreciation for all she'd done. He'd had no idea how much work maintaining a home and child was. He wished he'd shown her more gratitude.

"People are touchy about *labels* these days," Roger said. "I don't get it, but Raven says *maid* isn't politically correct. I guess it's like calling someone a servant." His gaze flicked up to the screen, which had switched to baseball clips. "Home run! The Angels are looking good this year." He looked back at Banks. "But, yeah, she's for helping you with Tommy."

Banks thought of the teenagers Helen had had come babysit Tommy and Smith over the years. It would be weird and definitely not socially acceptable to have a young girl in his house without a woman there. This was Helen's department.

"She's a grandma. And a widow." Something like amusement flashed in Roger's eyes before he turned serious again. "So she'll be able to relate to what you're going through."

Banks's shoulders loosened, and hope sprouted. An old woman would be all right. Perfect, actually.

"She's an amazing cook. Her apple pie is inimitable. Believe me, Raven has tried to make it."

Banks's mouth watered at the thought. Helen had spoiled him. And disabled him. He'd spent the first month after her passing just trying to find where all the stuff in his house was located. Since Ivy went home, he and Tommy were surviving on toast and takeout.

"She lives in Emerald Bay. Across PCH from you," Roger was saying. "So local and flexible."

"When can she start?"

Roger chuckled.

Banks was not joking. "How do you know her?"

"She's a friend of the wifey."

"Why is she interested in the job?"

Roger shrugged, finishing his beer. "Her youngest daughter went to college last month, and now she's got too much time on her hands. I think she needs the money. Raven said she's lived in the same house for years and owns it outright, but bills are tough."

"Have you met her?"

"Yes, of course. I'm not invited to their girls' lunches, but I know her well. She was always my Jimmy's favorite babysitter. He loved going to her house, even before he started dating her youngest, Edith. I would trust her with anyone's life. She's raised three amazing daughters in a situation that was less than ideal. She's honest and kind."

Banks was intimidated by the process of trying to find and vet a good nanny. Roger had just done all that background work for him. And she lived in his neighborhood. She sounded too good to be true. "Can she come tomorrow?"

Roger grinned. "I really like her, and so will you. She's kind and *still spry.*" He winked and scrunched up his round face, and Banks knew there would be a plethora of grandma jokes in his future.

"She'd better not smell elderly," Banks said.

"Classy." He bit his lips but couldn't hold back laughter. "Don't worry, Raven likes her a lot."

Roger's wife also liked black licorice.

"Her name is Clara."

"That's a nice old lady name."

"I think of *The Nutcracker.*"

"Not a great association," Banks said, voice flat. He'd only made the mistake of going to that men-in-tights production with Helen *one* time.

"I took the liberty of scheduling her to show up at your house tonight at five fifteen. Since she lives in E. Bay, too, you can't keep her out of the gate. There's no pressure on either side. You can see how it goes meeting her and then decide."

Banks wondered if he should pretend to be mad at the intrusion, at the obvious setup, before begrudgingly accepting the gift. Instead, he stared at his friend's deep laugh lines and rich brown eyes. Gratitude wrapped him like a blanket, and he had to force the lurking tears back. "Thank you." Damn his raspy voice.

Roger stood, thumped him on the back, and steered him toward the sunny front entrance without another word.

Banks needed help. The past four months of single parenting had almost killed him. The in-laws had offered to move in, but he would never be that desperate. How had he lost Helen and still gotten stuck with the Shellburgs? He could only hope Clara was as sweet a little old lady as his own mother had been.

Chapter 3
SMITH

Smith Sexton swallowed his frustration and maintained his placid smile—a skill he'd honed to perfection over his years as a successful real estate agent in Orange County. He'd also sharpened his client-interest meter. And this man wasn't going to buy this house either. Smith had been showing properties to this Texan for three months. Nothing was good enough. Smith had been more than happy to sign him when he'd heard the house budget was ten million, but he was about to sign off. It sounded like this cow wrangler should stay in the Lone Star State.

Smith closed the lockbox on the $9.4 million beauty in lower Emerald Bay. Fortunately, the malcontented client had insisted on driving to the house separately. It was with pleasure that Smith waved goodbye and watched the gleaming Ford Raptor drive away. He shrugged out of his coat and tore off the pale-blue tie. It was way too hot for a suit. Too hot for fruitless work. He opened the back door of his Range Rover Sport—he needed a nice car for his job. Important to have a classy ride for when he had to drive high-end clients around luxury neighborhoods. It was all part of the experience.

He laid his navy coat across the back row. Since he was already in the neighborhood, he'd stop by Dad's house before heading home. Maybe he'd take Tommy down to catch a set of waves, then grab tacos. Smith was really trying to be there for his little brother. He'd seen more of his dad and brother in the last four months than he had in the last four years.

Of course he missed Mom, but Smith was thirty, not five. Those extra twenty-five years he'd had with Mom left a greasy feeling of guilt in his belly. Helen wasn't his biological mother, but she was his *mother*. The female who'd birthed Smith in college had only agreed to not get an abortion on the condition that Banks would take the baby and she could disappear. Nana had helped raise Smith until Dad married Helen when Smith was four years old.

Smith unbuttoned his collar and pulled at his shirt to let the welcome breeze cool down his chest before climbing in the front seat. He drove the familiar streets of his childhood to the north end of the view lots to his parents'—his *father's* home. It was a main-floor master, panoramic-view two-story that Dad could probably get sixteen million for with the right buyer. Not that Dad would ever sell.

Smith pulled onto the side of the wide driveway. He strode up the shaded walkway and let himself in the unlocked front door. Dad hadn't touched Mom's decorations or furniture. The house was the same as it had been four months ago, except the large blank space on the entry wall. Mom's sister had taken the horse painting when she'd returned to Indiana after the funeral. Mom had said she could take it. And Aunt Jennifer had taken it.

"Tommy Boy? You here?"

A yelp issued from the kitchen, and seconds later Tommy appeared, running full tilt. Smith swung the boy up, blond curls flying.

"How you doin', big man?" Smith put his brother down. "How was kindergarten today?"

"Good," Tommy said.

"Beach and tacos tonight?"

Dad rounded the corner. His hair glistened from a shower, and he'd trimmed the short gray beard he'd started sporting these last few months. Mom hadn't liked facial hair, but Smith thought it looked good on Dad, made his fine features more rugged and manly. Dad looked nice today. It was Thursday. Golf with Roger must have done him good.

Smith suffered a flash of remorse. Should he be doing more for Dad and Tommy? Sometimes it was just too hard to come over here. They were like three fish in a pond without water. Sometimes he wasn't strong enough to carry their burdens when his own grief was so heavy. He'd been better since he'd broken up with Ella last month. Mom's passing had changed Smith, made him reevaluate his life. Time was fleeting. Ella wanted fun and freedom, not a family. Smith hoped those things weren't mutually exclusive. He wanted it all.

He'd been close with his mom, talking to her a couple of times a week. They used to go on a dinner date every Wednesday. He valued her opinion and advice. Now when the desire struck to call her, he forced himself to try and reach out to Dad instead, to strengthen that bond. Dad wasn't anywhere near as cool as Mom, but Smith was trying.

"Smith," Dad said. "I'm glad you're here."

"He's taking me down to the beach," Tommy said. "Then tacos." Blue eyes turned imploring as he looked up at Smith. "Can we go to Asada and get the queso?"

"Absolutely." As if there were any other answer to that question.

"Wait," Dad said. "There's a woman coming over." He glanced at his watch.

Dread crept over Smith, replacing the September heat stroke with a frosty chill. Not a *woman*. Not so soon. They did not need a strange female barging into their boys' club. Was this why Dad had put on a collared shirt? Was he already smitten?

"She's supposed to be here any minute. And I really want her to like us."

Us? "Who is she?" Smith's tone came out too aggressive.

Dad's distracted gaze sharpened on his oldest son. "Clara. She's supposedly a very nice grandma in the neighborhood whose husband died and children have moved out and who we might be able to talk into helping us. She comes with a golden recommendation from Roger. Also, apparently, she's a great cook and makes a killer apple pie." Dad looked at Tommy as if willing him to already like the woman.

A massive wave of relief loosened Smith's spine. "Oh. That's great!"

"Hopefully, she'll be just like your nana."

That would be a dream. Dad's mom had been barely five feet tall and maybe one hundred pounds, but every ounce of her had been pure goodness—a woman crafted from gingerbread and feathers. "She's not going to be able to replace Nana or Mom," Smith said, looking with worry at the eagerness, the sheer wanting in Tommy's eyes.

Dad caught the glance and quickly said, "Of course not. No one can, but let's hope she's kind and happy, and let's do our best to give her a good first impression of us." He checked the collar of his shirt.

"What's not to like?" Smith kept his voice light, and Dad sent him a nervous smile.

Smith had been trying to get a nanny in here since Mom's *first* heart attack, eighteen months ago, but Mom wanted to do it all herself. She wanted to be strong enough, so she refused the help.

This widow sounded like the perfect nanny. A sweet little old lady to take care of them—make them crumpets and pinch their cheeks. A grandma was just what Dad and Tommy needed, just what the whole family needed.

A strong fist knocked on the heavy front door three times, and Smith's optimism shifted into a strange sense of foreboding. Were those knocks too assertive? Nana hadn't pounded the door like an FBI agent. She hadn't had the strength, for one thing . . .

Dad opened the door, revealing a beautiful woman who looked to be in her thirties, with sparkling eyes, a willowy figure, and olive skin. Smith's lungs froze, and every ounce of anxiety rushed back. She was *nothing* like Nana.

And this was a terrible idea.

Chapter 4
CLAIRE

Nerves made Claire smile too big—as she stepped onto the entry rug of the gorgeous home. *Ah.* And they were liberal with the air-conditioning. She hadn't allowed herself to spend money on air-conditioning for years.

Two men and a boy stared at her as if she had three heads. As the moment of silence stretched, she made her own snap judgments. Young Tommy was adorable—golden skin, blond curls, and blue eyes that melted her heart. It was the yearning and blatant hope shining in those depths that worried her. This boy had just lost his mother. How could she offer to help a few hours a day knowing she couldn't come close to healing his wounds or replacing what he'd lost?

But as she fell for Tommy's bright gaze and perfect features, she didn't see how she could turn away from such adoration and need. She could see right through to his tender heart. And it was broken. She'd only seen him for a blink, but she knew in that pulse she wanted to help him. Forget the money, the reason she'd even agreed to consider working for this family. Now she wanted to be there at the bus stop when Tommy came home from school. She wanted to make him lasagna and read him stories. Her blood rose in the excitement of her unexpected feelings. She had three daughters and one grandbaby—also a girl. They loved her and she them—with all her soul, but they didn't need her like this little boy did.

She winked at him.

Tommy grinned, showing a neat row of baby teeth. "I love apple pie," he said.

Claire smiled as her heart dissolved a little more. She opened her mouth to tell him she'd make him some, but low uncomfortable laughter interrupted. She lifted her face, remembering there were others in the world besides her and this shining boy. She looked at the two men flanking Tommy. They both seemed to startle when her focus landed on their faces. The younger one recovered first, settling his handsome features into a welcoming smile.

He held out a hand. "Hey, Clara. I'm Smith."

His handshake was strong and comforting—a well-developed skill. And it worked. His warm palm against hers put her at ease at the same time his charm had alarm bells ringing.

"And my dad, Banks, and my main man, Tommy."

"Just Claire, please," she said.

"That's not an old lady name," Banks said.

Smith's brow furrowed at his father, but Banks didn't seem to notice. He was still staring at her.

"Roger said your name was Clara." He frowned.

She forced a lighthearted smile even though he was being weird about her name. "At the beginning he thought it was funny to call me the wrong name. He likes to tease me. Now I think he's forgotten it's not right. He can get away with it, but I hope you won't follow suit."

"He also said you were a grandma." Banks had a dumbfounded look on his otherwise-pleasing features. "But you're . . ."

"I know." A familiar warmth rushed to her cheeks. Better to just explain what they were seeing now and answer the question they were both too polite to ask. "I'm forty."

Banks's eyes widened.

"I had my oldest daughter when I was eighteen. And she had her baby at twenty-one, just seven months ago. So, I get that I'm not quite what you might have expected when Roger told you I was a grandma."

Banks coughed in what Claire assumed was agreement.

"You're way prettier than my Grandma Shellburg," Tommy said.

Banks jolted at those words, seeming to snap back to himself. "Please excuse us." He stepped back and motioned her to come in farther over the blue oriental rug. He closed the door behind her. "Thank you so much for coming and considering helping us." He gestured to himself and his sons. "As you can see . . . we need help."

Besides the lost look in the father's eyes and the wanting in the youngest, they appeared anything but helpless. Boys straight out of a magazine feature.

Banks looked younger and fresher than most fifty-year-olds she knew. He had the same blue eyes as Tommy. The fine wrinkles could have come from years of smiling . . . or squinting. He had tanned skin with a nicely trimmed beard that shaped his face and a thick head of gray hair. He was a couple of inches taller than her five foot eight. A handsome widow. He looked like a man who could get a younger woman. The kind of man her friends had been trying to set her up with since Stevie had died five years ago. Her friends claimed that not all men were the same. They insisted she'd married so young that she'd never gotten out there and tasted the variety. Claire had finally agreed to go out on a setup. That horrible night she'd realized she could have done much, *much* worse than Stevie. She hadn't been on a date since then. It had been over four years. She called herself a spinster now. And couldn't be happier about it. She'd take plain over pain.

At least that's what she always told herself.

She sized up the thirty-year-old son. Smith looked like the kind of man who could get any woman—golden skin, lean muscles. She knew what lay under that shirt. She'd never spoken to him before, but she recognized him from seeing him down at the beach over the years.

Yes, she'd noticed him. He knew how to dress to advantage too. Those pants accentuated his long thighs and strong backside quite nicely. His eyes had green mixed in with the blue, like a frothing ocean. His nose, cheeks, and clean-shaven jaw were sharper, straighter than his father's, and he was a couple of inches taller. He broke six feet. Smith's hair was a rich caramel, cut long enough to show off how thick it was. Her oldest daughter, Mona, would like this boy. Hell, Claire kind of wanted him too. She was way too old, she reminded herself. And here on business. And not interested in romance anyway.

Claire took all this in in an instant. "I think you all look great."

Tommy beamed. Banks stood a touch taller. Smith looked her straight in the eyes. The kind of steady gaze that struck her core and had her staring back. Her belly warmed. Smith was attracted to her. She decided to be flattered and move on because it did *not* matter.

"Let me show you around the house," Banks said. "Or maybe Smith should." He let out a nervous chuckle. "He gets plenty of practice as a Realtor."

Smith put his hands in his pockets. "If you have questions about the age of the oak floors or the counter stone in the bathrooms, I'm your guy."

She chuckled—for their benefit—wishing she could do something to get rid of the awkwardness, their nervous smiles and too-long stares. So, she wasn't the poster grandmother. They could get over it.

"I'll show you my room." Tommy grabbed her hand and tugged her along.

The men were wearing shoes, so she left on her platform sandals. Banks and Smith straggled behind as Tommy led her downstairs. There was a game room, cozy couch, massive TV, foosball, and pool table. Great for after school hours. It would make her job so easy. She surprised herself by how much she wanted to do this. She'd always wanted a son.

Tommy pointed to a door across the open space. "That's Smithy's room."

She startled at that, looking over at the full-grown man. She'd been married twelve years and had three kids by the time she was thirty. His mom had just died, though, so maybe he'd moved back to help?

Smith flushed. "It's just for when I come visit. I live in Corona del Mar."

She was oddly grateful. She didn't think she wanted him around all the time. And she was not ready to review why she might even care about that.

Tommy ran through the first doorway on the right. "I sleep there." He pointed to a nautical-themed queen bed.

Vacuum lines striped the plush carpet. Good. Claire didn't want to be expected to deep clean the house.

"Those are my toys." Colored bins lined the shelves against the wall. "And my desk." He turned to her. Waiting. Expectant.

"What a perfect room. I love it in here." She peered at a framed child's painting of what looked like a car. "Especially this masterpiece." Then she moved on to the photo of Tommy with a smiling blonde woman. Before Stevie died, Claire might have ignored the photo, ignored the hippopotamus of pain in the room. Now she knew better. Talk to people about their lost ones. "Your mother is beautiful, Tommy. She looks very, very nice. I wish I could have met her."

He looked at the photograph with so much wanting that Claire's ribs pinched. "I'm sorry you can't."

"I hope you'll tell me all about her."

"Okay." Tommy picked up a model truck and held it up for show.

The two men stood by the door. Watching.

"What kind of truck is this?"

"It's a skid-steer loader."

"Wow. You must know a lot about trucks."

"My mom bought me the *Big Book of Trucks*. It's my favorite."

"I'd like to see it." How long was she supposed to play with him while Banks and Smith watched like creepers? Was this her job interview?

"Tommy," Banks said. "Let's show Ms. Claire around the rest of the house and save the *Big Book of Trucks* for another time."

Disappointment lowered Tommy's facial features, but he put the massive tome down and didn't argue. He slipped his hand into hers again, and they followed Banks back into the game room.

"Game closet there. And that's a third bedroom Helen set up for guests." Banks pointed to the last unexplained door downstairs.

"That's where Aunt Ivy stayed," Tommy said. "But she left. She had to go back to her house in Vegas. Are you going to sleep there?"

Claire's cheeks pinked. She wasn't usually a blusher, but there was something about these two men that had her thoughts moving into long-restricted areas. She wasn't sure if it made her feel better or worse that the men looked as uncomfortable as she with the idea of her sleeping in their home.

"No, Tommy. I have my own house. It's very close by. You know the Emerald Bay park on the other side of PCH?"

He nodded.

"My house is right by there. Maybe you can come see it sometime."

"Today?" He looked to his dad. "Can I?"

Banks did the awkward chuckle he'd already employed a couple of times in these last fifteen minutes. "Not today. Let's take this tour upstairs."

The kitchen was appropriately dazzling. She would have a delightful time baking biscuits in that oven. So much counter space for prepping. The ocean glittered outside the wall of windows. And he had a pool. She eyed a leather chair near the window. What a spectacular place to watch the sunset, curled up in an oversized sweater with a cup of tea. She could get used to that.

"Want me to show her your room?" Tommy asked his dad.

That nervous chuckle sounded again. "How about you and Smith get ready to go to the beach while I have a grown-up talk with Ms. Claire."

Claire didn't like that phrase, *grown-up talk*. It sounded condescending. And unpleasant.

"Come on, Tom. Get your suit." Smith turned his charming face to her. "Nice to meet you, Claire." At least he wasn't going to call her miss. Like she was *his* governess.

"Likewise."

The sons went downstairs, and Banks motioned her into his dark, wood-paneled office. She sank into a leather buster. Banks made to sit in the ergonomic chair behind the desk, hesitated, then walked back around the desk to sit in the twin to Claire's chair.

"How do you know Roger and Raven Char?" he asked.

"Raven and I met at early-morning Pilates probably twelve years ago now. We immediately became close. Their son, Jimmy, dated my daughter Edith for a few months last year. They were seniors together, which was fun."

"They are good people. They speak highly of you."

"And you."

Banks gave her a handsome half smile. "Roger and I have been friends for a long time. When Helen and I moved here from New York twenty-five years ago, he lived on our street in Irvine. I was working eighty-hour weeks back then, but somehow he still insisted on being my friend. And I'll be eternally grateful to Raven for being there for Helen when I wasn't." He stopped talking and swallowed. Sadness seemed to weigh him down.

After a heavy pause, she spoke softly. "I'm sorry about your wife. No one should have to bury their spouse so young."

Banks inhaled, blinking rapidly.

"Especially when you're left with a child to raise."

He lowered his brow. "I'm worried about him. My sad little boy."

Claire's heart hurt.

Anger flashed through his grief. "Tommy needs his mom. It isn't fair. But all my pleading prayers were for nothing." His face turned stricken again as his gaze ran over her face, her low dark ponytail slung over one shoulder. "And now I find myself in the position of beggar again." Blue eyes turned piercing. "Honestly, I've been hesitant to find a nanny because I don't want to bring someone unknown and unvetted into my home and give them charge over my greatest treasure, but with Roger's trust in you and my initial feeling that you are a deeply good person and a great fit for us, I hope you'll take the job."

His words had her sitting a fraction taller.

"I couldn't bear to see the look on Tommy's face if I have to tell him you're not coming back. The boy up and fell in love with you already." He spread his hands out, palms up. "Please."

She knew the moment she saw Tommy that he'd be the kind of boy she could never say no to, but now, looking at Banks's fine face and pleading eyes, she realized Tommy had inherited the irresistibility trait from his father. The day that had started so empty was now full of interest and purpose. "I can't replace his mother. I will never be Helen . . . but I will do what I can to help. I can come weekdays after school until you get home from work—late isn't a problem."

"Thank you, Claire."

The depth of his honest gratitude pulled a generous smile over her face. Banks sat up straighter when he saw it, his features shifting from desperate to . . . she wasn't sure what. But he seemed to be having a hard time looking away from her mouth. She'd been complimented on her smile all her life—straight white teeth, wide lips that curved up toward bright eyes. She frowned. The last thing she needed was to have to tell her new employer her rule: *absolutely no dating*. "Walk me through the details and your expectations of me," she said, voice professional.

He cleared his throat, his features shifting into the steady face she imagined he employed at his private-equity firm. "Tommy is the job.

Playing with him after school. Reading to him. Taking him to parks, the beach, anything you might have done with your own children. I'm not hiring you to clean—they come on Tuesdays—but I'm hoping you'll feed him, make him dinner most nights. Or take him out for a bite."

"I can do that."

He pulled out a wallet from his pocket and slid out an American Express. "For the groceries, restaurants, activities. Any charges you make on our behalf."

She took the card gingerly. It was heavier and thicker than her credit cards. She felt as if she'd stepped into a dream.

He stood and moved behind the desk. "I'll print out Tommy's bus schedule." He clicked the mouse. "And I'll have my assistant reach out to you about employment paperwork. He'll take care of paying you weekly or whenever you want. What do you want to be paid?"

Claire blinked, and no words came.

"Fifty an hour? And do you need health insurance? I don't know how this works. I've never hired someone outside the office. Helen always took care of the house domain."

She stared in shock.

"You can talk to my assistant, Sal, about it. Whatever you need, he'll see to getting it set up." When she still hadn't spoken, he looked up from his screen. "Is that all right with you? Am I forgetting something?"

She swallowed with effort. "That's too generous. I was going to ask for twenty an hour. I'll take twenty-five."

His lips curved up, revealing straight teeth. "I've learned not to play games when it comes to the important things. When there is something worth having that I want—a company for sale, a house with a view"—he motioned to her—"a friend for my son. It's best to come out with a strong first offer."

She wasn't sure how she felt being compared to one of the companies he acquired at his firm, but it did feel amazing to be wanted, *valued.*

She hadn't felt this good in a long, *long* time. Her shoulders pulled back as her chest filled with warmth.

"Then I accept your offer with my thanks and a promise to do my best for Tommy and do right by you."

He grinned. "You see. Already worth it." He leaned forward across the desk and whispered, "You should have negotiated. I would have paid double that."

"Then I'll expect a raise by Christmas."

He laughed. A real laugh that was nothing like his previous grating chuckle. This sound was deep and musical and made her very proud of her little joke. He opened a drawer, and pulled out a key on a bronze key chain. It was heavy in her palm. Real bronze? She looked closer and saw the ball was an intricately etched globe. Her personal key chain was a tiny superhero from her middle daughter, Indi, many Mother's Days ago. The Sextons were fancy. What was she getting into?

"House key," Banks said. "And the garage code is seven six five zero." He handed her the paper from the printer tray.

Claire slipped the tiny world she'd just accepted into her purse along with the bus schedule. They exchanged phone numbers.

"When can you start?" His voice came out tight with hope.

"I'll be at the bus stop tomorrow after school."

"Truly." His shoulders relaxed with a shudder. "Thank you."

"You'll need to reach out to El Morro Elementary and give permission for me to pick him up since he's in kindergarten." Claire had dealt with the local schools long enough to know the drill.

Banks opened a leather folder and wrote a note at the top of a legal pad with a bold cursive script. "Thank you for the reminder."

She stood and held out her hand. "Thank you for the job."

He shook her hand, holding a second longer than felt professional. But what was professional in this context? He wasn't hiring her at the office. He'd given her his house key and his son. He was practically family now.

Chapter 5
BANKS

Banks showed Claire out and shut the door before she reached her Honda. It felt creepy to watch her leave. He didn't watch people at his office come and go. Looking at the swirling wood knot in the back of his front door, he hissed out a pent-up breath. Then another. He returned to his office and picked up the note card she'd written her number on. She had lovely penmanship, a thin italic script, a trait few people possessed in this digital world. He found it very attractive. He wanted to take her out on a date. And that made him feel weird—wrong. Alive.

Helen had been gone four months. She wasn't coming back. But was it really okay for him to *want*?

The card in his fingers had a romantic edge to it. He imagined he'd met Claire at a party and she'd slipped it into his coat pocket. He'd call her later, talk to her while she was getting ready for bed. Arrange a candlelit dinner. He cut off the spiraling thoughts. She was an employee now.

He plugged her number into his phone. He made to toss the card, but instead of dropping it in the bin, he slipped it in the back of his folder. He snapped it shut as Smith and Tommy appeared at the door in their swim trunks.

"So?" Smith asked, his brows annoyingly suggestive. He adjusted the towel that hung over his bare shoulder.

"Is she coming back?" Tommy asked, his voice high with hope.

"Yes." Banks grinned. "She's going to meet you at the bus stop after school tomorrow."

Tommy raised an excited fist. Victory.

It sure felt like that.

Banks laughed as gratitude filled his heart. He never could have guessed when he'd woken up this morning heavyhearted and full of discouragement that today would end with such a bright turn. "She said she can play with you every weekday after school."

Tommy whooped. His elation made Banks feel a tad guilty. Was it so terrible for Tommy when it was just the two of them?

"How do you know you already like her so much?" Smith asked his little brother.

"I could feel it," Tommy said, touching his chest. His gaze went soft. "When I looked into her eyes. I could tell that she was meant to be mine."

Smith blinked down. He seemed as speechless as Banks felt. Kids said the damnedest things.

"Are you coming to the beach with us, Daddy?" Tommy's tone was impatient, as if he hadn't just spoken such heavy truth with cutting precision.

"Go ahead without me. I need to get some work done." And he needed a minute to process.

They left, and he leaned back in his chair. He exhaled another pent-up breath. His cell phone rang. He leaned forward, picked it up, and chuckled as he answered. "Still *spry*, huh?"

"So, you met Clara," Roger said.

"Her name is Claire."

"Oh, she's still trying to cut the *a*, is she?"

Banks rolled his eyes. "Forget the name. You intentionally misled me. You described her as a widowed grandmother."

Roger's deep laughter rolled through the phone line. "Both true. I can't help it if your own narrow worldview didn't come to pass."

"You are enjoying this a little too much." Banks grinned.

"Me?" Roger's voice was mock offense. "You can't tell me you're not enjoying it far more than I. Admit it. She's stunning."

She was. But it wasn't just her looks. There was something magnetic about her. He couldn't wait to have her back in his home. "She's my employee."

"Tommy's nanny is not the same thing as a subordinate at work. The line gets fuzzy."

Banks had to stop his imagination from jumping back down that hole. "Tommy is smitten. And I'll do nothing to jeopardize his after-school help or a home-cooked dinner." He could hardly believe he was having this conversation. "I have zero interest in her outside of the job I hired her to do." It wasn't even a good lie.

"Fine." Roger sounded disappointed. "At least you can enjoy a pretty face while she's at it. Nothing wrong with that."

Yeah, Banks thought with sarcasm. *What could possibly go wrong?*

Chapter 6
CLAIRE

Claire stepped out of the shade when the yellow school bus pulled around the corner. She waved to the driver, then squinted at the little faces in the rows beyond. She couldn't see him yet. The bus stopped at the curb, and the doors hissed open. Two kids climbed out and behind them, Tommy. He scanned the sidewalk with an injured frown, and then he focused in on her face below her wide-brimmed hat. As recognition hit, his whole body changed from gray to golden.

Yes. She was doing the right thing. All last night she'd fretted about her decision to work for Banks Sexton. He was handsome, wealthy, and widowed. And he was obviously used to getting whatever he wanted.

"You came!" Tommy ran into her legs and wrapped his arms around her rear.

She sidestepped to stay standing and dug her fingers into his curls, tilting his head back to look at his face. The smell of sweat and faded shampoo assaulted her. "Yes, I did. And you'd better get used to it."

He was a ray of noonday sun. It had been so long since she'd picked up Mona, Indi, and Edith from the bus. Edith was the one who sometimes ran to embrace her, but her girls most often came home tired and hangry. Claire hadn't always been cheerful either.

This felt like a do-over.

Tommy pulled back and tugged off his navy canvas backpack. He unzipped it and pulled out a wrinkled folder.

She took it. "And what's this?"

"My Friday folder. There's some work I did and some notes for Dad." He squinted up at her eyes. "Or maybe for you?"

She peeled the folder open and pulled out a painting of red blobs. She loved it. Abstract was her thing, but she couldn't risk guessing on this one. "Tell me about this."

"Autumn harvest. Those are apples. Pomegranates. And those are pumpkins. They are supposed to be orange, but Sawyer used it all."

"Red pumpkins are even cooler. Kinda spooky for Halloween, right?"

"I love Halloween. I haven't decided what to be this year. Mom usually helps me, but Dad and Smithy said they would dress up with me so we could go together. I want to do something matching." Tommy started walking toward home, talking a thousand miles a minute about past costumes.

Claire flipped through his folder. There was one school notice, a fundraiser from the PTA, amid the stack of schoolwork. She instinctively reached for Tommy's hand as they crossed an empty residential street. She'd forgotten how grimy little hands could become after a day at school.

"What are you going to be for Halloween?" he asked.

She exhaled. "I don't know. I have a witch hat I like to put on when I answer the door for trick-or-treaters."

He looked extremely disappointed in that answer.

She chuckled at his honest expressiveness.

"You can be something with us. I'll just have to think up a girl part."

"Maybe." She tried to make it sound more like maybe *not* than maybe yes.

He dropped her hand and jogged to a nearby flower bed. He plucked two purple blossoms right at the head. The flower in full bloom he gave to her.

"Oh, thank you."

He kept walking, head down, twirling the second flower in his fingers. It was still a tight bud. His voice came out so quiet she had to lean over to hear him. "This one's not done growing. I shouldn't have picked it." His sweet, sad voice wrapped her heart like a heavy fist.

"It's all right, Tommy." She put a hand on his droopy shoulders as he dropped the bud in the gutter.

They didn't talk the rest of the way to his home. She'd come early to put the groceries away and make him blueberry muffins as an after-school snack. She let him put in the garage code. He kicked off his shoes and thrust his bag against the garage wall. It almost snagged on the hook before thumping to the epoxied cement.

"Is that where you're supposed to put your backpack?"

He stopped on the threshold into the house and circled back. He lifted his crumpled backpack up to the hook. "And I'm supposed to take my lunch box to the kitchen for Dad to fill, but we only remembered the first day, so I've been eating school lunch." He took out a flattened insulated bag with parrots embroidered on it.

"Do you like school lunch?"

"Not really."

"Shall I pack a lunch tonight for you to take in the morning?"

Blue eyes brightened. "Can I help?"

"Yes, sir. We can pack it after a little snack. Are you hungry now?"

"Yeah."

"Wash your hands, and you can have a blueberry muffin in the kitchen."

Tommy darted inside, leaving her bracing against the swinging door and carrying his folder and empty lunch box.

Claire had her muffin drizzled with honey. It was breakfast for her. Most mornings she didn't have much of an appetite. It used to be three square meals a day for her girls, but she didn't bother with that now. Eating alone wasn't fun. She thought that maybe it wasn't such a healthy thing to skip so many meals, but she also loved fitting in her size-two jeans. She thought that maybe wasn't such an important thing to care about, either, but she wasn't concerned enough to change her mind about it. Obviously, she wasn't staying skinny for a man. She liked the feel of being lean and lithe. She stayed trim and toned for her own health and pleasure.

Tommy had two muffins with extra, extra butter. Claire wrapped one for Tommy's lunch tomorrow and put the rest in the fridge.

"Wow." He peered around her hip to investigate the stocked fridge. "There's so much stuff in here." He opened the fruit drawer and pulled out an apple. "Can I have this?"

"Of course. Want me to cut it?"

He shook his head and bit into it, juice spitting onto his chin.

"Let's talk about lunches. What do you like?"

"Ham sandwiches, quesadillas wrapped in foil so they're still warm, pepperoni pizza, no bananas, but yes to grapes, but don't cut them in half, I'm not two anymore. Oh, and the pretzel-and-cheese-dip things that Liv takes in her lunch."

She had no idea what those were, but her lips curved up. Packing her daughters' lunches had never been this fun. She'd been tired and rushed. Why was she eager about it now? Did that make her old—that prepping lunches seemed like a joy instead of a chore? She didn't think she wanted another child, but Tommy was already making her reconsider that. She felt lit up inside. Needed again. His hugs were shockingly potent. "We don't have those options today."

Tommy opened the fridge and surveyed it like a conquering hero. He pointed to the pineapple. She cut it, and he got a container for the slices. He put a string cheese in his lunch box. Together they made a trail mix in descending order of deliciousness—Tommy's idea. Five chocolates, four raisins, three pistachios, two peanuts, and one lone almond. With the kitchen cleaned up and tomorrow's lunch in the fridge, she set out Tommy's folder for Banks, along with a note reminding him that he needed to send Tommy's lunch to school tomorrow morning.

"Oh no, Tommy."

He looked up from where he'd doodled on extra Post-it notes and stuck them to the cabinets. Misshapen faces all over the kitchen. "What?"

"There's no school tomorrow. Tomorrow is Saturday."

He shrugged. "Let's leave it for Monday." He pulled up his fingers and ticked off Saturday and Sunday. "It's only three days until I'll get to take it to school."

"Well, the muffin might not be so good by then. What if we freeze it and then you can pull it out on Monday and put it in the lunch, and it will keep the pineapple slices and cheese cold until you eat."

His lips twisted. "You'll have to remind me. That's too hard for me to remember."

She smiled and crumpled the paper to Banks. "I'll write your dad a new note."

"He's not good at remembering that stuff either."

"Let's try it and see." She finished the brief instructions. "Now. I've been waiting to see that *Big Book of Trucks* . . ."

Tommy was down the stairs in a blink.

For the rest of the afternoon, they read and played games. When Tommy got hungry again, they made spaghetti with garlic and parmesan and peas. Claire also had a green salad, but Tommy politely declined that course. She put what they didn't finish in the fridge. She'd find out soon enough if Banks was a leftovers type of guy. Probably not. He was too fancy for that. She loved leftovers. Two or three meals for the effort of one. Her late husband had hated them.

Stevie had grown up without much, and he'd had to eat leftovers constantly as a child. As soon as he started making money, he refused to eat reheated food on principle. He'd done well enough as a public relations–and-marketing consultant to buy their little cottage in Emerald Bay, but there was never anything in the savings account. A good plan for him since he'd died young. But not such a great situation for Claire now. And she hadn't sold a painting in months. She closed the fridge. So far, she'd made two hundred bucks this afternoon, though. Things were looking up in her personal finance department.

Her phone vibrated in her pocket. "Hello?"

"Claire. Hi. It's Banks. How are things going?"

"Great. Tommy and I just finished dinner. We were planning to take a walk down to the beach before he showers and gets ready for bed." She glanced at the oven clock: 6:22. "But if you're headed home and you'd like us to stay here . . ."

"No. Please. Oh, Claire. I can't tell you how much I appreciate you being there. I hadn't realized how much I've been putting off things at work while I worried about home. I'm playing serious catch-up today. And I'm hoping you really meant it when you said late would be fine."

"Yes. Totally fine. I have a book to read after Tommy is asleep."

A grateful gush came through the phone. "Make yourself at home. Please. I'll text you when I have a better estimate of when I'll be back."

"Don't worry about it, Banks. We're fine here. I'll see you when I see you."

"You're a dream." And with those parting words, the line went dead.

She looked at the beautiful boy. "Well, time for shell hunting?"

He grinned and ran for his bucket.

A contented filter seemed to gild the rest of her evening. The house was peaceful and luxurious. Tommy was so happy to have her company that he was affectionate and easily persuaded. With excitement he shared his glittering world with her. She became privy to his secret rock at the beach, his favorite pajamas, the expensive-smelling perfume in his shampoo. She loved it all. She wanted more.

"Where's your floss?" she asked him as they stood together in his bathroom.

Tommy looked at her with so much guilt she chuckled.

"Come on. It's good for you."

"I hid it under the sink."

She dug around the extra rolls of toilet paper and came up with a little blue box.

"I really don't want to."

"Would you rather floss or have no teeth?"

Tommy's eyes went wide. "Is that what happens?"

She hesitated. When Mona was little, Claire would have said yes, end of story. Now, she said, "Floss protects you from getting holes in your teeth. I suppose the sugar bugs could eat the holes so big they consume your whole teeth in the end. That happened in the olden days."

Tommy flossed.

After a story, they lay together on his bed, his night-light a dim presence in the corner.

"Are you coming back tomorrow?" Tommy asked.

"Tomorrow is Saturday, so no. I won't be here on the weekends. I'll stay tonight until your dad gets home, but I won't be here when you wake up in the morning. Your dad will be. But I'll be back on Monday at the bus when you get home from school. Just like today."

He snuggled against her arm. "I'm glad."

"Me too." And she was. Tommy made her realize how dull her life had become since she lost Stevie, and then Mona moved away and then Indi, and finally Edith had left too. "Good night, Tommy."

"Night, Ms. Claire."

Heart swollen to bursting, she kissed his brow and left his room, leaving the door open a crack—as directed. She climbed up the stairs and stood before the wall of windows. The last shimmers of orange streaked the darkening sky. Tonight, the ache in her breast wasn't from loneliness. Tonight, she floated on clouds of hope and optimism. And it hurt just as much.

Chapter 7
SMITH

A few bold stars winked to life above an inky ocean. Smith found his focus drifting far too often from his pretty date to the mysterious expanse just beyond the restaurant patio. He thought he'd recognized Claire from seeing her around the neighborhood and the beach over the years. Why was she snagging his attention so completely now? It bothered him that he couldn't stop thinking about the forty-year-old.

Smith could always tell when he was attracted to someone, because he saw them in details. Claire was hazel eyes shot through with honey. Rich brown hair highlighted with auburn. High cheekbones and a square jaw. She was lean muscles and delicate ankles. And that mouth. Wide as the outside edges of her irises and lips as thick on top as on the bottom. He'd refused to sketch her when he'd gotten home last night. She was ten years older than he, a full decade, not to mention she was Tommy's now. Claire was untouchable. Yet her intriguing image remained in his mind. His fingers twitched for a pencil.

The woman across the two-top table batted her eyes at him. Claire hadn't given two shits about impressing Smith. She'd seem him stare, and she'd essentially shrugged. As if he were a child—less than a child, because for Tommy, she was all charm and smiles. The lucky bastard.

Claire had a self-assured aloofness that had completely hooked his interest, like she knew who she was and she didn't need outside approval.

Smith smiled at the memory of shaking Claire's hand and feeling a warm spark. His date's gaze dropped to his mouth. Yes, it was all about the game. And Claire had made an expert first move. She was pretending she wasn't even interested in playing. The opposite of the overt interest of the petite blonde in front of him.

He felt tired and old. Jaded. He was sick of first dates, the small talk and forced manners. The facade young singles all put on to appear perfect. He didn't want to go to loud, touchy parties anymore. When was he going to find a woman to settle down with? He wanted a partner, a best friend to make peanut butter–and-honey sandwiches with to take on a sunset hike in their sweats together. He'd carry their baby on his back. More and more now he wanted a child. The hunger had strengthened after Mom's death. He regretted she would never know her grandchild.

Problem was he had to find his baby's mama first.

The twentysomething in front of him wasn't thinking *baby*. She'd spent the first half hour of dinner talking about her roommates, their living habits and pet peeves. Smith couldn't bring himself to be interested. He sagged against his seat, feeling out of sync with her exuberant, party-seeking vibe. More and more lately, he'd been craving quiet connection.

Mom's declining health and untimely death had aged him. He felt his old heart sink like a stone in his chest. He imagined Mom telling him that his maturity was a good thing. He should embrace the wisdom and shift in priorities that had come from this painful experience.

Easier said than done, Mom.

He missed her. He'd lucked out with a mom like Helen. She'd welcomed him fully as her own and had loved him with a steady, attentive, and unassuming love that his father, with all his expectations, had never achieved.

Claire seemed like the same kind of mother. In his few minutes watching her with Tommy, he'd felt her nurturing, tenderhearted energy. In addition to Roger's recommendation, he'd felt deep in his belly that she was safe and good. He was protective of Tommy, but he'd left the house deeply relieved and grateful that Dad had found Claire.

Now he was annoyed that she'd stuck to his thoughts like the nasty burrs on his favorite trail run.

He'd met her once. He was being ridiculous. These feelings obviously only meant that he'd changed this last year. He needed to devote more time and energy to finding a woman who was ready to build a family and grow old together.

"Excuse me." His date leaned forward enough to give him a glimpse of enhanced cleavage. "I'm going to slip to the little lady's room."

He nodded and turned to the ocean again, thoughts still stormy. He slipped his phone from his pocket and pulled up his dad's location. At work.

Tommy would be in bed by now. And Claire was at Dad's home. Alone.

Did he have any excuse to stop by? Feign surprise at finding her there?

His date returned with deep-red lipstick on. It looked hot, but not kissable. The server swung by, asking if they'd like dessert.

He cocked an eyebrow at her in invitation, but hoped she'd decline.

"If you want," she said. "But I don't need any."

Smith paid the bill and slid a hand on the small of her narrow back as he led her out. The chemistry wasn't there. He removed his touch. The car ride to her house was quiet. His mind was on another woman, and he found he lacked the energy to pretend tonight. He walked her to her door—old habits.

"I have ice cream in the freezer if you want dessert." The way she said *dessert* did not make Smith think of food.

"Maybe another night."

She puffed her lips into a pout.

Another time he would have kissed that pucker. A younger, hornier Smith. But tonight he stepped back. "Thanks for dinner." He turned and walked to his car.

He resisted the urge to drive to his dad's, but he couldn't help checking his phone again. Dad was still at work. Smith reluctantly pulled up to his tiny cottage near Cameo Shores. The silence loomed over him, menacing and eternal.

After a shower, he stalked around in his boxer briefs. Finally he picked up the sketchbook that lay on the end table. Paper and pencil and black marker. That's all he ever used. He sat at the dinner table, hunched over. Intent. He drew her as an ancient huntress with a quiver of poisoned arrows and a scandalously low neckline on her fighting leathers. Hair loose and long, dancing with an invisible breeze. A knife strapped to a lean thigh. Willowy curves. Come-get-me eyes and full lips.

Smoking hot.

Finished, he dropped the pen with a determined sigh. Good. Done. Claire was now out of his system.

Chapter 8
BANKS

It was nearly 11:00 p.m. when Banks pulled up to his house, praying that Claire really was okay with a late night. Best to find these things out right away. Expectations and everything. He pulled his Beemer into the garage and let himself into the house. It was quiet and dark except for a lamp in the family room. He slipped off his shoes and tiptoed inside. She was asleep on the couch, *his* couch. *Hell.* Heat spiraled down his groin as he scanned the curve of her waist, her smooth cheeks, and thick lashes, magnified through the lens of her reading glasses. A novel lay open over her gently rising and falling chest. Dark hair swirled around her face like a velvet frame. He missed coming home to a sleeping woman. Holy shit he missed it.

He'd worked like a twenty-five-year-old today, aggressive and productive. He'd plowed through a backlog of emails and fixed several festering problems. He'd left the office feeling like the emperor of the world. And then to come home to bed a beautiful woman . . . he closed his eyes and swallowed the unwelcome thought away.

"Claire," he whispered and gently touched an elbow.

Her eyes flew open as she jerked. She blinked up at him.

"I'm sorry I'm so late."

She sat up. "It's fine."

Damn her sleepy, husky voice. "How did it go?"

"Great. Tommy is a sweetheart." She took off her glasses, stood, and closed her book. "His school papers are on the counter. And he drew you a truck. He really knows a lot about those."

"Yes." Banks chuckled. "He thinks being a trucker is the epitome of a career."

Her low laugh rang through his bones. "We made him a lunch for school because we forgot it's the weekend, so if you can remember for Monday. The muffin for it is in the freezer."

"I can handle that." As if saying it made it true. Banks would prove he was a great father, and he would remember.

She ran a hand through her tousled hair. "I'll be at the bus for Tommy at Monday pickup."

"Thank you."

She lifted her purse, slipped on her sneakers, and walked out. He locked the door behind her.

"I think that went very well," he said to the fig tree by the window. He cringed at the inappropriate thoughts he'd had about a woman who was not his wife and was his son's nanny. "Well, it went well enough." He padded downstairs to check on his sleeping cherub. He kissed Tommy's brow. "I love you, son."

Back upstairs, he readied for bed and, for the first time in four months, went straight to sleep.

Chapter 9
CLAIRE

Claire let herself into her small home, wrapping herself in the familiarity of it. Banks's house was bright and sexy, but her cottage felt like a warm blanket, like an old friend. She sighed as she peeled off her clothes. Wearily she picked up her toothbrush. She'd forgotten how tiring children were. No matter how wonderful, they sucked her energy. She didn't often think about those years when her three girls were little. When things had started to sour with Stevie.

It wasn't her girls' fault, but it all seemed to happen at the same time. Those tiny-children years that should have been beautiful were tainted by their association with sorrow. Potty training messes and late-night arguments with Stevie. She'd blocked out the exhaustion, the way a day could feel like forever, the isolation. When she'd watched her daughters in ballet class, she'd often wished she'd learned how to dance through the pain of her life with such grace and poise. Her painting series titled *Ballet* had sold incredibly well.

She washed the day off her face and padded toward her dresser, pausing to view the framed photo of high school graduation. Stevie had one arm about her shoulders and the other around her round belly. She'd gotten pregnant as a senior. It was hard—no, it was brutal—to go to class with her growing belly, but she'd done it. It was like the other students didn't know the difference between a leper and an expectant mother. They'd certainly acted like they'd gotten the two confused.

But Claire had finished her classes. Mona was born in late June, just after high school graduation and the shotgun wedding. Claire didn't regret marrying Stevie. She left no place for that kind of bitterness to rot her mind. She'd loved Stevie. She still loved Stevie, but she'd often wondered over the years, what if? What if she hadn't gotten pregnant?

She wouldn't have married Stevie.

It was a hard day when she realized that. At age eighteen, she'd thought getting married was an exciting adventure. They'd made their vows in a whirl of eagerness and optimism.

She'd been so naive.

Now she knew marriage was like a game of Texas Hold'em where you go all in before the flop. No matter how good the starting pair of cards were, you couldn't know what cards would come out next. You didn't get to see your final hand before risking *everything*.

And with Stevie, she'd ended up with a losing hand. The loss of her innocence had been the first thing to go.

She wasn't naive anymore. Now she was *free*. She had grown children to enjoy. She was forever grateful to Stevie for giving her Mona, Indi, and Edith, but she'd never lock herself up again and risk not just a broken heart but a friendship soured. Stevie had been a dreamboat at the beginning. She'd had no way of foreseeing that he would turn into a miserable drunk who dragged her down and kept her aching for scraps of affection and praise. She learned the hard way it was better to be alone than to feel so stuck. Better to have total independence than to have a bedmate who took advantage of her, told her how to spend her money, and left tweezed eyebrow hairs in the sink for her to clean up.

She slipped into one of Stevie's soft T-shirts—she'd kept a stack of them for sleeping—and crawled into her favorite place, her fluffy bed.

She fell asleep with a prayer of gratitude in her heart for little Tommy and for the well-paying job.

In the morning, she woke to her phone vibrating. Mona.

"Hello." She eyed her clock: 8:02 a.m. She hadn't slept this late in a long time.

"Mom. Hey." A pause. "Did I wake you?"

"No. Just lazing about a bit."

"What are you doing today?"

"I've got a meeting at the gallery this morning, then nothing this afternoon. Do you need me to watch Millie?" Claire felt a tiny stab of guilt that she hoped Mona would say no. She loved Millie, but she didn't feel like bouncing a baby on her hip today. She'd given all her energy to Tommy yesterday.

"I was thinking we could all go to the beach this afternoon. It's such a perfect day for it."

"Love to." She meant it. Mona would take care of her baby, and Claire would enjoy their company.

"Great. Millie and I will come to the house after lunch. Love you." She clicked off without waiting for a reply.

Mona lived in a condo in Ladera Ranch with her seven-month-old. She'd graduated from hair school and now gave discounted cuts and colors to the neighborhood moms who were willing to come to her house and overlook the baby. She had quite a business going. Mona hadn't married her baby daddy. Claire wasn't sure how she felt about that. Resentful, jealous, glad, disappointed, angry, proud?

Claire was grateful she could give her daughters a good dad—no, Stevie had been a great dad. Whatever had gone on between him and Claire, he'd given his best to his daughters—at least up until the last few years there, when he didn't have much love left in his heart to give anyone. Even then, every last drop went to the girls. Claire had done everything she could to give her daughters a stable homelife, even if it wasn't perfect. She'd stayed with Stevie because she believed it was the best thing for her girls. Life was sacrifice. No roads were easy.

After a tall glass of lukewarm water, Claire put herself through her own Pilates class. She hadn't spent money on a gym since before Stevie died. But she did turn her air-conditioning on. *Thank you, Banks.* She stood over the vent and giggled at her good fortune. She was surprised to find herself hungry, so after a quick smoothie, she showered and put on makeup, slacks, and a collared blouse. She'd been dreading this appointment with Sheila all week, but now that she thought about how much money she'd made yesterday, she felt a pleasant calm.

She'd started painting twenty-two years ago, when her whole world had changed. She'd needed an outlet for her confusing and overwhelming emotions. Before Stevie, she'd felt like she'd been on a fast-moving train headed for greatness. When she'd married and had a baby at age eighteen, it was as if she'd fallen off into a ditch.

She couldn't complain to her parents; they'd kept saying she'd made her bed and slept in it. It was so annoying. She couldn't talk to Stevie. He didn't seem to get it. Everything was going great for him: career, wife, cute baby. So she'd picked up a canvas and brush, and she'd poured out her feelings in colors and shapes. She didn't think while painting. She'd started to add things like lace, paper, wax, wood, and shells. Whatever felt beautiful and dynamic and authentic. During those sweet escapes, she'd lose herself to intuition and emotion and creativity.

And her paintings had sold.

People liked to see the riot of color and texture. People liked that when looking at her art, they felt that they were understood. Someone else had expressed the chaos and struggle they felt inside. And it eased their burdens.

But sales had steadily declined over the last five years. She knew it was her fault. She'd closed off inside. And the hollowness showed. Her latest paintings were bland and lackluster—just like her calm life.

Claire breezed into the Main Street Gallery and smiled at Sheila Rivers. They'd done business together for fifteen years.

Sheila truly looked sorry when she said, "We need the wall space. We have to move your pieces."

"It's all right," Claire said. And it was. She had money coming in now. Her whole income didn't depend on this fickle business or her unreliable emotions. "I know this batch is crap. I'm sorry I wasted your time with it."

Sheila's shoulders lowered in relief. "You'll find your stride again."

Claire wasn't so sure. The angst and emotional highs and lows that had powered her artistic career weren't there anymore. The roller coaster that was her life with Stevie had long since stopped running. She'd never seriously considered leaving Stevie. Okay, maybe she'd planned her departure in her head every time he came home stinking of booze and lashing out at her with contempt. But she'd continued to believe his good outweighed the bad, especially when it came to her daughters, her priority.

Her life was easier now, certainly, but it was also far less interesting and eventful. She wondered if that made her a bit sick in the head. To miss someone who had continually caused her so much hurt and anxiety couldn't be healthy. She and Stevie had been through so much together, sicknesses and job changes and birthdays. Months and years of familiarity. That bond ran deep. But he had been so much work. She hadn't realized how heavily the mantle of marriage to Stevie had weighed on her until she'd buried him and the burden had slid off and into the ground with him.

The lightness in her chest, the absence of that tight knot of worry she'd hauled around for so many years, was the reason she refused to date.

Sheila took her to the back room of the gallery. Six paintings lay on the table. They really were vanilla. She couldn't imagine what had compelled her to use that pastel purple or pair it with such a shiny yellow. Claire stacked them up, heedless of the banging. Sheila jumped forward.

“Let me help you. We can pack them.”

“Not worth the Bubble Wrap.”

Sheila opened her mouth, closed it.

Claire balanced the garbage in her arms and started for the door. “Good to see you, Sheila.”

“Let me know when you have something new.”

Sheila had always been good to her. “Thank you.” Claire didn’t mention it might be a long while. She waltzed out. There was a dumpster at the end of the block. Perfect. Her heart lightened as she tossed the paintings in.

Chapter 10
SMITH

Tommy sat on Smith's lap, helping him drive the golf cart down to the beach. Smith had had showings all morning, but no one, not even house buyers, wanted to be looking at homes when it was eighty-seven degrees and sunny. From the passenger seat, Dad pointed to an open parking spot. Smith bit back annoyance. He could park without instruction. At what point would Dad stop backseat driving? Smith, thinking himself the bigger man, pulled in where Dad indicated. He helped Tommy hop off and handed Dad the keys.

"Busy today," Dad said.

If there was another person at the beach, Dad thought it was busy. But this smattering of umbrellas was nothing like the crowds at the public beaches. One reason Smith preferred to come here on hot Saturdays.

Dad handed Tommy his shovel and bucket and picked up two beach chairs. Smith adjusted his baseball cap, slung a towel over his shoulder, and lifted his surfboard. They all left their sandals in the back of the golf cart and walked together past the volleyball court to the sand. Smith was checking out the swells when he heard Tommy, ten paces ahead, exclaim, "Ms. Claire!"

Smith's focus snapped to the figure sitting under a blue-and-white-striped umbrella.

Claire stood and stepped out of her shade. She wore a wide-brimmed hat, sunglasses, and a white long-sleeve dress that fell to her knees. He had no idea how Tommy had picked her out under all that gear.

Tommy wrapped his arms around her waist, setting his face against her belly, and Smith felt a flash of jealousy. He pictured her as the huntress he'd drawn.

So the attraction was still at high voltage. Annoying, but he'd get over it.

"Hey, Tommy. It's so nice to see you today."

Banks and Smith came up behind Tommy as a young woman stepped up next to Claire. She wore oversized sunglasses and a bikini. She had big boobs billowing out of the red band, softness around her middle, and solid thighs. She stood with a hand on her hip. Her confidence was attractive, and she had a very nice smile.

"You're Tommy?" The girl pinched her voice in the irritating manner people sometimes do when they talk to babies. "My mom's been telling me all about you. She said she had so much fun with you yesterday."

Tommy beamed.

Claire's daughter. How crazy she had a grown-ass daughter. And why wasn't it repulsive to Smith? She didn't seem ten years older. Why was he wondering what swimsuit Claire had on under that muumuu? He'd have to draw something later, but if she'd give him a peek, he wouldn't have to make it up.

He really needed to get a grip.

Claire looked up, welcoming Dad and Smith into the conversation. "Meet my daughter, Mona." She motioned to a baby carrier set in the shade. "And that's her little one, Millie. Napping."

Dad set down his chairs, leaned them against his leg, and held out a hand. "Mona, I'm Banks Sexton."

Mona shook his hand, and then faced Smith.

"Smith." He nodded his head, but didn't come forward, didn't want to knock anyone with his board. Didn't want to get sucked further into *this*.

Mona's shoulders shifted back slightly, and her chin tilted as her assessing gaze raked over him. "Hello."

He knew that *hello*. That was a hello with an invitation if he'd ever heard one—and he had.

"How is it we've been going to the same beach for years and never met up before?" Dad asked.

"I recognize you guys," Mona said. "Well, I've seen Smith down here before."

Everyone turned to look at Smith. Dad had an annoying tilt to his brow. *Leave it alone, Dad. It's nothing. Don't try to set us up.* "Yeah, I've seen you around. Nice to finally meet." He did not remember Mona at all.

"Want to dig a hole with me?" Tommy asked Claire.

"Sure," Claire said at the same time Dad said, "I will."

Claire smiled as she tilted her sunglasses toward Dad. She motioned to the sand. "There's plenty of room by us if you'd like to set up here."

"We don't mean to intrude," Dad said.

Tommy plopped down, deciding it. Dad unfolded his chairs, leaving three feet between them and Claire, close but not too close.

Why was this so weird right now? Smith dropped his towel and hat on the end chair. He was even feeling a bit shy about taking off his shirt—what with Mona spying on him from behind those monster lenses and Claire clearly not even noticing him. He was not a child. He was too old to be her son, at least. That had to count for something. She couldn't put him in Tommy's category.

It bothered him that it bothered him.

He lifted his T-shirt off with a quick motion, picked up his board, and made a beeline for the waves.

Chapter 11
CLAIRE

Claire sat in her beach chair. Tommy and Banks dug a monster hole ten feet in front of her. She watched them, horrified by how often her gaze tracked past them to the man on the surfboard. Smith's tawny hair hung in heavy wet locks over his neck and forehead. But it was that body. She chided herself. This was Southern California. She saw toned abs, golden skin, and muscled arms all the time. No biggie. So why was she watching the cut of his thighs when he caught a wave, the ripple of abs as he stood up in the shallows, the brightness of his teeth when he laughed with another surfer?

"He's hot."

Claire jolted as if caught red handed. She swiveled toward her daughter. "He's fifty. A little old for you."

"Ew. Not him."

Obviously Claire knew who Mona was talking about. And Banks wasn't *ew*.

"Although Banks is totally perfect for you."

Claire's teeth clamped together in annoyance that her daughter was trying to pair her up. As if *she* needed a man.

"We've all moved out now, Mom. You're out of excuses."

Claire had told her daughters she didn't date because she wanted to focus on raising them. True, if not the whole story. She'd read too many articles about the horrible things creepy stepdads did to unfortunate girls around the world. Claire had refused to risk it.

Mona was right—her daughters were grown women now. Maybe they didn't need her protection as much anymore. But she still needed to protect herself.

Millie cried, distracting Mona. Mona pulled the chubby baby, now red and sweating, from the carrier. After a quick glance around, she tugged down the top of her suit and stuck the baby on. Millie sucked. Loudly.

"How's work?" Claire asked.

"It's okay. Millie is napping less, so it makes it harder, but I found a sixth grader down the street who comes over after school for a couple hours and plays with Millie while I do appointments."

"Good for you."

"Yeah, it's been a big help. Especially since Carl keeps canceling his Monday mornings on me."

Carl was the baby daddy. He worked at the Lexus dealership, and Monday was his day off. Carl and Mona had broken up before Millie was born. Because he didn't have enough invested in the baby, it was easy for him to duck out. He didn't sacrifice like Mona did for Millie, so he didn't love her like Mona did. He wasn't committed. He hadn't even been there at the delivery. He'd come with bagels the *next* day. People sucked. "That's hard, honey. How frustrating."

"At least he pays his child support."

Expectations were everything.

Tommy skipped over and handed Claire a seashell.

"It's beautiful," she said.

He trotted away happy.

"Wow," Mona said. "He's really into you."

"The boy just lost his mother. He would have latched on to any woman who smiled at him." But Claire liked to think that wasn't totally true. She felt that she and Tommy already had a special connection. A connection she hadn't realized she'd been craving.

"Ow." Mona pulled Millie off her breast with a frown. "Speaking of latching on. She's got a bottom tooth growing in, and she keeps grinding it into my nipple." Mona covered said nipple and unveiled its twin. Millie went back to sucking. "She's literally biting the boob that feeds her. If she keeps this up, I'm going to cut her off."

"Better that than she cuts you off."

"Gross, Mom."

"Not to mention dangerous, she'd probably choke on it and die." Claire chuckled, relaxing for the first time since the Sextons had interrupted her peaceful afternoon with their white smiles and fancy beach chairs.

And then Smith appeared in front of her feet with his chest dripping wet and his arm flexed around the surfboard at his side. He practically glowed with endorphins and sunshine. "Nice day out there. The water is so warm and clear."

"You look like you know what you're doing," Mona said, a touch of flirt in her tone.

"Nah. I'm just playing . . ." The words faded when he looked down and noticed what Mona was doing. His eyes bugged out slightly when his gaze landed on the baby's head and the pillow of cleavage behind it. He recovered quickly, though, brightening into an easy smile. Good for him. "Even saw a pod of dolphins."

"Yeah," Claire said. "I've been watching them."

"I love seeing them." Smith looked out at the cerulean blue.

"Me too. And the seals and the whales." She loved all the wildlife.

Smith sat in the chair closest to Claire. Good, it was much easier not to look at his naked torso this way.

"It's the best taking the boat out in the winter and getting up close to them," he said. "They're incredible."

"That sounds amazing." Claire didn't have a boat.

He glanced sidelong at her. "You'll have to join me this year." His face faltered for a moment after he'd said it.

Was it because he'd accidentally said *me*, as in a date with Smith, instead of *us*, as in the entire Sexton family? Obviously he didn't mean anything by it. To prove it, he turned away from her, showing off a rippling deltoid. He put on his baseball cap and closed his eyes.

All righty then.

She was sweating. Late summer brought warm water and few clouds. The kind of day she went swimming in the ocean. She'd been about to go in when the Sextons had arrived, but then she'd suddenly felt thirteen and embarrassed to take off her cover-up. Why? The more she thought about it, the more it bugged her that she was being stupid.

Obviously Mona was super into Smith. He seemed like a good guy. A great guy for Mona. She wanted him checking out Mona. Not her. At least that was what she kept telling herself. She didn't want him to be comparing mother and daughter. But that was dumb. And unavoidable. Claire was leaner than her daughter, but weren't kids these days into bigger butts? That's what she'd heard her daughters talking about. Something about more cushion for the pushin'.

Calling Smith a kid didn't seem quite right, though. When she'd met him that first day at the house, he'd seemed more mature than she'd expected. If she hadn't known better, she'd have assumed he was Tommy's father. And a great dad at that.

If he decided to go for Mona and her youthful curves and strong legs, great. Yep, super great. She wasn't getting in their way. It had nothing to do with Claire walking down the beach and dipping her skinny ass in the water. In fact, she'd be getting out of their way. They could talk without her in the middle.

She did wait for Mona to put her boobs away, at least as far as her small top could be considered away. While Mona burped Millie, Claire stood. Feeling weird and then feeling weird for feeling weird, she took off her hat, her sunglasses, and finally her cover-up. She wore a black one-piece that was admittedly a little low in front and high on the hips for a widowed grandma. She glanced at Smith. It was too irresistible not to see if he was looking at her.

He was.

A flash of satisfaction hit when his blue-green eyes caught hers. She could feel good about a thirty-year-old appreciating what he saw. And, boy, did it feel *good.* It scared her a little how much she enjoyed the petty, carnal satisfaction. She'd sworn off men! She was a committed old maid.

She turned and glided toward the water and past Banks, who was also peeking. Well, these boys did know how to make an old gal feel pretty. She wasn't as austere as she'd planned, because she was grinning by the time her toes hit the water. Even the chill didn't faze her. She marched right in and dived under a cresting wave. The cool water tickled her scalp and face. She popped up, the vibrancy in her veins making her giggle. Feeling refreshed and alive, she stayed in the water until her fingers turned pruny, far longer than usual. After diving under one last wave, she stalked up the sand.

Smith was down the beach talking with a group of young people. Claire toweled off and sat back in the shade with Mona. She took Millie onto her lap and kissed her toes. Banks and Tommy came over and sat in their chairs.

"I'm hungry, Dad."

Banks opened a small Yeti cooler. "Thanks to Claire, we have good stuff today." He looked up at her. "These blueberry muffins are dynamite."

The warm bliss of being appreciated flowed through her. So much better than baking for only herself. "Thank you."

He held a plastic-wrapped muffin up. "Would you like one?"

Claire was sure they hadn't packed enough for her. She'd just opened her mouth to politely decline when Mona reached over and accepted it. "I would. Thank you. I love these things."

Banks dug out another and offered it to Claire. She shook her head. He grinned and handed her a cold sparkling water instead. That she did take with thanks. They sat together in companionable silence. He was a pleasant man to be around. She'd been so worried about taking this nannying job at first. But these boys . . . these boys were delightful. This situation with the thoughtful and generous Banks and the tender-hearted Tommy really was lovely.

Chapter 12
BANKS

When Claire and her daughter packed up their belongings, Banks jumped to his feet to help take down their umbrella.

"Would you like help to the car?" He looked pointedly at the heavy baby seat. He hadn't forgotten what a pain those were.

Mona looked like she was about to say yes, but Claire said, "No, thank you. We can manage. It's my workout for the day." She slung the diaper bag over her shoulder. "It was nice to see you down here. Thanks for sitting with us."

"Same," Banks said. "Enjoy the rest of your weekend. See you Monday."

She looked down at Tommy. "I'll be at the bus stop after school."

He grinned, showing all his tiny teeth.

"Any requests for an after-school snack?"

"Macaroni and cheese."

Banks sent her an apologetic look, but she chuckled. "All right."

"Thank you for stocking the fridge," Banks said. "That was above and beyond, but I appreciate it. It's hard for me to remember that he expects a meal every three hours."

Claire smiled, full and eclipsing.

He couldn't remember what he was going to say next.

"Nice to meet you," Mona said. Her face was flushed with heat, and that carrier wasn't getting any lighter. She lumbered away toward the parking lot.

"See you later, Banks." Claire followed her daughter.

When Banks turned away and sat down, the beach didn't seem quite so bright. "You about ready to go, buddy?"

"Not yet." Tommy rummaged around the snack bag and pulled out a granola bar.

Banks rested his head on the back of his chair. It wasn't like he should be in a hurry to go home. No one would be there waiting for them. Helen was gone. A wave of darkness flooded through him, burning his eyes and tearing at his heart. The grief took his breath away. It was like that, striking without warning and stinging like hell. He was grateful for his sunglasses. He counted to five, then forced a slow exhale. *It's all right. I'm all right. We're all right.* He put his hand in Tommy's hair just to feel the realness of him. He leaned over and pressed a kiss to his son's forehead and tasted warmth and salt. Life.

His voice was mostly steady when he said, "Should we do a movie night tonight?"

He smiled at Tommy's giddy squeal. Oh to be five and get such a thrill from the simple things. He could take a lesson from Tommy in that.

Smith's shadow fell over Tommy. "What have you got there, Tom Bomb?"

"The blueberry muffins are really good," Banks said. "There's one left."

"Hit me with it."

Tommy dug around the cooler, surely getting sand on everything, and handed his big brother the last muffin. Smith spread out his towel and sat down with his treat.

"So they took off?" Smith asked.

Obviously. "Yeah," Banks said.

"They seem like a nice family." He peeled off the top of the muffin. "It is still crazy to me that Claire is Mona's mother."

"They look like sisters," Banks said.

"Yeah. And that was her grandbaby." Smith coughed out a laugh. "Hilarious."

"I love Ms. Claire," Tommy said.

Smith chuckled, a low sound that rippled his abs. Banks used to look like that. Now his muscles were made of dried-out clay instead of iron. When did he get so old?

"This is good." Smith looked at the plastic wrap for a label. "Where is it from?"

"Claire made them," Banks said.

He nodded as he looked it over. "So, she's a great find. And I might be coming over for dinner more often."

Something about the way he said it sent a chill down Banks's back. He shrugged it away. It was nothing, just his own attraction to Claire making him weird. Maybe it was time for him to start dating again. He had a stack of phone numbers that brazen acquaintances had given him over the last four months.

"She's making me macaroni and cheese on Monday," Tommy said.

Smith mussed Tommy's hair. "Let me know when she makes crab cakes."

"Ew." Tommy stuck out his tongue.

Yes, Banks would set up a date for next week. Hiring Claire and seeing Tommy's reaction to her had made one thing clear: Tommy needed more than Banks could give. Banks wasn't a good single parent. Helen had done it all. She'd raised both his sons. He'd paid for everything and shown up for games and events, when possible, but he hadn't done the real, gritty work of raising the children. Banks couldn't do what Helen had done and what Claire was doing.

Tommy deserved a mother.

Chapter 13
CLAIRE

The next week flew by as Claire's new life shifted into a comfortable rhythm. She and Tommy cooked, played, swam, and went to the park. Tommy pulled Claire out of her shell, and she was smoothing balm on his broken heart. Banks worked late all week, and Claire didn't mind. She enjoyed the Sextons' quiet house in the evenings, watching the sunset and tidying up the games and books. And seeing her paycheck increase.

Friday afternoon found her and Tommy at the kitchen table, painting. She'd picked the activity, hoping it'd be a quiet project and they could sit for a while. She was tired. She needed to increase her child-caring endurance.

Tommy smeared paint over his paper in three dramatic sweeps. "Done."

Claire looked up from where she'd started making pale circles. She'd been thinking how nice it felt to use the brush again. Her fingers had tingled a little, as if maybe some of the creative juices were coming back. Or maybe that was a hopeful illusion. "Done?"

"Yes."

It had taken her ten times as long to set up the jars of water, paint palettes, and drop cloth.

"Let's do another one." She set out a new paper.

He grumbled but dunked his brush in the watercolor tray.

"Try a few more colors this time. Try making different marks, like dots and wiggles and lines."

He did everything she said—and was finished in eleven seconds.

So painting was not his thing. Bummer.

"I messed up right there." He pointed to where a splash had landed on one of his blobs.

She picked up his sheet. "Who said it was a mess up? See how the drop of water is spreading through the paint, changing the color and texture?" They watched the slow magic. "Some people don't like water spots in their paintings. I love them. I think they're interesting and beautiful and uncontrolled. I like to make them on purpose."

His eyes turned wide and eager. "Yeah. And look how the colors are mixing where they touch."

"Blue and yellow make . . ."

"Green." He grinned. "I like green."

"I love green." She set his paper down, and he started dropping water over it with a heavy hand.

She thought back to years ago. It had been a Valentine's Day morning. She'd made tiny love notes for the three girls and Stevie and set them out at breakfast. She was in the middle of making heart-shaped pancakes when Stevie marched in.

"What the hell happened to my sweater?" It was pulled tight around his chest and hung four inches too short in the torso and sleeves.

Claire laughed.

He did not. "I told you not to put it in the dryer."

"I didn't."

"Then why is it shrunken?"

"It's the style now, Daddy," Indi said, trying to lighten the mood. "Go for it."

He ignored her in favor of glaring at Claire. "You ruined my best sweater."

She set a pancake on Edith's plate. "If I did something wrong washing it, then I'm sorry. It was an accident."

He growled and left the room, yelling about her incompetence, yelling about her lack of concern for his maroon sweater, yelling about her wastefulness.

Claire made a smiley face out of blueberries on Edith's pancake.

"Thanks, Mom."

Five minutes later, Stevie came back to the kitchen, kissed their daughters, and told them he loved them. Jaw tight, he ignored Claire as he turned toward the door.

She lifted the valentine she'd made him and held it out. A watercolor heart and a chocolate bar.

He lifted his chin and spoke with scorn. "Do what you want with it."

Claire braced against the slap of rejection.

"Accept your valentine, Dad." Mona's voice was displeased. She was thirteen now and becoming more protective of her mother, more aware of the discordant notes. Claire wished she could protect her daughters from this.

"I don't want it." Stevie walked out.

The girls looked at each other. Claire forced a laugh. "Extra chocolate for the rest of us." Her whole body felt like Stevie had poured acid over it.

She kept it together until she got her girls out the door for school. Then she went into her garage and let the pain rage through. She painted a series that looked like acid-washed skies. With each drop—a mix of water and the salty tears streaming down her face—onto the paper, she'd imagined the pain leaving her and going into her paintings. She'd used watercolor like Stevie's valentine had been. Incorporated the reds and purples of bruised love. As she'd added the corrosive-looking streaks to the pages, it made something intensely beautiful. Beauty for pain. She could only hope the same might be happening to her heart.

"I'm hungry." Tommy's voice snapped her back to reality. His art had turned into a puddle of gray.

"Okay. Let's just get this cleaned back up again, and we can start on making dinner together."

He watched her pack the supplies into the bin she'd brought. She set it by the front door before heading to the kitchen, her mind running through the steps to make fajitas. Tommy was responsible enough to help her toast the tortillas, and he'd do well smashing the avocado.

He put a hand on her thigh. He was always touching her, reaching out, drawing close. She leaned into the tender connection.

"Can you make my mom's chicken and rice?"

Her heart sank. She set the cutting board and knife down and crouched so her face was level with his. She spoke softly. "I don't know how to make it."

"So I'm *never* going to have it again?" His eyes welled with tears. They spilled over in a river of grief. She drew him against her shoulder and brought a hand to his silky head. She didn't say anything while he sobbed. She held him for a long time, her own eyes hot and wet. It had been the same with her daughters after their father died. When the pain would strike, she did her best to just *be* there. They didn't want to cry alone.

She did her best to share Tommy's loss, shoulder it like she did his body.

When he finally pulled back and wiped his nose on his shirt, she said, "Tell me about the chicken and rice. Did you make it with her?"

He nodded. "Sometimes. She'd let me mix the seasonings into the rice."

"That sounds really fun."

"She kept the recipe in her book." He walked over to a cupboard, opened it, and pointed to a binder. Claire tentatively approached. Was this a good idea or not? She took the binder and set it on the counter. She lifted Tommy up to sit next to it. The binder had a photo of the Sexton family in the front plastic. Helen was smiling, her arms around Smith and Banks. Infant Tommy was in Banks's arms. They looked so happy and perfect. Claire opened the binder.

"What does that say?" Tommy pointed to the first page.

It was handwritten. The woman *handwrote* her recipes. WTF. "Baked eggs with feta."

"*Not* that one. Gross." He reached over and grabbed the page.

"Careful. We don't want to rip anything." There were food stains and smudges, but she felt like she was handling an original manuscript from before Gutenberg. She lifted the next page. "Quiche lorraine."

"Not that one."

Claire's lip turned up. Together they went through each page until they came to "Tommy's Chicken Bake."

"Yes." He pumped his fists as if he'd won the lottery. "It's that one."

"She even named it after you."

He beamed. "It's my favorite."

"Well, let's see if we have the ingredients. Chicken breasts. Butter. Cream of mushroom soup." She cringed inwardly. She was not a fan of canned creamed soups. "Rice. Salt and pepper. Dried garlic and parsley." She'd planned to make fajitas, so she had chicken. "Let's check the pantry."

They had all the ingredients.

"So can we make it?" The hope of the world lit up his eyes.

She stepped up close to where he sat on the counter and looked him in the eyes. "Tommy, we can make it. I'll follow your mom's instructions as best I can, but it might not be perfectly the same as your mom did it. She might have had a little bit of magic that I don't have."

His brows creased. "Okay."

She found an apron and tied it on, then pulled out a baking dish. She really hoped this would work out well.

She followed the directions with the precision of a nuclear chemist. Tommy shouted out encouragement. "Yes, just like that . . . no, cut it smaller . . . stir . . . now you wash your hands from the raw germs . . ."

Once the chicken made it to the oven, she took several yoga breaths. Tommy ran around the house while she made sautéed zucchini to go on the side and cut up fresh peaches. She opened the freezer and rummaged around to see if there were any garlic rolls left from the dinner she'd made three nights ago. That's when she found the blueberry muffin intended for Tommy's lunch from her first day here. It wasn't a surprise Banks had forgotten, but she hadn't expected to feel so disappointed about it. Was she upset Tommy didn't get to eat it and he might have felt bad when he opened his half-empty lunch, or was she upset that Banks wasn't better? It was a simple mistake, she told herself. Anyone could have forgotten the muffin on a busy Monday morning.

She warmed the muffin in the microwave and cut it in two. Tommy helped her set the table by getting two forks. She did it up nice; it seemed appropriate to go with Helen's recipe. She even found a couple of squat candles. Her hand over Tommy's, they lit them together. Once everything was on the table, they stood back and looked in appreciation at the candlelit table set for two.

"I think we did very well," she said.

"Can we eat now?"

"Of course."

He buzzed forward at the same time she heard the garage door open. He changed direction on a dime and tore toward the entry. He reappeared in his father's arms.

"Hello, Claire."

"Nice to see you, Banks." And he did look striking in his business suit. Trim waist and square shoulders. Bright-blue eyes and shining silver hair. The clincher, though, was the boy wrapped around his neck.

Tommy adored his dad, which made her feel adoration for him too. Apparently, Claire was a sucker for a loving father.

Banks looked at the dining table, eyes bright with appreciation and possibly a hint of longing. "I see I'm interrupting."

"Come eat with us," Tommy said. "Ms. Claire made Mom's chicken and rice."

"Did she?" His gaze tracked to her.

She hoped she wasn't overstepping. "I did try. I'm sure it's not as good as the real thing."

"That was very nice of you." Banks's voice was genuine. "I didn't dare attempt it." His gaze dropped to her apron, and he got a funny look on his face.

Claire glanced down. The words across her chest read **Kiss the Cook**.

His focus lingered on her lips, and she imagined whenever Helen wore this apron, Banks enjoyed following the instruction. Quickly she untied the apron, slipped it off, and crumpled it in a heap on the counter. He'd probably bought it for his wife as a charming little gift. Adorable. But Claire was not Helen.

And Stevie was no Banks. On the Valentine's Day before his death, Claire had made an extra effort to have a positive night together. She'd bought him the fancy sausage he loved and a new shirt for work. He'd come home only half drunk. How considerate. After he'd eaten the lobster sandwich she'd made him for dinner, he'd stood and held out a hand. "Come over here for your gift." She'd approached with a spark of hope. Until he'd said, "It's going to be the best fuck of your life."

If only that had been true.

As the memory slid through her thoughts, she invited it to pass all the way out. *I see you, I learned from you, and now I let you go.* That's what her therapist had taught her to do when a painful memory surfaced. She'd spent money on a therapist for a couple of months after Stevie's death. Then life had gotten busy—that was the excuse she'd used for ending treatment. In truth, it had been overwhelming and scary and excruciating. She hadn't had the strength to work completely through her trauma. She wondered why now it felt not only freeing but pleasurable to use the healing tools she'd ignored for so long. She looked at the beautiful Sexton boys, wondering if it was their loving energy that was the difference.

She smiled at Banks. He would never know the effect his compassionate character was having on her, but she was grateful.

His gaze narrowed on her mouth.

"Come on, Dad." Tommy tugged his tie.

Banks jerked his attention away from Claire and put Tommy down. "I wish I could." And as he looked over the meal, and the candles, and their faces, he looked like he meant it. "But I can't tonight, son. I have a meeting."

He had a date, Claire knew. He'd texted her earlier asking if she'd stay while he went out.

"You two eat. I'm going to change."

Claire motioned Tommy over, and they sat at the table while Banks strode out of the room. But she was conscious that he was *here*. She wasn't as comfortable as she'd been just five minutes before. Tentatively she helped Tommy cut his chicken—by doing it entirely for him.

She held her breath while he took his first bite. He chewed. He swallowed. He looked up at her. "It's the same! You must have magic too."

Be still her beating heart. Her hand rose to her chest as she melted.

She put some peaches and zucchini on her plate but was too anxious to eat, preoccupied with watching the happy child shovel in food and wondering when Banks was suddenly going to appear again.

Tommy was on his second helping when Banks strode into the kitchen, hair wet and combed and face freshly shaven. No more beard. He'd unearthed a handsome face, high cheekbones and smooth skin.

He wore black chinos and a collared shirt. He looked very nice. Almost tempting. His date was a lucky woman.

"Have fun tonight," Claire said.

He got a rueful grin that was very cute on him. "Wish me luck."

"I don't think you'll need it."

She was just trying to be polite, but his face changed when the compliment registered. Maybe she shouldn't have said it?

He kissed Tommy's head. "Good night. I'll see you in the morning." He looked to her. "I have no idea how long I'll be. Probably not very long." He did that awkward chuckle she'd come to recognize as nerves. She felt for him. Dates were tough. First dates as a widow or widower . . . brutal. She didn't have the courage to try again, but good for him. He was getting out there.

She gave him an encouraging smile. "Whenever will be fine." As long as he didn't bring his date home.

Now why had she thought that? Was it because she felt she was the woman of this house now? The fridge was organized per her whims. The key was in her purse. Or did she feel territorial of Banks too? She wasn't okay with either option.

Chapter 14
BANKS

Barbara was a short, blonde woman with kind eyes and puffy hair. She exited her house while he was still walking up the path to her door. Was that weird? Did she not want him to see inside, or was she that eager?

He stopped in front of her. His first reaction was to hold out a hand. His date didn't stop; she strode straight into his chest, her arms going around his back. He got a whiff of perfume. It was an okay scent, but too floral to be sensual. She felt good, soft and warm, but he was very aware she was not Helen. Not his wife. Not her familiar frame, the body he knew as well as his own. Helen had narrow ribs, round shoulders, a short waist that had made her pregnant belly stick out nearly as far as she was tall. She'd had narrow wrists, tight little biceps, and strong legs. Small soft breasts and the most perfect handful of ass. He missed his wife so much in that moment it took his breath clean out of his lungs.

Barbara, a complete stranger, sent him a toothy smile. "Banks. It's so nice to meet you."

He didn't want to be here anymore. He wanted to be home with Helen. He swallowed the desire to scream and cry and said with a smile, "Thanks for hanging out with me tonight." He turned and motioned her toward his car. He opened the door for her, wondering if that was old fashioned or antifeminist. But she seemed to like it. He walked slowly around to his side. Deep breaths. In, out. In, out. *This sucks, Helen.*

He'd gotten Barbara's number from a partner at the firm. She was forty-seven and divorced. He wondered why it hadn't worked out. Did she give up on her marriage? Even the greatest loves took work and commitment. And loads of forgiveness. Claire was a widow, not divorced, which was better because she didn't have a failed marriage on her track record. He stopped by the back wheel, ashamed of his judgment. That wasn't fair.

Give Barbara a chance. Give her a chance.

He slid into his seat and turned on the purring engine. "Have you lived in Laguna long?"

"I grew up in Nashville, but I've been here twenty-four years."

He could hear it now, the tiniest southern accent. It was cute. They made small talk until he pulled up to Mastro's Ocean Club.

"Is this okay?"

She pulled a face that he thought was supposed to be coy, but a simple smile would have served her better. Man, he was being a dick. "Looks divine."

"They do have a good steak." He got out of the car.

She walked very close to his side as they went in. Did she want him to put his arm around her? He didn't, instead feeling awkward and uncharming. "Banks Sexton for two."

The host led them to a table with a view across PCH and over the ocean. Banks sat with his back to the west so Barbara could watch the sunset.

"This is beautiful." She fluttered her lashes in the direction of the living mural. "I never get sick of seeing that ocean. My sister keeps at me to move back to Nashville, but how could I leave this?" Golden sunlight gilded her brown eyes in warmth.

Banks softened toward her. *Give her a chance.* She was cute and seemed genuinely kind. A happy person. He could use more of those around. "I know what you mean. The ocean gets in your blood, hooks you."

The server approached and told them about the Maine lobster and the Wagyu specials and then gave them a minute.

"What looks good?" Banks asked.

"I'm a vegetarian but allow myself one cheat meal a month, so I'll get the filet."

He stared, not sure if he should chuckle. "Okay, but they also have vegetarian options on the menu that are good, too, if you'd prefer that."

"I don't want to make a thing of it. People can be weird about it. And I'm not."

Seemed she was the one being a bit odd. He couldn't care less what she ordered, but if she hadn't eaten any meat since last month, he hoped she wasn't going to have gastric issues later.

The server returned, and Barbara ordered the eight-ounce filet.

He suddenly found he didn't have much of an appetite. What sounded really good right now was Helen's chicken and rice. And those peaches Claire had cut into perfect slices would go down easy right now. He ordered a salad and a sushi roll. And a bottle of wine.

"Do you have children?" Banks asked when it was just the two of them, staring at each other. So awkward.

"I have a son." She scrunched her face into a huge smile. "He's twenty, studying business at Berkeley."

"Good for him."

"It's just me at home now. Except Migzey, who keeps me sane."

"Who's Migzey?" He wasn't sure he wanted to know. It was too much work. It would be impossible to get to know someone else as well as he knew Helen. Overwhelming. He tugged at his collar, but the strangling tightness remained.

She pulled out her phone and showed him a picture. The photo was of her holding a cat. She was wearing a tiny camisole. Did she realize how much boob was showing in this? Of course she did. How could she not? They were her best asset. So, lead with it. And it was sort of working. He was a bit turned on. Oh, right. The cat. He didn't like cats.

"How old is Migzey?"

"He's two. My son got him for me when he moved out so I wouldn't be alone."

"How sweet."

"Yes. He's such a wonderful man."

Did she say that with a weird tone? Was Banks overanalyzing everything? He was, but he didn't know how to stop. He automatically compared her to Helen, and she didn't come close. It wasn't her fault.

He'd met Helen in Central Park. It had been a meet-cute for the movies. The sleet had hit suddenly, leaving people rushing for cover. He'd welcomed the weather. It echoed his mood—stressed from work and worried that Smith would pass his cold along to Nana. A woman had slid on the ice and fallen directly at his feet. A gift. With her blonde hair and bright eyes, she'd been the sun breaking through the storm. He'd helped her to her feet, teased her about the lack of traction on her fashionable boots, and taken her for Irish coffees to warm up.

Barbara swiped to more photos, leaning over so he could see the phone better, but then his gaze slipped past the screen to the breasts she'd set on the dinner table. He missed sex.

"Handsome." He couldn't have even told her what color her son's hair was.

She smiled at the compliment. He supposed he could see how she rationalized taking the credit for her son's good looks.

"And you have two sons?"

"Yes." He didn't want to talk about them. It felt like too much work. He sipped his wine, feeling discouraged. Sipped it again. "So what do you like to do with your free time?"

"I love to embroider."

"What's that?"

"Needlework." She pointed to a row of tiny flowers on the edge of her low-cut top. "I stitched these on."

"Wow. Very impressive." Okay. That was kind of pretty and unique.

The server brought their meal, and Banks gratefully turned his attention to his salad. Dating was a lot of work. And he'd had business meetings for hours today. He was old and tired. And he wanted to go home and curl up with Helen in his bed. His eyes watered.

"Oh, this steak is amazing," Barbara said with a slight moan. "This is what I've been missing in my life." She looked at him with a hint of seduction in her eyes.

"How long have you been vegetarian?" He stabbed a piece of tomato. "Not including your cheat meals, of course." There was a touch of mocking in his tone. He knew his sadness wasn't an excuse for him to be such a bastard to this perfectly nice lady—who was not Helen.

"Ten years."

"Good for you."

"Can I try your sushi?"

He put the plate in the middle of the table. "Help yourself."

She ate about half of it. Which was fine. Except now he was still hungry. He couldn't drink another glass of wine because he was driving. Damn it. She finished the bottle too.

"Can I interest you in dessert?" The server held out two small menus.

Banks didn't want dessert. He wanted chicken and rice with Tommy. And Claire.

"Yes, please." Barbara accepted it. "Everything has been amazing."

He looked over the menu. The butter cake here was good. Everything, really, except the key lime pie; it was way too tart.

Barbara made another little moan of pleasure. "Oh, I love key lime pie. Will you share it with me?"

"Of course."

He ordered a coffee. Full strength. He ate the smallest, slowest bites of pie he thought he could get away with. Barbara didn't seem to notice. She closed her eyes every time she took a bite herself.

He imagined kissing those puckered lips. As needy and alone as he was, he wasn't all that excited about the prospect. Was this his new life now, judging everyone by how they compared to Helen and finding them all lacking? He hoped the sarcastic, critical voice in his head wasn't here to stay.

He paid the bill and stood.

"Thank you for dinner," she said.

With the coffee perking him up and the evening breeze a welcome cool, he gave her a genuine smile. "I had fun."

She beamed. He checked out her round butt as she walked out in front of him. He sighed. She wasn't Helen. She wasn't Claire, but she wasn't unattractive. They were quiet on the drive back to her house. She seemed nervous. He definitely was. What now? He pulled up to her curb. She reached over and put a hand on his thigh. He jolted at the touch. Maybe there was more chemistry here than he'd thought. Or maybe he was that pent up.

"Do you want to come in?"

Just like that? Did he want to come in? Did he want to go have sex with this strange woman? What about birth control? He felt like a teenager, except even dumber. Maybe he could go in. Feel it out a little. Talk. No, he didn't want to do any more talking. Dinner had been long enough.

She lifted her fingers off him when he didn't answer right away. "You could meet Migzey."

That settled it. Hell no to the cat.

"I'm sorry," he said. "I have to get home to my son. I'm still dealing with babysitters." He gave her a grimace, but inside he could not have been more grateful for Tommy and Claire right now. His get-out-of-dates-free card. When disappointment flashed over her face, he said, "I'll walk you up."

They both got out. Slower than a funeral march, they walked side by side. He stopped before the bottom step leading to her door.

"Thanks for taking a chance on me tonight," Banks said.

She turned and gave him a hug. She pulled back but kept her arms around his neck. Her face was inches from his. He could smell the wine and lime on her breath. She pressed her lips to his. He froze at first. Then relaxed into it. His hands shifted to her lower back. Her soft boobs smooshed against his chest. He deepened the kiss. Habit, and also, it was fun. *I'm so sorry, Helen.*

She finally pulled back, her eyes dark. "Are you going to call me again?"

He swallowed. That was frank. He thought of the rest of the women's numbers he had. A whole list of potential. Barbara wasn't the one for him. He thought of Claire. Stop thinking about Claire. "I had fun tonight. And you're a wonderful woman, Claire."

"Claire?" She stepped back, brows tight, eyes blazing.

Heat roared to his face. "I'm so sorry, Barbara. I'm terrible with names."

She softened, looking ready to forgive him. He didn't really want that either. He was a mess.

"I think I'd better go before I make more of an ass of myself. Thanks again." Without waiting for her reply, he turned and strode to his car. She was still standing at her doorstep when he got to his door. He waved, a stupid little wiggle of his fingers. He hated himself for it. He got in the car and drove away.

As he drove, he thought over the date. Replayed the conversation. The kiss. He got hard thinking about it. Maybe he should have slept with her. It had been over four months now. But that would not have been fair to her. There was zero future with that relationship. And he wasn't really a one-night-stand kind of guy. Maybe he could be? He blew out a breath so hard he did a raspberry with his lips. He did it again because it felt good, kind of shook off the kiss.

When he pulled into his garage, he felt suddenly guilty, like Helen would be in there and he'd have to go confess. In all his late nights at the office and work trips, he'd never come close to cheating on Helen. She was his queen. Sometimes he'd felt like her king. Other times her knight. And even at times her court jester. But when he returned home to his castle, it wasn't Helen's face that greeted him. It was Claire's. And he wanted to apologize to her too.

She sat in his high-back chair facing the ocean. She closed her book, took off her brown-rimmed glasses, and swiveled to face him. The lamplight accented her high cheekbones and straight nose. Damn she was beautiful. And he was still horny.

She checked her phone, and he saw the time light up: 9:02. "You're back before I expected." She sent him a rueful grin. "Not great?"

He dropped onto his couch with a chuckle. "She has a cat named Migzey and is a vegetarian who ordered steak."

Claire laughed out loud.

It was a magical sound. So bold and deep. He wanted to make her do it again. Wanted to listen to it forever.

"How exotic." Her eyes twinkled.

"She was perfectly nice. Nice personality, nice looking. And I was not interested. It wasn't her fault, and I feel bad about it." He shook his head. "Is dating always this hard?"

She shrugged. "I don't know."

"What do you mean? You've been at this for what? It's been five years since Stevie passed?"

"I don't date." She said it like a prison sentence.

He went cold all over. "Ever?"

"Ever."

The word dropped like a punch to the groin.

"I'm a committed spinster."

He leaned forward. "Why?" She must have men lining up to take her out. He wanted to take her out. He could no longer deny it.

She opened her mouth, hesitated, closed it. Studied him.

He tried to relax under the scrutiny. Could she tell that he wished he'd been with her tonight instead? Could she tell he was already getting used to coming home to her face every evening? He wanted to lead her to his bedroom right now. *Sorry again, Helen.* He leaned back and cleared his throat. His voice came out in his professional tone. "Excuse me. That's none of my business. Thank you for staying late on your Friday night."

Her face softened. "Give yourself time. I think one of the weaknesses in our culture is we try to rush grief. We expect people to bounce back way too fast. Let yourself feel the sorrow move through you, change you, heal you. You'll know when there's space again for love to take root. You're still in the cleansing-fire part of the story."

Banks blinked at her. She spoke truth. She spoke from experience. "You are incredibly wise, Claire."

She gave him a sad smile. "I'm not. I've just been where you are. Maybe not exactly, since things were different between me and Stevie than the lovely marriage you clearly had with Helen, but grief is universal. Everyone gets a turn with it."

Stevie had hurt her; Banks could tell. The realization made him spike with anger and a desire to protect her. He wanted to make it better.

"I spent too many years fighting against feeling any of the pain." She fiddled with her readers. "I shoved it all away, determined that would make it disappear. Obviously, that doesn't work." She shrugged with a self-deprecating chuckle.

He leaned forward, chest tight with empathy. "Claire—"

She held up a forestalling hand. "I'm not telling you all of this for sympathy, but to say that now, for some reason, it seems that I'm finally surrendering—er, maybe it's more like I'm accepting the experiences of my past instead of denying I was hurt—and I'm feeling healthier and happier than I have in years. You might as well learn from my mistakes." She put a hand on her chest. "I'm sorry if I'm being too personal."

"No, not at all."

"I just want you to know that your family has taught me a lot by your kindness, and I wanted to say I'm grateful." She looked out the windows as if shy of her confession.

Banks held his breath, not knowing what to say and wishing Helen were here. She would know how to help Claire, who was so obviously being brave in her honesty, who was carrying a lot more than she let on. Why did it all have to be so hard?

"I thought after all these years, I would have healed automatically. Time would be the cure. Space definitely helped, but I was avoiding tending to my grief. Now, I can feel the shift toward healing happening much faster." She sighed. She looked as tired as he felt. "I know that part of it is that my youngest daughter moved out, leaving me alone, with little choice but to look inside myself, but I also know that a big part of it is your family being so welcoming."

Banks's heart swelled. Her words were like healing balm over his anxieties. He'd been so worried that without Helen he was failing entirely, but Claire made him feel useful. He sparked with hope. *We did something good, Helen.* He felt the memory of his wife wrap his chest with the warmth of approval. Heat built behind his eyes.

Claire stood.

He didn't want her to go. Her presence was comfortable and pleasurable and interesting. This bit of connection she'd forged tonight felt like she'd thrown him a lifeline. He didn't want to be left alone.

"Someday you'll find another great woman, Banks. And when you find her, she'll be lucky to have you."

The words were meant to be kind, but coming from her, they felt like cold rejection. "Thanks."

Claire left, and Banks told himself he was glad he wouldn't see her until Monday. He needed a little break, some space between her and his rising interest. And resentment. She had certainly implied that she thought he was great, but she didn't want him.

After all his bravado, when Monday evening came, he couldn't help being eager to see her again. Unfortunately it wasn't only Claire and Tommy who greeted him as he strode into his kitchen after work.

His in-laws were here.

Tommy sat next to his grandfather, playing with a new puzzle they must have brought him. Claire sat in a chair across from the coffee table, looking uncomfortable. Helen's mother stood up from the couch when she saw Banks. She checked her watch.

He gritted his teeth against what would come next.

"It's nearly seven. Quite a late night at the office. You missed dinner." Jan reached out for a hug, and he forced his arms around her soft torso.

"I didn't know you were coming down." He was unable to completely hide the irritation in his voice. No text or call?

"Well, dear, we were already down this way and couldn't leave without stopping by."

"What brought you down here?" he asked. They lived north of LA. It was a two-hour drive . . . without traffic.

Neil, Helen's father, stood and strode over, holding his hand out. "You look well."

"Thank you," Banks muttered.

"Much better than when we saw you six weeks ago," Jan said.

The two in-laws were gathered around him like carrion birds over a carcass. He couldn't breathe.

"This must be Claire's doing," Jan said, motioning toward the woman now tidying books on the coffee table. Banks did not like the look in Jan's all-seeing eyes, even if she was right and Claire had worked magic on him.

He could only pray they hadn't been picking her apart. "I see you met Tommy's *nanny*."

"She's wonderful," Neil said. "She's not Helen, but I'm glad you've gotten some help."

Of course, she wasn't Helen. Helen was dead. *Thanks for the reminder.*

"You were really struggling on your own," Jan said.

True. But, rude. Banks didn't need to be told point blank he didn't make a great solo parent. He'd learned it the hard way. Twice. When Smith was born, and now this.

Claire stood and walked around the couch. "Welcome home, Banks. If you don't need anything else tonight, I'll head home."

"Of course. I'll walk you out."

With epically long strides, she beelined toward the door.

"I'll be right back," he said to his in-laws.

Jan nodded knowingly.

She didn't know anything. Banks scowled at her before he followed Claire. Outside, he closed the door on prying ears and touched Claire's elbow, stopping her on the step. "I'm so sorry. I didn't know they were coming."

"It's fine. They were nice."

"Really? They didn't ask you a lot of personal questions?"

"They did."

His belly clenched. "I'm sorry. How long have they been here?"

"About two hours."

He leaned back in dismay. His in-laws had obviously stopped by to wait for the traffic to die down. No sane person would drive through LA at 5:00 p.m. if they could avoid it.

"They told me I could go, but I didn't want to leave Tommy with anyone else without getting your okay first. And it was fine, really."

Banks exhaled. She was amazing. "Thank you, Claire." The words didn't feel like enough.

Smith pulled up and parked at the curb. He strode over, his face grim. "Gramps and Gran are here?"

Claire chuckled at Smith's serious tone, and he gave her a small smile.

"They let you know before me," Banks said.

"I got a call twenty minutes ago demanding I come say hello."

"How delightful." Banks frowned.

"I see you're fleeing the scene," Smith said to Claire.

"I already did my time." She matched their locker-room tone.

He cringed. "You brave girl."

"They are perfectly nice people." Her chuckle undermined the words.

Smith tilted his chin. "You must not be talking about *the* Neil and Jan Shellburg, founders of the stare, champions of the guilt trip, experts at the passive aggressive . . ."

She pulled a face that made her look spirited and very young. Good thing she was focused on Smith, because Banks couldn't stop ogling the vibrant woman.

"Get in there and play the doting grandson." Her voice was teasing.

Smith doffed an invisible cap, and with a wink, he dashed inside.

Banks rolled out his neck and followed his son into battle. Moments later, they were all sitting on the couch, staring at each other in silence.

"Smith, you're not married yet?"

"No, Gran. I broke up with the last runner-up, so it'll be a while. I'm taking a bit of a mental health break from dating."

Jan frowned, and Banks had to bite back his smile. That kid knew how to needle her.

She turned to her son-in-law. "Are you dating?"

Banks shook his head and looked pointedly at Tommy, who'd lifted his gaze from his puzzle to focus on the conversation. Kids only listen when you don't want them to.

Jan's lips turned so far down, the corners disappeared into her wrinkles. "He needs an m-o-t-h-e-r."

Banks swallowed back his rising temper. He was a fifty-year-old man, responsible and successful. He should not feel like he was twenty again and first meeting the Shellburgs, desperate to make a good impression. "We are doing just fine. Better than fine. And we have help now."

"Yes," Jan said. "About *her*."

"Put a ring on it," Neil said, making the motion of sliding a wedding band on.

"It?" Smith's voice was a sudden pop of incredulity.

Jan and Neil ignored him, turning to Banks.

"You need to catch her and keep her," Jan said.

Banks hated, *hated*, that he might agree with Jan on this. "Before you get your minds set on this unauthorized setup, you should know that she's committed to never date or remarry. She is off the table."

Smith's eyes turned intense. "Are you serious?"

Banks nodded. "Not that it's our business, but I get the impression her husband wasn't a nice man."

Emotion darkened Smith's face. Banks wanted to ask what he was thinking.

"She did seem flighty," Neil said.

Smith's nostrils flared.

He hadn't expected it from Smith, but he appreciated that he wasn't the only one incensed on Claire's behalf. "Why are you so eager for me to move on from Helen?" Banks asked.

"Obviously you'll never find anyone equal to our daughter." Jan puffed with pride. "But you need a woman, Banks. You're not suited to bachelorhood." She looked at Tommy. "Or single parenthood."

His temper spiked white hot, but since he didn't know how to argue that, he said, "I don't appreciate you coming here without telling me and hounding my employee with personal questions."

"Watch your tone," Neil said.

Banks chewed his tongue. Smith's lips thinned to a hard line.

Silence pulsed. One beat. Two.

Jan bobbled her head. "So, are you going to ask me how my hip is doing?"

"How's your hip?" Banks's tone was flat.

"It hurts."

"I'm sorry to hear that," he said.

"Thank you, dear."

Chapter 15
SMITH

Smith said goodbye to his clients and walked to his car. He couldn't stop smiling. This deal was the best one he'd brokered this year, and it had closed this morning. Money was in hand.

Back at the office, he floated through paperwork and emails. He was still beaming when he left work and drove south to Emerald Bay. He was having dinner with Dad and Tommy tonight to celebrate his big commission. As he pulled up to the house, he took off his tie and unbuttoned his collar. He let himself in through the front door with his key.

"Hey-o. Tom? Pops?"

No answer. He tracked through the kitchen and noticed the side door was ajar. The pool water rippled outside. Were they seriously swimming? It was only five thirty, but Smith was hungry. He was hoping they'd leave ASAP for dinner. He stepped outside and stopped as Claire emerged from the pool like a sea siren, her eyes closed and her dark hair slicked back with water.

"Marco," she said.

Tommy, sitting on the stairs, looked at Smith and held a finger to his lips. "Polo," he whispered.

Eyes still closed, Claire smiled, her white teeth shining in the sunlight. Her collarbones glistened as she rose higher, revealing a low-neck blue one-piece. Rivulets coursed over her breasts as she stood.

Smith stared.

These last weeks when thoughts of Claire had invaded his peace, he'd reminded himself that she was too old for him. But with her fresh face and energetic tone, the age gap seemed to fold up and disappear entirely.

Claire waded toward Tommy. "Marco."

He giggled and dived.

She opened her eyes and looked at the now-empty stairs. Her gaze tracked the little boy's movement through the water. Then she looked up and saw Smith. She did a double take.

"You're cheating." Smith grinned.

She laughed, her face like sunshine. "And I still can't win." She turned toward Tommy, who'd popped up behind her. She reached for him, and he latched on.

Smith couldn't fail to notice that Tommy's arm pressed across Claire's chest, his legs tight around her waist. Punk. And Smith was the idiot jealous of a five-year-old. But a koala-bear hug wasn't exactly the embrace he wanted to be sharing with her. Instead of getting over his crush, he found his interest was rising. She was calm, steady, responsible, genuine. Traits that he found more attractive even than her almond eyes.

"Look who's here," she said to Tommy.

And Claire was off limits. Irritation flared. "What are *you* doing here?" Smith's voice came out cold.

Her head snapped toward him, and she blinked at his tone. "Um."

"My dad said that he was getting Tommy today." Smith had talked to him just hours ago. Dad had said he was surprising Tommy at the bus. They were all going to dinner. Just the boys. Claire was *not* supposed to be here. And certainly not in that damn swimsuit, with wet hair and bright energy.

Dismay darkened her face. She held Tommy a little tighter. "He called me to come over an hour ago. He said there was a last-minute emergency at the office, and he needed to go in. I'm sorry." She looked like she wished she could teleport herself away from him, melt into the water, and hide from his meanness.

Smith deflated into regret. "No, I'm sorry." His voice was heavy. He didn't ever want to cause her pain. "I was rude and totally in the wrong." He sighed, embarrassed and annoyed with himself, disturbed by how much he wanted to kiss her all better. Yikes. "We had dinner plans, and I guess I'm upset he didn't tell me the change of plans. You are very sweet . . . er . . . accommodating to come last minute."

Her face brightened like a bud suddenly blooming. She waded closer and stopped at the edge of the pool. He crouched so he wasn't looking directly down her swimsuit. "I'm sure it was an honest mistake. But that's frustrating. I'm sorry."

As he fell headlong into her warm hazel eyes, all his irritation dissolved to nothing. Actually, it seemed kinda lucky for him that he got to hang with Claire. She was a lot more fun to look at than Dad. And a good listener. She looked at him like she cared. Like he was important. Danger.

"I know it's not dinner with your dad, but Tommy and I just ordered pizza. Do you want to stay and eat with us?"

Yes. Yes, he *really* did. "I don't want to intrude."

"It's just me and Tommy." She said it as if obviously there was nothing to intrude on here.

"Come swimming," Tommy said. "Claire's still Marco."

"Doesn't look like that's going to change anytime soon." He sent a twisted half grin at Tommy. "I'll go get my suit."

Tommy dived underwater.

Smith hesitated. "Thanks for being so nice to us."

Her eyes seemed to expand, deep as the sky. Her lips parted. A drop of water ran the length of her fine jaw.

He stood abruptly and strode to the house. He felt her gaze burning his back the whole way.

Back inside the safety of the house, he snagged a banana. He ate it as he went downstairs to his old room and changed into a blue plaid swimsuit. Was it really creepy to go swimming with his little brother and the babysitter? It's not like she was a teenager. Was a grandma worse? Whatever. She'd invited him, and he wanted to. There was no talking himself out of this bad idea.

Upstairs and back outside, to keep from looking at Claire, he scanned the ocean. The view really was spectacular. And that did include Claire. She was sitting on the steps, throwing toys into the shallow end for Tommy to retrieve.

Smith did a cannonball as close to her as he dared without hitting his butt on the bottom of the pool. She was wiping her face when he came up. He grinned. She splashed him. He swam over to Tommy and picked him up. Tommy giggled and hugged his neck tight.

"Did you have a good day?" Smith asked.

"Regular. Which means great."

"Well, that's a lesson for the ages."

Tommy squinted. "Whatever that means."

"It means I want to be just like you when I grow up." Smith tousled his little brother's wet hair. "Nothing can keep you down, big man."

Teeth tight, Tommy flexed his skinny arms. He looked like he might hurt himself with the effort.

Claire chuckled.

Tommy sent her a betrayed glare.

"You're very strong," she said.

"As strong as Smith?"

She glanced at Smith's bare shoulders and chest, and he suddenly felt feverish. She looked away. "If you keep eating your spinach, I think you will be one day."

Tommy pursed his lips, unsatisfied for one second before he brightened again and looked up at the queen. "Can we finish our game now? You're still it."

She seemed to flush a bit when she looked at Smith. "You don't have to play."

"How could I not?"

Her cheeks were definitely pink when she turned around. Adorable. "Okay. Ready, go. Marco."

Tommy dived under the water so he didn't have to answer. Smith said, "Polo." He backed up.

She giggled like a schoolgirl as she turned. She slowly reached, but he'd moved. "Marco."

Tommy came up spluttering, and she veered in his direction. She caught him easily. Then Smith let Tommy catch him. When it was Smith's turn, he pointedly only went after Tommy. He couldn't grab at Claire. And what kind of pervy game was this? Groping at barely dressed people with your eyes closed?

After Tommy, it was Claire's turn again. She walked across the middle of the pool, her arms out. "Marco."

"Polo." Smith whispered it from three feet in front of her. Tommy yelled it from across the pool.

She hesitated. Smith was so close. And she knew it.

"Marco?" Her brows creased in question.

He was happy to have the answer. "Polo." He hadn't moved. He didn't want to move. He wanted to see whether she'd be bold and take the next step. He was so used to seeing women with tons of makeup that her natural face felt intimate. Like he was seeing a part of her naked. She looked so young and vulnerable. It was a *very* attractive look.

She was relaxed, unassuming, easy to be with.

She stepped forward. Both her hands landed on his chest. Her eyes flew open. The pupils dilated. His nipples went hard under her touch. A spark crackled through the connection as they stared at each other for a pulse.

Whoa.

She jolted and lifted her fingers as if burned. She tried for a smile and failed. Her bottom lip curled between her teeth. For a flash she looked almost scared. His hand lifted to an awkward hover at her side, not touching, but wanting to help, as if he could protect her from her invisible demons.

She whirled toward Tommy. "Let's play a new game. Actually it's probably time for dinner to get here. Let's get out."

"Hot tub first." Tommy's voice was high with a tinge of whine. "Please."

"Just a quick warm-up." Claire's hips swayed as she marched up the stairs. One side of her swimsuit had ridden up, revealing an extra two inches of her right butt cheek.

Smith buried his face in the water. He stayed under until he was burning for air instead of something else. He blew bubbles as if he could exhale his unwelcome crush. That's all it was. Inconvenient, but not a big deal. It wasn't even a good lie. He might have been crushing on her the first day they met, but not anymore. Now he was noticing her humor and kindness, and he was deeply enjoying her pleasant company.

He stalked over to the hot tub and climbed in. Tommy came over and sat on his knee.

"What'd you learn today in school."

"Nothing."

"Nothing? I think I'd better talk to this teacher of yours."

"Stop it," Tommy said.

"You're not supposed to learn nothing in school."

Claire chuckled from across the square spa. "You told me you learned about things that float and things that don't."

"Well, that's learning something." Smith lifted Tommy off his thigh. "Let's see if you float."

Tommy lay on his back. And sank.

Smith pulled his brother back up. "I would say that's a no."

He giggled. "My teacher has a rock that floats because it has air bubbles in it."

"That's cool." Smith gave him a fist bump.

"I'll get my pool toys. They sink." He scrambled out of the hot tub.

And then it was just Claire and Smith. Together, nearly naked in hot water. She looked at him with a boldness that all but paralyzed him. "He's lucky to have a brother like you."

Her kindness struck deep. "He's lucky to have you." He said it with a touch too much sincerity. But she was a godsend. She'd been here less than a month, but Smith couldn't imagine what Dad and Tommy would do without her. He only hoped Dad wasn't going to take the Shellburgs' advice and try anything funny with Claire. "I don't know what my dad had to sacrifice to what gods to get such a tenderhearted, patient, steady woman to save us."

"You give me too much credit." She dipped her head modestly, but he could tell his words had touched her.

He wondered about his dad's declaration that she would never date again. He wondered if she'd been lonely much. Her quiet wisdom made him think maybe she had. "Has working here been going okay for you?"

Her eyes sparkled. "Yes. It's been really great. I was nervous, at first. I'm not trained to nanny or anything."

"I think raising three kids makes you a little overqualified."

Her smile turned grateful, and it hit something in his belly. "Tommy is a sweetheart. I'm just glad he likes me."

"Of course he does. Who wouldn't?" Smith turned to watch the little boy diving for rubber fish. Had he said too much? She put him at ease in a way that loosened his tongue. "It was good of you to come in last minute today. Obviously, this wasn't what you expected to be doing with your Friday night." He wondered what she would have been doing. What was her life outside his family? Disconcerting how much he wanted to know. Everything. He wanted to know everything.

She smiled at Tommy and then out at the sunset. "Nothing I would have been doing could beat this."

She was more beautiful than the multimillion-dollar view.

And then she looked at him, and her gaze struck like an arrow.

He wanted to be part of her statement. Did she know what her welcoming eyes did to him? She didn't look away. She didn't play games or act coy. She was real and vibrant.

"I hope you didn't have to cancel on a boyfriend or something." Yes, he was obviously fishing, but he wanted to know.

She looked down at the water. "No."

He was disappointed when she didn't elaborate, but then she looked up at him and let out a self-deprecating chuckle. "I've only been on one date since Stevie died. It was a disaster, and I haven't tried again."

His jaw dropped.

"I know. It's weird . . ." Her voice faded away.

He leaned closer, not sure how to ask for more. "May I ask why?"

She held his gaze, then squinted out at the ocean view. She looked to Tommy, who was still happily diving for toys. She exhaled. "Yeah. I guess the truth is. Which I can't believe I'm going to admit this. But. I guess the truth is, I haven't given love a chance, because I've been too afraid." She speared him with her hazel stare. "It didn't end well the first time around. I've been happy on my own for years. I took care of my daughters. I took care of myself. Being alone was better than being hurt."

Smith's body went still against the desire to wrap her up in his arms. His voice came out low. "He hurt you?"

She twitched. "Not physically like you're thinking. He didn't hit me. Sorry. I didn't mean to get so personal. I just. You are so . . . I. Sorry."

"You can get as personal as you want. It's nice. Makes me feel less alone in my own problems." They sat in silence for a moment. "How about I tell you a deep truth and then you can have another turn if you feel like sharing?"

She raised an inviting eyebrow.

"My birth mother didn't want me."

Claire's hand slipped into his, and she held his fingers under the water. He barely knew her, but he felt a powerful desire to draw her close.

"My dad had made an agreement with her that if she would give birth, he'd take the baby and never contact her. But when I was in college, I wanted to find her. I just needed to know. To see. I snooped through my dad's files until I found her name." His voice wavered. "Angelica Robertsville. I tracked her down at a law firm in Denver. I flew out and stalked her for an entire day. I could tell that she was the correct woman. I could see shadows of my features in her face, in her green eyes and straight nose, but she was just a regular lady. She wasn't my mother. I didn't feel hatred or desire. I didn't try to speak to her. I just left."

Claire's face was soft with compassion. "Her loss, Smith."

He smiled and forced himself to let go of her hand. He marveled at himself for sharing that story. She'd completely dismantled his defenses. "Actually feels better to let it out. I've never told anyone that. Dad has no idea I made the trip."

"I'll be your safe space."

That. That was the hottest thing anyone had ever said to him. And he felt the truth of it through his whole body.

"I want to be a father, but I want to be married first. My dad and Helen have been amazing parents to me, but I always know in the back of my mind that I'm a bastard. Maybe it's old fashioned and most people don't care about it, but I can't help feeling at times like that title is branded on me. And now that Mom died, I regret that I never gave her a grandchild."

He gazed up at Claire, but she appeared speechless. Had he said too many deep truths? He tried to lighten the mood. "I've never once had sex without a condom."

She coughed.

He grinned. "Your turn."

It was several seconds before she spoke. "Stevie died in a car accident while driving drunk. When I got the call that he was gone"—she swallowed—"the very first emotion that hit me was relief." She looked sidelong at him to see his reaction. Smith hoped nothing but empathy showed on his face. "Horror and sadness and grief came after. I felt guilty about my relief for a long time, but it's my dark truth. I was relieved my husband of seventeen years had died. I was freed from being married to a mean drunk. Since then, I haven't wanted to put myself in a position where I could feel stuck or hurt or the focus of someone else's short temper."

Whoa.

She looked nervous. "Too much deep truth?"

He shook his head. "Maybe we should call it deep shit instead."

She let out a grateful snicker.

He grew somber as he recalled her words. All that, yet she'd come out stronger. He saw it in the softness of her eyes. She'd been through a hell he'd never understand, and still she'd carried on with kindness and goodness. She drew him right in. His voice came out low. "I'm sorry that happened to you." He truly meant it.

"You're right. It does feel nice to admit it. Air out the old hurt. Thank you." She shook her arms and her shoulders as if shrugging it off.

"Claire." He waited until she was really looking at him. "Not all men are controlling and cruel. You do have more options than being alone or being with a mean partner."

She looked from his eyes to his mouth and back again. Her throat bobbed, and her eyes looked watery as she nodded.

He was way too hot in here. But he didn't move. Their knees were almost touching. She'd held his hand. It was time for him to pull way back on the personal stuff. She worked here. She was on the clock. "So, what does Grandmother Claire like to do in her free time?"

She looked relieved at his change of subject. "Knit socks for the grandbaby."

"Seriously?"

"No."

He chuckled. "Not that there's anything wrong with that. I love a good hand-knit cap." He had one from his nana he pulled out when he traveled to colder climates. Or when he especially missed her.

Tommy scrambled up and dropped his toys into the hot tub. He adjusted his goggles and jumped in.

"So if knitting is out, what do you do? Play with your cats?"

"Cats?" She affected outrage.

"I'm sorry, was I wrong? Pet lizard? Snake?"

"I don't have any pets," she said.

"I knew it." She did not seem like an animal person.

"Neither do you."

"How could you tell?"

"Your clothes are too clean and fresh and furless for a pet person. You're too fastidious, I think."

"That was incredibly judgmental and offensive to pet owners. Also, potentially to me. However, I will take it as a compliment." And he did. She'd noticed his clothes. Noticed him. He beamed at her.

She rolled her eyes.

"So no pets, no knitting. Movie buff?"

"I'm working on a painting." She looked down as she said it.

He got serious. "You're an artist."

"I'm no Rembrandt, but I like to splash paint." She spoke to the stairs.

"That's really cool." His voice came out more genuine than he'd intended. Too deep and low for talking with the babysitter. He needed to get those walls back up.

"Do you paint?"

"No." He shrugged. "I like to scribble little drawings sometimes. Helps me relax. It's very therapeutic, I think."

She leaned back and tilted her chin toward the sky, exposing a long creamy neck. His tongue was jealous of the dribble of water that traced the curve of her throat. He swallowed.

"Yes. That's exactly how I feel."

"So, when can I see your paintings?" It just popped out. It wasn't appropriate to ask her that. This wasn't that kind of relationship. They'd already gotten too familiar with each other tonight.

"Hmm." She closed her eyes. "I'll let you know." Her body floated up in the water, and her knee bumped into his thigh.

"That doesn't sound too promising."

"Don't hold your breath."

Seemed like good advice on several fronts.

Tommy walked along the bench to Smith's side. "Throw this for me."

Smith chucked it into the main pool. Tommy needed to cool down anyway; little kids weren't supposed to be in the hot tub for long. Smith was long past overheating himself. He'd surely cooked all his sperm. Good thing he wouldn't be needing them anytime soon. The sarcasm didn't sound great inside his head.

His little brother scrambled out of the hot tub and down toward the pool.

Claire sat up, her knee lifting away from him. "I lied."

"What?" His voice was total surprise.

Her gaze flicked away from him as if embarrassed. He braced himself for something horrible. Veronica had lied to him. Lying was a deal breaker, a heartbreaker.

"I *should* have been painting this afternoon. But I wasn't. I'm not. I've had a blank canvas on my easel for months now. In the morning, I stare at it for a while, but I don't paint." Her voice was soft as a feather. "I'm not painting."

He felt as if she'd trusted him with something intimate, given him something more fragile than even the truth about her asshat husband. He wasn't sure what to do with it, but he didn't want to hurt it—her. She was a real artist with real artist problems. He had no idea how to help, how to protect this trust. He wanted to take away the grief she'd shared, draw her close and hold her. The setting sun highlighted the flecks of green in her vulnerable eyes. He thought of Tommy's poetic words that first day: *I could tell that she was meant to be mine.* A few of his own choice curse words followed the heavy feeling of wanting that settled in his core. He forced his voice to sound casual. "When did you first start painting?"

"Twenty-two years ago."

Wow. Okay. He was going to google her the second he got home. He couldn't believe he hadn't yet. He hadn't because he'd forced himself not to, but this was too much. "Has this ever happened before?"

"Not bad like this."

"I'm sorry. I imagine that's frustrating. Maybe all you need is a little break. Sharpen the saw, as they say." And now he was the dork for saying it. "Clean the brushes, maybe?" Even dorkier.

She didn't look as though she agreed, but she said, "Thanks." Her fingers played with the ripples in the water. "What else does Smith like to do besides surf and sketch?"

"Eat."

She startled. "Oh, the pizza. It should be here by now."

"Daddy!" Tommy yelled from where he stood on the pool steps.

They both looked over to where Banks was standing in the doorway, two pizza boxes in hand. He wasn't looking at Tommy. He was looking at Smith. His gaze could have cut steel. Heat crawled up Smith's already warm neck. Yeah. Maybe it didn't look so good to be caught in the hot tub with the babysitter.

"Banks." Claire was already out of the hot tub. She whipped a towel around her torso with lightning speed. "Thank you so much for getting the pizza. I didn't hear the door."

He finally tore his gaze away from Smith. His face softened when he looked at Claire. "It's fine. I pulled up to the house at the same time as the delivery guy, so I thought I'd bring it in." He set the stack on the teak table.

"Tommy," Claire said. "Come dry off. I'll get you a drink."

Smith didn't want to get out of the hot tub. He wanted to drown in it. He felt like he was sixteen again and Dad had caught him kissing Tia in the basement after midnight. But that's not what was happening here! And Smith was thirty freaking years old. When Claire went inside the house, Smith regretfully dripped out of the water. It had been such a nice few minutes: swimming with Claire and Tommy, visiting with her, feeling connected and heard. Seen. Sheesh, the way she'd looked at him. Not like an object, but like an interesting man.

Dad's angry eyes cut right through that happy bubble. Pop.

Dad set Tommy up at the table with a fat slice of pepperoni and pineapple, then marched over to his oldest son. Smith was hungry, and it looked so good. Could he please eat before the lecture?

"What are you doing here?" Dad's jaw twitched. "I'm not paying her to flirt with you."

The words landed like a slap to the face. Smith's nostrils flared. "Are you kidding?" In high school he would have told Dad to kiss his ass. Now he chewed back the profanity and settled his tone. "I'm here because I closed the Crosby house, and we had dinner plans. Remember?" That last bit came out sharp. Old habits die hard.

Banks hissed out his breath, the fight leaving him as embarrassment rushed in. "I'm so sorry, son. I meant to call you. And then this report came out about an acquisition, and there was a problem, so I had to go in. I thought I'd be back before you got here."

Smith exhaled, forcing Dad's accusation about Claire to roll off his back. They had not been flirting. They had *not* been flirting. Be calm. "It's all right. It happens."

"I shouldn't have said that to you. I know you wouldn't hit on Claire." Dad was always proclaiming things like an emperor, as if he could make it true by decree.

Smith bit his tongue. Normally he wouldn't go for Tommy's babysitter, or a forty-year-old, or a grandma. So many things, yet . . . dammit, he wanted to. Dad telling him he couldn't made him want to revert to a rebellious teenager.

Dad raked a hand through his hair. "I don't know what came over me."

Smith nodded magnanimously, his guts in knots. Dad turned back to the house, toward the beautiful woman wearing only a tight-as-hell swimsuit and a towel around her waist. Smith knew exactly what had come over his dad—jealousy.

Dad was falling for Claire.

No.

Revulsion washed through him. Gross. Dammit. No way. Smith and Dad were attracted to the same woman. They both wanted to have sex with the same woman. Smith swallowed bile. He pushed it all away as if ridding himself of toxic goo. It didn't matter if Dad was interested in her, because starting right now, Smith was 100 percent over Claire. She said it herself; she didn't date. Although a good part of him found the challenge of that appealing. Nope. He'd never think of her as more than Tommy's kindly old babysitter.

And good for Dad if he could snag Claire. Dad had good looks for a fifty-year-old. He could be charming. And he had money. Claire would be all over that. Maybe wooing Dad was the real reason Claire had taken the job. Sneaky little lady.

Then he thought of the heat in her eyes when she'd touched him. Could almost feel her fingertips brushing his nipples, her palms flush over his pecs. Nope. Never. Those thoughts were now off limits. Fantasy officially dead.

He picked up a towel and rubbed it over his wet hair.

"Here. Drink this, Tommy." Claire set a cup of water by his plate. "And here's some apple slices. If you eat them after the pizza, it'll help clean the tomato sauce off your teeth."

Smith couldn't help grinning. The woman was low-key amazing. Never thinking of her again was going to be harder than he thought. And if she was constantly here, tempting him with her understated charm, chill quality, and damn sexiness . . .

Claire straightened. "I'll leave you gentlemen to your dinner."

He was annoyed and glad at the same time.

Dad stopped the pizza halfway to his mouth. "You're not staying?"

Her brows furrowed. "Do you need help with Tommy?"

Dad leaned back slightly at the reminder that she was an employee here, not his wife. "Oh. No. We're good here. I just thought you might like something to eat."

Dad might have his work cut out for him with this one after all. And that made Smith like her even more. Double dammit.

"I'm okay. Thanks. See you next week, Tommy."

"Bye, Ms. Claire."

She didn't say another word to Smith or his dad. She'd obviously caught the tension. She'd have to be senseless not to, but hopefully she didn't know she was the cause. She was too watchful and discerning than was helpful at the moment. The Sextons stood there awkwardly and watched that incredible woman walk away. Smith had a feeling his dad enjoyed the view as much as he did. Shit.

Chapter 16
CLAIRE

Claire lay sprawled across her Pilates mat on the floor of her family room. Her muscles were warm and soft, her mind clear. It had been a great month. She had money building in the bank, and things were going well with Tommy and Banks. She felt awake. Alive.

Her phone buzzed. She rolled over and picked it up off the carpet. Text from Banks.

> Your costume came. We're all set for tonight. See you at six.

Dammit. She'd really been hoping she could weasel her way out of trick-or-treating with the Sextons tonight. Another text came through.

> Tommy is so excited you're coming. Thank you for doing this. I owe you big.

She sighed. Well, that was that. Anything for the golden boy. See you tonight. She twisted her knee across her body in a spine stretch as she called Mona. No answer. She got a text in reply.

Can't talk. Happy Halloween. Have fun tonight.

Claire replied, Send me a picture of Millie in her costume.

She got a thumbs up. She called Indi, her twenty-year-old daughter at Boise State. Indi had wanted away from the nest ASAP. She'd insisted on going out of state for college. Her name suited her. Or did the independent streak come because of her name? The call went straight to voice mail. Indi was rarely available to chat, even on a Saturday at 11:00 a.m. If the girl wasn't in class or with friends, she was working to pay her half of the tuition. Claire tried Edith, her eighteen-year-old daughter at UCLA. Also no answer. She texted out her love and tossed the phone away.

She was suddenly very grateful she had a nice family to spend the holiday with, to share her chili and cornbread with. When Stevie died, she still had three girls at home to love and tend to. With Edith in college, *now* Claire was truly alone. As she stared at her ceiling fan, the cold emptiness of her isolation settled around her like a frozen tundra.

It took her breath away. Was this really what she wanted for the rest of her life?

It's all right, she told herself, gasping. She'd adjusted to Stevie's death, to Mona leaving, and then Indi, and now Edith. They'd all left, one by one. She'd recover. She would be fine. She *was* fine.

And she wasn't alone. No matter where her girls lived, they were her daughters. She had friends. And Tommy and Banks. And maybe a little bit Smith. He was more attentive and genuine than she'd expected. His trials had aged him, given him wisdom and maturity that Claire was having a hard time ignoring.

She didn't have many male friends, certainly not single ones. In the past few years, she'd found that if she didn't let potential suitors get too close, she didn't miss being in a romantic relationship too often. She'd gotten good at blocking that part of herself off.

But Smith had snuck in a side door. One minute she was babysitting, the next she was sharing her intimate details and imagining what it would be like to climb onto his lap and run her hands over his glittering shoulders. She'd accidentally let her guard down, and now she was feeling things again. Her core contracted at the memory of his heavy chest muscles warm against her palms. The soft look in his beautiful eyes when she's shared ugly bits of her past. He'd made her feel important. It was intoxicating.

She thought about her advice to Banks. *You'll know when there's space again for love to take root.* Her words had snagged her then, and they continued to hound her. Now that her daughters had moved out, she felt the space they left yawning open. A darkness that threatened to devour her. It scared her. Her pulse rose.

She faced her fear and whispered, "I see you, I learned from you, and now I let you go."

The shadows in her mind retreated, and her ribs loosened. She breathed slow and deep. *I am everything I need.* She believed that, had proved it to herself for years, but she couldn't help thinking there might be more she now *wanted*. She forced the image of Smith from her mind as she stood, rolled up her mat, and put it away in the basket by the couch.

She cleaned her house for an hour before starting her chili. Tommy had told her she was going to be a medieval lady, so after her shower, she twisted her hair into intricate braids that fell down her back and put on red lipstick. Yes, this was fun. She was very grateful for Tommy and Banks.

At six minutes to six, wearing leggings and a T-shirt, she packed up dinner and drove south through her neighborhood to the now-familiar house with the killer ocean view. The jack-o'-lanterns she'd made with Tommy lined the walkway. But clearly, this morning, Banks had gotten to work because there was an inflatable ghost on the lawn and purple lights draping the front step. She'd done nothing to her house. Why bother? She had no kids, and she wouldn't be home to pass out candy by herself. Yes, she was glad to be out among others tonight.

Very glad.

Banks came out the front door while she was gathering dinner. She chuckled when she saw him. He threw his velvet cape over his shoulder and struck a pose. The plastic crown on his brow twinkled in the sunlight.

"Your majesty." She bowed.

"I could get used to that." He strode over, his toy sword banging his thigh. "Cool hair."

"Thanks." It was very nice to be noticed by this man.

"Can I help you?"

"Please." She pointed to the chili. "It's hot and heavy."

He raised an eyebrow.

She chuckled, heat licking her cheeks. She had not meant *that*. Had she?

He hefted the pot, and she followed with the bread and toppings.

"Ms. Claire!" Tommy ran up the stairs as they set dinner on the kitchen counter. His helmet dropped over his brow in his rush. He stopped in front of her and twirled, not exactly how she imagined a real knight would present himself.

"Sir Tommy," she said. "You look very bold and brave."

"Can we go trick-or-treating now?"

"Dinner first," Banks said. "Then candy. And we want it to get dark." He wiggled his fingers. "So it's spoooooky. That's when the monsters come out."

Tommy paled, then giggled. "Stop it, Dad."

The front door opened and closed. Seconds later Smith rounded the corner. Her heart reached out at the sight of him. He wore all black: black pants, boots, and belt and a sleeveless black hoodie. Over his shoulder, he held a massive axe with a leather safety case over the head. Fake tattoos ringed his biceps. She hadn't seen him for over a week, and she didn't like how she'd noticed his absence and how she was reacting with interest now.

"How did she get away with not having a costume?" Smith's voice was low and full of jest.

"Oh." Banks set down the soup ladle. "Let me get it."

"We can eat first," Claire said. Anything to delay dress-up. She was too old for this holiday.

"All right." Banks headed for the cupboard and pulled out four bowls. "Thanks to Claire for bringing us dinner and joining us boys for Halloween."

"Thank you for having me." She wasn't here for work; she was here as a guest. She'd made new friends, valuable treasures at this stage in her life. It was nice to be with these people she cared about. Hopefully it didn't turn into a bad idea.

Banks helped Tommy take off his breastplate so he wouldn't spill on it. Claire made the boy a bowl of chili, with cheese and chips, no avocado or scallions, just the way he liked it. When Tommy was situated at the table, Claire got herself dinner. She sat with the three Sextons. There was a moment of awkward silence, except for Tommy's slurping, before Claire spoke.

"What are you?" She looked over Smith again, allowing herself one brief moment to check out the brightness of his sea-green eyes and the stripes on his toned arms.

"The executioner. Of course."

"Of course." It did seem obvious now. Lady-killer.

"I wanted him to be the dragon," Tommy said. "He refused."

Smith nodded, a lock of dark blond falling over his forehead. "I did refuse the large-lizard option. But I'm here on a Saturday night with you. I think you should take that as a win, Sir Salami."

"Your parties don't start until after he's in bed," Banks said.

Smith winked at Claire.

Banks rolled his eyes.

She wondered what kind of party Smith would be going to. Did he have a date? She felt ancient and unhip. She didn't have any parties. Smith's dinner with his baby brother was her big event.

"And now I'm dressed for whatever the night brings." His full lips curved up. "Including criminals in need of beheading."

"Just don't steal my candy like you did last year," Tommy said.

"I most certainly will."

Claire caught herself grinning. She looked down at her chili. She liked this family too much. She swallowed away the sudden anxiety at the realization she could lose them. People didn't nanny forever. She inhaled. Exhaled. Nothing she could do now but enjoy the night.

"Soup's very good," Smith said. "Thanks."

He sat on her right. She cocked her chin and sent him a half smile.

And that was the moment he looked her in the eyes for the first time since the hot tub. Her mouth went dry. The connection stretched and warped and crackled.

"So did Tommy talk you into the dragon suit instead?" Smith asked, his gaze still hot on hers.

"No." Claire looked to Tommy. "I am his lady."

Smith held out a fist bump to his younger brother. "Well played, my man."

The doorbell rang.

"Trick-or-treaters already?" Banks strode to the entry, his purple cape fluttering behind him. She listened to him pass out well-wishes and candy. He returned with a childish smile. "I love this stupid holiday."

Smith snorted.

"The kids are so cute and eager."

"They all come here because you pass out king size."

The king bowed at the waist and did a flourish with his arm.

Smith stood. He picked up Claire's empty bowl and his and walked to the sink. He rinsed them and put them in the dishwasher.

Banks handed her a package. "You can change anywhere."

"Not in here," Smith called from the kitchen.

Banks's eyes widened.

Claire chewed on a giggle as she took the costume and slipped into the guest bathroom down the hall. She held up a dress that looked too small by half and more of a milkmaid fantasy getup than the fine lady's gown she'd had in mind. She peeled off her leggings and shirt, folded them, and set them on the marble counter. She loosened the laces on the corset-type bodice and stepped in. The dress ended inches above her knees. It tied in the back, which she couldn't manage on her own. She had the pitiful thought that if she'd been home alone, she'd never be able to get this on. But if she'd been home alone, she never would have worn it. She looked at her front in the mirror and started to sweat. It *barely* covered her bra. Nope, it didn't. There was a little lace frill there at the top. Cleavage pillowed out of the dress like an overstuffed double-scoop cup of caramel ice cream. Was this made for a twelve-year-old? Should she refuse to wear it? But what about Tommy's Halloween?

The irony was that she'd gotten these boobs only three weeks before Stevie's accident. He'd been wanting her to get them ever since Edith had weaned. Her children and the years had sucked her dry. She'd finally given in, and now she had large—Stevie's influence again—squishy boobs that Stevie never got to play with and that currently didn't fit into this dress.

Oh, what the hell.

She cracked open the bathroom door. "Excuse me?"

"Yep."

She didn't know if that deep voice had been Banks's or Smith's. Did it matter? It shouldn't, but it did. She wanted Smith. He was the one she felt more comfortable being uncomfortable with. "Can you come help me . . . please?"

Smith appeared at the door. She sent silent thanks to the Fates as she opened it wider. His focus dropped, and then his eyes bugged. His cheeks flushed.

She grimaced at the same time her core pulsed at the heat in his eyes. He desired her. She'd forgotten how good that could feel. Long-forbidden pleasure rolled through her, nearly knocking her off her feet. She sucked on her bottom lip to try and squelch the sudden fire roaring through her. Smith's focus snapped to her mouth. His gaze could have melted metal. It was certainly turning her into a dripping mess.

"We have a problem," she whispered.

And not just the one.

He snapped his jaw closed and looked her in the eyes.

She was toast. Sheer force of will had her swallowing the desire to drop the dress entirely and slam him into the wall. She shocked herself with the thought of it. What the hell was happening to her? "Maybe if you can help me tie it up in back, it will pull it up in front?"

"Um. Yeah. Okay." He forced his face into a decorous expression. Professional.

She turned to face the mirror as he stepped into the small room. *Breathe, Claire. Calm the crap down.*

His fingers trailed along her neck as he brushed her braids out of the way. A simple touch he probably didn't notice, yet she was hyper-aware of every cell that connected with his fingertips. She watched him in the mirror. Fantasy made real. His furrowed brow. He chewed on his bottom lip as he tugged the laces. She imagined pulling that luscious lip between her teeth, tasting salt and male, his hand sliding under the dress . . . she cursed internally and shook herself out of the downward spiral of thoughts.

He looked up in concern. "Did I get you? Was that too tight?"

Her face flushed an embarrassing shade of red. What was happening to her body right now? Why was it betraying her after all these years of cold indifference? "No. It's fine. Sorry."

She took satisfaction in the fumble of his hands and the darkened color of his face. He tied the laces into an uneven bow. "There."

She turned to face him and looked down at her chest. He did too.

"It didn't help much," she said. It was definitely worse now. Flesh shoved right up and out.

"You don't have to wear this. You should not feel uncomfortable."

"Not a good look for me?" Her voice was teasing, but her insides had tightened in defense. Stupid girl to ask that.

"Quite the opposite. You pull it off like a fantasy, but—"

Tommy appeared at the open door. "Ready? Can we go?"

Claire couldn't breathe, caught between sweet, innocent Tommy and his seductive older brother, a man who'd put her and fantasy in the same sentence. Her veins sparked and sizzled.

Banks stepped up behind Tommy. Now everyone was looking at her cleavage. Great.

Tommy's lip quivered. "Now we can't go because Ms. Claire's boobies are showing, and they're private."

She was speechless. Three adults turned to statues around one crying child.

Banks's voice came out gravelly. "They're not showing all the way."

She could only imagine her face was the same color as her lipstick by now.

Tommy assessed her again. She resisted the urge to try and cover herself with her hands. "You mean because her nipples are covered?"

Smith choked.

Banks, blushing like a teenager, reached for the clasp of his cape. "Here. She can wear this."

"But that's part of your costume," Tommy said.

"But it's more important for her to be comfortable," Banks said. His hands shook on the clasp. "Claire gets to wear what she wants. Maybe she'd like to change into her own outfit. It's her decision." He turned an apologetic face her way. "That is definitely not the costume I ordered. I am so sorry."

Tommy looked stricken.

"I have an idea," Smith said. "Come with me, Claire. If you please." He swept his arm dramatically. "My lady."

Tommy looked a bit better after hearing that.

Nerves on fire, she trailed Smith to Banks's bedroom. She halted by the door, suddenly very aware of the large bed with the navy sheets.

"In here."

She hesitated, then followed the voice into a massive closet. She'd never been in here. Why would she? Half of it had women's clothes. He hadn't gotten rid of Helen's things. Poor man. And here she was intruding on his private affairs. She felt as if she'd stomped on his battered heart by invading this bastion of his private grief.

Smith rifled through a shallow drawer.

"Ta-da." He pulled out a linen handkerchief. "The old man keeps telling me these come in handy. And today, they finally are." He held it out, his gaze dropping again. He snapped it back up. "Maybe you can just put it across there." He did a weird little wave of his hand and looked away.

She grabbed at the cloth. As she tucked it into her bra straps, her heart hammered against her fingertips. Her skin was warm and soft, hypersensitive to the touch. "Is that good?" Chin down, she looked up at Smith through her lashes. Her face was hot, her body near boiling point. It wasn't from embarrassment. The problem was the rest of the surging hormones mixed in.

"Um." He took a step closer, and her toes curled into the soft carpet. "There's a gap at the bottom still. You can see . . ." He reached out his fingers, realized what he was doing, and retracted them.

She barely stopped herself from leaning into his touch. "Shit, Smith. Just fix it before I die of awkwardness."

He startled. Then he laughed. A low delightful sound that had her biting her lip and failing to hold back her bubbling giggles. If they could already be laughing about it, everything was going to be okay.

His shoulders relaxed as he bent down and took a closer look. "It's like peekaboob."

Her body trembled with laughter.

"Hold still." White teeth flashed as he grinned. With two fingers, he gently tucked the linen into the top edge of the bodice.

Yep. His middle finger was touching her breasts. And she liked it. Wanted a whole lot more. The dam she'd built around any romantic feelings exploded. Desire spiraled through her body, stirring up long-suppressed emotion. She closed her eyes to hold back the torrent. She swayed with want, unmoored. When she opened her eyes, he was looking at her face, his hands clasped in front of his belt. His breathing was heavy and unsteady, like her pulse. His dark gaze tracked down to her mouth.

A sudden tidal wave of need crashed through her body. She wanted him to take her right here in this cedarwood-and-jasmine-scented closet.

Fuck.

Without saying a word, denying the pulsing ache, she turned and walked away. The short, fluffy skirt caressed her thighs. She exhaled everything out. *I let you go.* She would ignore these feelings, and they would pass.

Better to be safe than sorry. Her motto from the last five years didn't have the same comforting ring to it tonight.

She found Tommy and Banks by the front door. Tommy had his helmet on and his treat bag in hand. She blinked as if coming out of a dream. Halloween. Little boy she tended. Regular stuff.

Banks saw his handkerchief and grinned.

"You don't mind if I borrow it?" She was grateful her voice came out steady because her legs felt like rubber.

"You can keep it." He looked inordinately pleased about it. She couldn't worry about that right now. "They come in handy, you know."

"Finally, you're proven right," Smith said, coming up behind her. He picked up his axe and grinned at Tommy. "Are you ready to get me some candy?"

"Let's go!" Tommy ran out the door and nearly crashed into a group of trick-or-treaters.

"Have fun," Banks said.

"Wait. You're not coming with us?" Claire turned to him with a tight brow. He couldn't leave her alone in the dark with Smith.

Again, he seemed overly thrilled by her words. "Handing out the candy is my favorite part. I won't desert my station." To prove it, he greeted the newcomers with enthusiasm.

"Don't even bother." Smith put a hand on her elbow to guide her around a pumpkin. She was disturbed by how much she wanted him to keep touching her. "He's never gone out with us."

"Mom always took us." Tommy grabbed her hand, pulled her out of Smith's warm palm, and urged her to walk faster.

Her stomach dropped. Was she Smith's mother in this situation? She had been starting to feel their age gap was closing, not growing. She sucked down the cool air, grateful for the breeze on her hot skin and the darkness that cloaked her rising dismay.

Smith thankfully—and regrettably—didn't touch her as they walked. She hung back in the street while Tommy ran up to doors. She wasn't in the mood to visit with neighbors or be seen in her tight minidress. She wanted to get away. Needed to rebuild her walls.

"Did you have any Halloween traditions with your daughters?" Smith asked as they watched Tommy race past a blow-up ghost. He shrieked when it moved.

She leaned closer, their arms an inch apart. "We used to watch old episodes of *Bewitched*. Edith, my youngest, refuses anything remotely scary. Indi, my middle child, would have gone full horror movie, but I was secretly grateful Edith was my excuse to not give myself nightmares."

He smiled at her, and her shoulders relaxed in response.

"I could never get them to wear matching-themed costumes like this either. Stevie refused to ever dress up, and I was pretty much a witch every year. Boring, I know. I would give the girls each ten dollars, and then they had to be creative with it."

"That's cool. Made for unique costumes, I bet."

She sighed at the happy images that came to her mind. Edith wrapped in an old sheet splotched with red dye—a pagan sacrifice gone wrong. Indi wearing a tropical shirt and a skirt of dried hay because she was a Hawaiian haystack. "Yeah. Mona was always annoyed because she wanted to buy something fancy. Indi loved the challenge and would go super out there." Claire chuckled. "One year she was zombie garbage. She saved up the cleanest trash she could find for weeks and then glued it to a trash bag she wore as a dress. Add crazy makeup and holding her arms out straight all night, no one wanted to get within six feet of her. She was so proud."

"Admit it." Smith sent her a lopsided grin. "You were proud too."

She poked his muscled arm. "Yeah. She's a good example to me of living authentically."

His voice lowered. "You miss them?"

She nodded, biting back emotion. "So much. This summer was especially hard when Edith moved out. I feel like Tommy has saved me. I never thought I'd want to raise more children, but I'm so happy with him. It feels like he's brought me back to life, made me feel young again."

Smith was staring with an intensity that had her wanting to hide and at the same time wanting to jump into those inky depths.

"Is that stupid?"

"No. I know the feeling. That desire to live life a little fuller, a little less alone."

Her body swayed toward him of its own accord, the attraction a tangible thing. She forced a teasing tone. "Executioner does seem a lonely existence."

He laughed. "Corpses don't make for the best company."

She glanced at the axe. "Especially headless ones."

"They're the bloody worst."

She giggled like a schoolgirl.

Tommy bounded up. "Come on, slowpokes." He hooked a hand through Smith's belt loop and started tugging him down the street.

Smith looked over his shoulder, reached back with the arm that wasn't holding the axe, and took Claire's hand. "Not very polite of a knight to leave his lady behind."

Warmth shot through her arm and pierced her core. He let go of her at the next house, and she tucked her tingling hand against her ribs.

After two long streets, Tommy tired, and they headed back.

Smith turned to Claire and held out his weapon. "I must axe you to hold this."

"Clever." She took it with a smirk.

"Why thank you, dear milkmaid."

She snorted.

Smith lifted Tommy onto his shoulders.

Tommy set his treat bag on Smith's head.

"Want me to carry that too?" Claire asked.

"Don't do it," Smith warned. "That's how they get you. You think she's just being nice, and then *bam*, she's eaten all your candy."

Laughter bubbled through her body.

Tommy tugged his candy a little closer to his chest.

"But I'm going to need some fuel if I'm going to carry you all the way home. You're heavier than my last kill."

Tommy rummaged through the bag and then leaned forward, held his hand to Smith's mouth, and shoved something inside.

Smith chewed. "That was a gummy bear. I hate those."

"I love them," Tommy said.

"Well, I appreciate the gesture." Smith swallowed. "I also think there was a hair on that one."

"Maybe it was mine," Tommy said. "I was just scratching my head."

Claire held her stomach against the giggles.

Smith's voice was full of amusement. "That's not all that comforting." When he sent a conspiratorial grin sidelong at Claire, she let herself bask in the pleasure of this moment. It felt so good. So deeply good.

She hadn't allowed a man to hurt her in years, but in the process, she'd protected herself from all the laughter and love too. It stung to realize how much she'd been missing.

When they neared Smith's car, he set his brother on the ground. "Thanks for a fun night." He bowed and lifted Claire's knuckles to his warm, soft lips. Her breath caught in her throat. He was joking around, but her body was seriously aroused. "Dear lady, I thank you for your condescension toward a lowly executioner."

She handed him back his axe. "I'm sure the kingdom thanks you for your grisly service."

He turned to Tommy and dipped his head. "Sir Knight."

"Bye." Tommy put his arm around Claire's leg, as if afraid she'd leave him too. She set a reassuring hand on his narrow shoulder.

Smith strode to his car, stopped, and turned. "One more thing."

"What?" Tommy asked.

"Snickers."

Tommy walked over, digging through his bag. "Here. Here. Here." He handed out all the Snickers he could find. "Those are gross."

"And you are welcome to keep all the hairy bears." Smith unwrapped a fun size and popped it in his mouth. "This is why we make such a good team." He looked up at Claire. "Have a good night."

"Yeah," she mumbled. "You too." She didn't stay to watch him leave. She turned Tommy and ushered him into his house. First things first, she changed. Fortunately she could reach the ribbon behind her back and untie it herself. Thank you, yoga. She would have cut the mini costume off before she asked Banks to undress her. She had been far, *far* too friendly with the Sexton men tonight.

While Tommy organized his candy on the floor, she cleaned up dinner. She packaged the leftovers and put them in the fridge. Turned out, Banks loved her leftovers. She smiled.

"Time for bed, big Tom." Banks took off his cape and crown and dropped them on the counter. "Come on. You get your pajamas on, and I'll brush your teeth. And you must floss tonight. Halloween rule."

"I want Ms. Claire to take me."

Banks looked over at Claire as if he were going to ask if she would do it, then he seemed to realize she wasn't here as a nanny tonight. And she wasn't the mother. He faced his son. "I'm going to take you tonight."

Tommy turned big wobbly blue eyes on Claire. "Please?"

This kid was going to be the end of her. How could she say no to that? It'd been much easier to deny her daughters. "Fine. Go get started. I'll come down in a minute."

Tommy ran off before she could change her mind.

And that's how Claire ended up putting Tommy to bed without getting paid for it. Just like a real mother would.

Chapter 17
BANKS

Banks picked up his cell phone and dialed the third number, listed under Helen and Smith, in favorites. He should really delete Helen's number. It was a little flick against his heart every time he looked at it.

"Hey, Banks," Claire said, her voice light and puffy, as if she'd been running. She probably had. With a body like that.

He needed to get to the gym more. "Sorry to bother your morning."

"No bother. Everything okay?"

"Yes. But I need to take a business trip. There's a company in San Jose we've been talking with, and I need to pop up there and do some due diligence. Meet with their people."

"You want me to watch Tommy while you're gone? Sure."

Man, she was an angel.

"When is it?"

"Tomorrow. I'll drop Tommy at school on my way to the airport. Then I'll be back late Wednesday. So it's only one night, but I'll need you to sleep at the house. We have that guest room downstairs."

"Okay."

Seriously, how had he gotten so lucky? "Thank you, Claire. Maybe I don't tell you enough, but I'm so grateful for you."

"You're welcome."

Could it be this easy? "I'll see you tonight. I should be home in time to put Tommy to bed myself."

"Sounds good. See you." She hung up.

He leaned back in his leather office chair, thinking about Claire. Tommy loved her. She was competent and beautiful. He trusted her completely. It would devastate them both if she quit. He had to make sure he didn't lose her.

His assistant poked his head through the glass doors. "Mr. Washbicker is in the conference room."

"Get Jill and tell her to meet us in there." Banks pushed Claire out of his mind and got back to work. He didn't think about her again until he arrived home and walked into a house that smelled like roasted garlic and melted cheese.

Yes, he really needed to keep her.

She sat on the couch with Tommy, a book spread over his lap. Tommy didn't even get up, didn't run full tilt at Banks, his eyes needy and his hands like claws. Claire had done this. Claire had taken a terrified, broken boy and started to heal him.

"Hi, Dad."

"Did you have a good day?"

He'd already turned his focus back to the page. "Read."

Claire smiled at Banks. "There's lasagna on the counter. You might want to nuke it. I put your salad in the fridge."

Marry me.

He balked as the words blasted through his mind. He'd almost said them out loud too. Horrors. He hadn't meant it. Had he?

"Read," Tommy said, voice more insistent.

"Manners." Banks frowned.

Claire tilted the book up, focused on the page, and cleared her throat.

"I'll just go get changed."

"The mighty duo waded through the marsh toward Rabbit's . . ." Her soothing voice faded as he shuffled into his bedroom. He loosened his tie as he entered his closet. His gaze traveled over Helen's side, her shirts, shoes, purses. All there in neat rows. Untouched. It wasn't as painful today to undress in here as it had been yesterday, or the day before that. Had Claire done that? Healed him a bit too?

He ran a finger down a silk sleeve. "It's time, Helen."

The words sent him spiraling back to when he'd asked her to marry him. After she'd nodded in agreement to his plea, she'd said, "It's time." Her response had struck him as odd, but he loved that about her. Her air of mystery and intuition. Banks was proud to call himself an intellectual, but she operated on a softer wavelength. She'd make pronouncements as if she could hear the whisperings of the universe. "It's the will of the ocean," she'd say when things didn't go her way. The sky was much more benevolent, and Helen often gave the wind credit for luck. "The clouds smile on us" or "The wind carries us."

Six years ago, when they'd finally gotten pregnant with Tommy—after twenty years of infertility and miscarriages—her response had again been, "It's time." As if it were all working out as it should, as if she'd known this one would succeed. And she'd been right. He had a hard time being so optimistic, especially those short months ago, when it wasn't Helen saying it, but the doctor. "It's time." It was time to pull the plug on a life. On his love. His wife.

It was never the *time* for her to die.

He leaned his head against the wall and let a few tears drop. *I miss you, my angel.* He lifted his head, wiped his cheeks, and swallowed his grief. Dressed in a T-shirt and joggers, he shuffled back to the kitchen.

"Now read this one." Tommy slapped a picture book on Claire's lap and climbed back up to sit next to her.

"I'll read it to you." Banks pulled the salad from the fridge. It had mandarin oranges mixed in with the lettuce and slivered almonds.

Looked good. "And Tommy, Claire is going to sleep over here tomorrow while I take a business trip."

Tommy beamed at her. "You can sleep in my room. I have a big bed."

"She'll sleep in the guest room, and you'll use your best manners. No more bossing her around. She's the boss of you." Banks used his emperor voice.

Tommy didn't argue.

She peeled herself off the couch. "I hope the trip goes well. Don't worry about Tommy. He'll be fine here."

Banks wasn't worried. For the first time since Helen's *first* heart attack, a year and a half ago, he wasn't worried about Tommy. He breathed easily into a chest no longer clamped tight. He breathed in the sky, as Helen would have said.

Claire let herself out, and Banks settled in her lingering warmth on the couch as Tommy handed him a book.

After he put his young son to bed, he ate dinner. The food was fantastic, but he wished Claire were here eating with him. Wished she didn't leave the second he got home. The house seemed so big and empty tonight. Too quiet. Stagnant. Not so much as a friendly breeze.

He texted Smith. Do you want any of Mom's clothes? I'm bagging them for donation. He'd give everything to the new gal in accounting who looked to be Helen's size—as long as she promised to never wear any of it to work.

No, thanks. Want me to come help you?

Banks's eyes watered. Yes, he really did. But he knew that wasn't fair to Smith. And Banks was tough. He didn't need his kid to hold his hand. No. I'm okay. It won't take long.

I'm proud of you, Pops. This doesn't mean you love her any less.

A tear rolled down. Banks pocketed his phone and snagged the box of black garbage bags from the garage.

It wouldn't have taken long if Banks had grabbed everything and shoved the piles in. He didn't. He went through each item. He smelled the shirts for her lingering scent. The perfume was detectable on only a few. Her favorites. He tried to remember her wearing each piece as he reverently folded it and placed it into blackness, burying it like he had her body.

He held up the oversized amusement park T-shirt he'd brought home to her last year when he'd taken Tommy for his first time. Helen had been to the park once as a child and never again. She'd hated it. The pressing crowds. Waiting in line for a ride she didn't enjoy. The dressed-up characters gave her the creeps. Once in a while, Banks would take his son on a date with the roller coasters, and Helen would stay home and garden. The shirt went into the bag.

He paused on a dark-yellow dress. She'd worn it on their last date. He hadn't known it would be their last dinner out together. Their final supper. Would he have done things differently? Ordered her a more expensive wine? Talked not of Tommy, work, and the PTA parents, but of grander things? He would have been gentler, kinder. He would have held her closer, tighter.

Well, that made it sound like he would have suffocated her. It wasn't fair to play this torturous game. He'd loved Helen as best as he knew how. He thought she'd been happy with him and the life they'd built together. She was joy personified.

Under Helen's stack of workout T-shirts lay a tiny pink dress. Ice slashed through his veins, and his ribs tightened on his heart like a vise. He hadn't known Helen had kept this. Of course, she had. He'd bought it at an overpriced boutique in Chicago. He'd been there on a work trip when Helen had called him after her ultrasound appointment and told him the news. A girl. He'd rushed out and purchased this dainty rose-hued treasure. He trailed a thumb over the delicate bow on the collar. Less than a month after that call, their daughter was stillborn at twenty-two weeks. Twelve years ago now, but the pain cut through him afresh.

He hoped his girls were finally together. He had to believe it.

He pictured them dancing together in the clouds.

The tears came in a torrent, aggressive and consuming. He didn't try to stop them, and it didn't hurt so bad this time when they passed through. When the shaking subsided and his vision cleared, he finished packing her stuff.

He left Helen's jewelry in the drawer. That was worth a small fortune. He took the heavy bags to the garage; then he stood at the closet door and surveyed the change. Helen's side was now bare shelves and rods, but it didn't feel as empty as it had before.

Banks did push-ups before he went to bed.

Chapter 18
CLAIRE

Claire met Raven Char at Maison Café in Dana Point for their monthly luncheon. She called it a luncheon instead of a lunch because that's what this restaurant was, pretentious. Tables of dolled-up females huddled together in tiny cliques. It was like middle school, but with money. Claire and Raven refused to go anywhere else.

They liked to women watch, and the chicken-arugula salad was worth the twenty-six-dollar price tag. And they were both in love with their waiter. Khalid. He always worked Tuesdays, and they always sat in his section. He had long curly black hair and tattoos ringing his bulging biceps. Over their many visits, they learned he was born in Jordan, then lived in Italy with his mother's parents through European grade school. He'd gone to high school in Nevada before moving to Southern California for college and then staying to surf. He was twenty-eight and always insisted he was single and available, but Claire and Raven had decided that was one of Khalid's tricks for getting amazing tips. He flirted shamelessly with all the middle-aged women who lunched and drank champagne in the middle of the week. He'd admitted once that he earned more money working lunches here than he had as a Hebrew and Italian teacher at Saddleback College.

"Claire. Raven. How are my favorite ladies?" Khalid asked as he approached their two-top. "Empty-nesting suits you both. You're glowing."

With a memory like that, the man deserved his tips.

Raven beamed, flashing her dark eyes. She insisted these lunches did more for her complexion than a spa day. Not that she needed help. She had gorgeous umber skin that Claire was perpetually jealous of.

"Claire isn't exactly childless anymore," Raven said.

Khalid looked down at Claire's trim waist. He raised an eyebrow. "Who is the lucky guy? I thought we had a good thing going, you and I?"

Claire sent him a coy grin. "I'm sorry, Khalid. I've fallen for another man."

He brought a thick hand to his broad chest as if he'd been struck.

"Claire is nannying the most adorable five-year-old on the planet," Raven said.

Khalid chuckled. "I see I didn't stand a chance."

"It's the father you have to worry about," Raven said. "He's fallen for our Claire too."

Claire cringed inwardly. She didn't want to talk about Banks. And she didn't want Raven putting such ideas out into the universe, where they could gain momentum and solidity, become real. As if Claire had any control in this.

Khalid nodded. "Him I might be able to challenge to a duel."

"If it makes you feel better." Claire looked at his muscled arms. "You would win."

"It makes my day." He winked, his rich eyes dancing. "I'll have them put extra cheese on your salad."

"You know I love the Manchego," Claire said.

"Of course I know." He stepped away without asking anything more about their order. He did know just what the women wanted. And he delivered every time.

Raven sighed grandly. "He never gets old."

"Do you think he thinks we're old?" Claire wondered if Smith thought of her as an old woman. She shouldn't care, yet here she was, caring a great deal. Crap.

"Of course he does," Raven said with an incredulous snort. She was forty-seven. "I'm old enough to be his mother."

Claire wasn't. Nor was she thinking about Khalid. She wasn't near old enough to have birthed Smith. Did that put her in his eligible dating pool? She was disappointed in herself for even wondering about it. She'd had a moment of weakness on Halloween, when she'd allowed herself to want, to fantasize about love and pleasure. "How's work?" Raven was an accountant for a law firm in San Juan Capistrano.

"It's got its assets and liabilities."

"Was that an accounting joke?"

"You didn't think it added up?" Raven chuckled.

Claire rolled her eyes and let out a soft amused breath.

"It's fine. They hired a new attorney last month. I like her a lot." Raven twisted her lips up. "I think I might break my rule."

Claire gasped with mocking shock. "Like you might be friends with her outside the office?"

Raven looked appropriately abashed at considering having a crossover work/friend friend. She'd had a bad experience before. "I mean, I think so."

Claire laughed. "Raven, you bold little devil."

"Eh." She shrugged. "Rules are meant to be broken."

Claire stopped laughing. That hit too close to home. *And* by Raven's sly grin, she knew it.

"You fallen for Banks yet?" Raven picked up her mint lemonade and took a sip.

Claire immediately thought of Smith's finger tracing along the low neckline of the milkmaid costume. She speared her friend with an accusatory glance to cover the heat rising through her torso. "You didn't get me this job as a setup, did you?"

Raven sat back as Khalid set her plate in front of her. "Thank you."

"Thanks," Claire echoed as he placed her salad.

Raven focused back on Claire. "I absolutely did not. But I thought it might happen." She picked up her fork. "You're a WILF. He's a WILF."

Claire pursed her lips.

"You know, a widow I'd like to f—"

"I know what WILF means." Claire kept her gaze flat and unimpressed.

Raven chuckled. "You seem like you'd be really great together."

"We are great together."

Raven's face brightened.

"But *not* like that. He's great to work with. Not date. You might be a rule breaker, but I am not." *Keep telling yourself that, Claire.*

Raven pursed her lips. She took a bite of roasted chicken. "Banks isn't Stevie."

Claire bristled. "No. I knew Stevie's vices and shortcomings. I don't know Banks's." That wasn't exactly true. She was coming to see that he could be impatient and arrogant. He thought because he was a fancy private-equity partner, he was a step above her.

"How cynical."

"How true." But it was also true that Banks was generous and handsome and could be quite charming and thoughtful. Her job was more enjoyable than she'd hoped. It wasn't fair to rank Banks anywhere near Stevie in the deficient category.

"How's the painting coming?" Raven asked.

"It's not." Claire frowned as she pictured the blank canvases in her garage. Yet again this morning when she'd picked up her brush in her limp hand, nothing had flowed through. She didn't even want to paint. "I am a dried-up well."

"We'll just have to figure out how to get you wet again." Raven grinned like a fiend.

"That was disgusting."

She cackled like a cartoon witch. "Maybe. But that doesn't mean there isn't truth to it."

Claire had no wisecrack comeback to what she was horribly afraid might be an accurate analysis. Maybe not in such a lewd way, but her art depended on depth of emotion—from her. And she'd closed off that deep well of feeling. Did she even dare to uncover it? Let alone dive in?

She thought of Smith again, of his sharing deep truths in the hot tub. He'd listened to her as if he cared. The attention was intoxicating. She remembered her hands spread over his warm chest in the pool, how that brief touch had flipped a switch inside her. It had been years since she'd touched a man. What had that kind of isolation done to her soul? She shuddered against the thought. She'd never worried about it before; she hated that the Sextons were making it suddenly seem like a problem.

"So." Claire stabbed arugula with her fork. "What are you reading these days?"

"I've got a biography of Amelia Earhart that's gripping."

"Does it soar?"

Raven speared a piece of cheese. "Don't worry, wiseass, I'll give it to you when I'm done. You can take the trip yourself."

Claire lifted her sparkling water. "To women who take the leap and fly."

"Amelia didn't leap. It was a complicated system of instruments and early aeronautical technology that got her airborne."

Claire lifted her drink higher. "To wiseass women."

"I'll drink to that," Khalid said as he walked by.

This time Claire joined Raven in the cackling.

After lunch, Claire went home and packed her overnight bag. She parked her car at Banks's house before walking to the bus stop. As always, when Tommy saw her, he smiled as big as the waxing moon, and it made her heart sparkle.

"Tonight is the sleepover," Tommy said as he put his grimy hand in hers.

"Yes, it is." Claire checked the street before they stepped onto the asphalt together. "So I think we should do something special to celebrate."

Tommy looked up at her, his eyes glowing with the exaggerated enthusiasm only the truly innocent can experience.

"Do you want to go on a fancy date with me to Javier's for nachos?"

He screamed, "Yes."

Claire made her voice deadly serious. "There's only one thing."

His brow creased with worry. "What?"

"We're going to have to have a paper-airplane competition to decide who gets to pick dessert."

His mouth dropped open.

"I think we'll need to send them off the balcony to see whose is the best."

Tommy squealed and threw his arms around her hips. She chuckled as he squeezed as tight as he could. "You're the best."

Her heart swelled. Sure, it wasn't literally true, but she still floated the rest of the way home—his home, not hers. The distinction was getting blurry.

After Tommy washed kindergarten off his hands, he ate blackberries while Claire set her laptop up on the kitchen table and got out the paper. She pulled up a video she'd found on how to make the best paper airplanes. Together they folded at least a dozen before Tommy hissed.

"Ow." He sucked his pointer finger.

"Paper cut?"

He pulled out his finger and glared at it. "Yeah. See, it's right there." A minuscule drop of blood slowly beaded on his skin.

"Let's wash the paper acid out of it so it stops stinging."

"Will you finish mine?" He held up the crinkled sheet.

Claire folded while he washed his hands. "I think it's time to try these bad boys out."

Arms full of homemade planes, they walked outside. To the right was the pool. Around to the left, there was a spiraling staircase that went up to a rooftop patio. They climbed, then stood side by side at the railing. Her gaze lifted to the panoramic view of boundless ocean. She inhaled, filling her whole body with the fresh air.

"What should we aim for?" Claire asked, feeling like she'd already reached the stars.

"The beach."

"Whoa." She laughed. "You think you can get yours all the way down there? That's a long way."

Tommy cocked an airplane back and let it fly. It spiraled down and landed on a lounge chair. He frowned.

"That's a good target. Whoever gets the most planes on that chair gets to pick what we have as a treat tonight."

She purposefully didn't aim for the chair, although it didn't matter since they had zero control over where the planes went. Tommy's first plane was the only one that hit the target.

"What's it gonna be, big mister?"

"I want cookies-and-cream ice cream from the store."

"Fair enough." And convenient. Claire wanted to grab what she needed to make him raspberry pancakes for breakfast. "We'll stop on the way home from dinner." She walked down the narrow stairs. They gathered the papers and stuffed them in the recycle bin.

"I'm hungry," Tommy said.

"Let's go get nachos."

At dinner, Claire couldn't stop smiling at Tommy over the candlelit tabletop. She marveled at her happiness. She hadn't wanted to take this job, and she'd nearly missed out on one of the best things that had ever happened to her. She found deep satisfaction in tending to this child.

And he wasn't even hers. What did that mean? How could she love him so much? Could she want another of her own? She didn't answer that question. It didn't matter. She was already done with that phase of her existence, with both the joy and pain of family life. And with that thought, her smile drooped.

She wondered what else she might be missing out on because she'd taken counsel from her fears.

"Your son is beautiful," the server said as she set down their shared plate. "He looks just like you."

"Thank you." Claire said it in regard to the nachos and not the wounding remark.

People should really not make assumptions. About anything. Ever.

Fortunately, Tommy didn't seem to have noticed, his focus entirely on the mound of melted fat and salt.

They giggled and talked about what superpowers they would need to rule the world. Invincibility, of course, was number one. Mind reading and the ability to shoot spiderwebs out of their hands came in as close seconds. Tommy wasn't convinced Claire needed teleportation. He was determined that sticky spider hands were somehow better than instant travel. Even when Claire said they'd be able to pop over to Italy for a pizza lunch anytime they wanted, he was unmoved. Claire laughed and let him have his theoretical victory. Also, Tommy wanted invisibility so he could sneak candies out of the pantry without getting caught.

They picked which animals they would choose to be able to turn into. Claire an osprey and Tommy a tiger. They discussed at length the merits of having large permanent wings attached to their backs. Pros far outweighed cons there. They compared candy to baked goods and could not come to an agreement. Tommy was as staunch in his defense of the gummy as Claire was for pie. He was cheerful and delighted with everything. In short, it was the perfect date—Banks even footed the bill.

And Tommy was the perfect son. Her thoughts sputtered again. He was not her son. She was done having children. No sense in starting to feel bad about it now.

Yet the wanting was there.

Back at home, after ice cream, books, and Tommy's bath, Claire pulled pajamas with tiny trucks patterned over them from his drawer and held them out to him. "Remember, if you need me tonight, I'm just across the playroom."

Tommy grabbed his pants. "Thanks, Mom."

Her body went still as ice burned through her veins. "Helen is your mom."

He stopped. His eyes held too many emotions for her to begin to work through. He looked so small in nothing but his underwear and his yearning. "Are you going to leave me too?"

Her heart dropped out of her chest. She couldn't lie to him, but she couldn't pour salt on his wounds either. She knelt in front of him and slipped his shirt over his head. "It depends on how long your dad wants me to keep working. I hope to be here for a long time, but you're getting older. You can do so many things without needing any help."

"Not everything. I can't drive for a long time." And he looked glad of it.

"I love you, Tommy. And even when I'm not your babysitter anymore, I'll always be your friend." She tucked him into her arms and soaked in his warmth.

He held tight. "I love you more."

"I love you most."

"I love you more than mostest."

She pulled back and pursed her lips in thought.

"You can't beat that," he said. "I win."

"All right, winner, get in bed."

He tumbled under the covers. She kissed his brow. She slipped out of his room with her heart in her throat and her mind fluttering. Oh, sweet boy. What had she done? She'd done good here. She knew it. But the fear that hit was cold and harsh. She really did love him. And how long would she be here? She hadn't thought it through before. One year? Two? Ten? That seemed like a very long time to nanny. But why not? She didn't plan to move. She could do her art in the mornings and on weekends, not that she was doing that anyway. At lunch with Raven today, Claire had gushed about how great this gig was working out.

But what if Banks got married? It was likely. Most widowers found another wife quickly. What if Tommy didn't love the stepmother like he loved Claire? What if Claire didn't get to meet him at the bus every day anymore? Her heart wobbled in her ribs as she tiptoed upstairs.

What if Claire became the stepmom?

Her immediate reaction was to shove the question away, but she forced herself to confront it.

Banks was interested in her. She pretended not to notice, but she was forty, not fourteen. And he wasn't exactly subtle about the puppy dog eyes he sent her when it was time for her to leave. Fortunately, besides the long looks and the personal questions, he'd been respectful and professional. She could be wrong, but sometimes when he smiled at her, she imagined he was waiting, letting her see all that he had to offer. And it was a lot. She couldn't deny it. Not the least was the money. Stevie and Claire had made a deal with their daughters. The girls could go anywhere they wanted for college, and their parents would pay half. Now Stevie's income was gone, but the bills weren't. Edith's next semester tuition payment for UCLA would drain Claire's account. And technically that money was already from Banks.

She cleaned up the ice cream bowls, pretending it was her house, her kitchen. She loved cooking in here. She knew the quirks of the stove and how to stack the pans to get them to fit into the drawer. What if it were her husband on a business trip? She snuck into Banks's bedroom. The cleaners had come, and the bed was made to five-star standards, not that she had much experience with fancy hotels. The furniture surfaces shined. She could sleep in that bed. She had the sudden urge to crawl into it. Try it out tonight. But that was cheating, she knew. Banks wasn't here. He was handsome, but could she sleep with him every night? Give him sex? Give him the rest of her life? Her mind rebelled against the thought.

She'd never remarry. She amended the statement. She'd never remarry unless she found a soul match like the tall tales—and those were all fiction. She had wanted romance, an epic love story, but marriage didn't come with that. With Stevie, the sex too often had felt like a chore.

She remembered one evening she'd been exhausted. An endless day of anxiety over Edith's croup, Mona and Indi turning into MMA fighters whenever they got within six feet of each other, and Stevie's cousin coming to visit. She'd finally fallen onto the bed facedown. She'd heard Stevie come into the house at that moment. One second after the work was done and the girls were settled at last. Resentment had swelled through her in a painful wave. He'd walked into the bedroom and started talking about work, complaining about a coworker and cooing about something he'd done well. Claire wasn't really listening. She was imagining telling someone who cared what a shitty day she'd had and how hard she worked.

Stevie came and stood at her feet. He tugged down her shorts. "Nice ass you've got there, my love." He climbed onto the bed.

Claire was so tired. Didn't have the energy to turn him away or rise to the occasion. Her muscles had gone limp. Her mind felt too clobbered to function. Down the hall, Edith's barking cough rang out.

When Stevie finished minutes later, she hadn't moved an inch. She wasn't physically hurt by the abrupt start, but by the end, she'd felt wounded and sad inside and, despite herself, unsatisfied down there now too. Miserable from head to toe. Edith coughed again. Maybe she should turn up the humidifier in there.

He leaned forward and kissed her cheek. "Looks like you could do with some sleep."

Screw you, Stevie.

He hadn't seemed to notice that he passed out that night without hearing an uttered word of reply from his wife.

Claire turned away from Banks's posh bed. She no longer wanted to get close to it now. She paused as she noticed herself shoving the past pain back down. Instead, she tried to breathe out the memory and focus on setting it free. *I see you, I learned from you, and now I let you go.* That felt a bit better.

She drifted into the closet and stopped. Helen's things were gone. The shelves were bare.

Waiting.

Her heart thumped. Thumped. Thumped.

The last time she'd been in here, Banks had been far from her mind. Her skin warmed as she remembered her ridiculous costume. And Smith. *Smith*—Banks's other son. That guy. She pictured his blue-green eyes. His thick hair. His laugh. His finger sliding along the curves of her breasts as he'd tucked in the handkerchief. Her body pulsed at the mere thought.

It didn't matter if she could *maybe* one day, eventually, potentially picture herself here with Banks. She could never be Smith's stepmother. Not when she was still rebuilding the walls he'd so quickly reduced to rubble. Not when his presence awakened a deep, primal part of her that was safer left untouched. Not when she wanted to get into *his* bed.

She felt the precariousness of the situation, like they all stood on the edge of a cliff. As long as no one made any moves or did anything stupid, everything would be fine.

Chapter 19
SMITH

Smith parked his bike in his garage and hung up his helmet. He peeled off his sweaty clothes and dropped them directly into the washing machine that was stationed in a tiny room by the garage entrance. Usually a hard ride cleared his head, but it hadn't worked this morning. He was still seeing Claire's paintings float through his head. She signed her paintings with her maiden name, but it wasn't rocket science to find her. Abstract was incredibly difficult to pull off, but her stuff was raw and intoxicating. Of her work, a critic online had stated, "She doesn't paint pictures. She paints emotions." And they were powerful.

Smith wished he'd never googled her, wished he didn't now know the depth of her creativity and complexity. He was utterly intrigued.

He turned the shower to lukewarm and stepped in. He'd gone out with Stacey three times now. Hadn't brought her home. Wasn't going to call her again. How could he when Claire had invaded his thoughts like a virus? She was a granny. He wasn't even a dad yet. And he wanted to have a child. She was in a completely different stage of life. Why the crap did he think about her all the time? Yet she'd mentioned wanting another child. She'd said it to him. An invitation? He rinsed the soap and dirt off and stepped out. Wearing only his boxer briefs, he ate scrambled eggs and drew Claire.

She was more stubborn than most, but he'd get her out of his system. Obviously nothing could come of his rising interest. She was Tommy's. She was too much older than he. She wouldn't be a good fit for him. He closed his sketchbook, disgusted with himself for not believing any of it.

His phone buzzed with a text from Dad. What do we do about holiday cards this year?

Smith rubbed the spot between his brows where the pain seemed to be coming from. Skip them. He'd assumed this was the one good thing about Mom being gone—no more family photos. No more adult son joining the picture like a creeper.

I need to send something out. I have my business list. Should we do a picture with just you, me, and Tom?

No. That would look so sad.

Should I ask Claire to be in it?

Smith startled. What in the world? He picked up the phone and called his dad.

"Hello?"

"You can't be serious. Claire? You didn't mention this to her, did you?" Smith's body had gone hot.

"No. Dumb idea, right?"

"Yes. It's so weird." Smith's voice was cold and firm. "She's not part of the family. You cannot put her in your Christmas card."

"You're right. I wasn't thinking."

Just the fact that Dad had considered it was disturbing. "Get some nice cards that don't have a photograph this year. There are some cool ones with artwork. It will look professional and masculine." He thought of Claire's paintings again. He wanted to study them more. He cringed.

"Good idea, son. Will you help me pick them out?"

Smith sighed. "Yeah. I can look up some stuff."

"Thank you. And, hey, what do you want to do for Thanksgiving?"

Smith didn't want to think about it until he showed up at the house for Mom's turkey. *Dammit. We need you here, Mom.*

"Ivy will be with her in-laws, so we can't go there. Helen's parents are going to Indiana to be with your aunt Jennifer. They invited us."

Smith grimaced. Visiting Mom's family without Mom. And he didn't exactly click with Aunt Jennifer. "That's a long way . . ."

"Good. I don't want to go either. Nothing sounds worse."

Smith chuckled. "We could still get out of town, but somewhere closer."

"Just the three of us?"

That's all there was. Three amigos left.

"I'll look around, but I'm swamped with work right now. Do you think we can manage making something ourselves?"

Smith groaned.

"Or we could go out. There are always places open."

"That will be fine, Dad. It doesn't have to be a big deal this year. We can keep it low key. I make a good spaghetti, and you can make your famous wings."

"I buy those."

"I know."

Dad's voice got serious and sad. "I'm sorry, Smith."

Smith was fine. He missed her, but he was a grown-ass man. "We'll just have to make it special for Tommy." This Christmas was going to be even worse.

"I don't know what I'd do without you."

"So glad you realize that." He kept his voice airy, trying to lighten things up.

"No, I'm serious. You've been really good to me this last year and a half."

Since Mom's first heart attack, Smith had started coming around more. To spend time with her, but he'd also tried hard to strengthen the bridge between him and his father. It had been awfully shaky at times in the past. It meant a lot that Dad had noticed.

"Your maturity and wisdom do you credit."

The compliment felt good. "Give the credit to Mom."

Dad chuckled before getting serious again. "I'm sorry I wasn't a better dad to you."

"You were a great dad. Are a great dad." And he was, especially because he'd kept Smith when his birth mother hadn't valued his life at all, and he'd given him every opportunity. And he'd given him Helen.

"You remember that time in middle school when you came to breakfast complaining of a stomachache?"

"Yes."

"You said you were sick, but I said you could tough it out. Real life didn't give you days off. Helen was visiting her sister, so I made you go to school."

Smith put a hand over his bare belly, remembering. It wasn't a painful memory but a sad one.

"You threw up at school."

Right in the middle of Ms. Rob's classroom. He'd been mortified and pissed at his father for days, but he'd long ago let the resentment fade.

"I never got you the dog you always asked for."

"Why you doin' this, Dad?"

"So I can apologize good and proper. I'm sorry I was so hard on you. I was gone so much. I felt like I had to be tough on you for you to turn out tough."

"Well, it worked."

"Yes. You are tough and so strong." Dad sighed, and Smith pitied his father the pain of regret that clearly chewed at him. "But again. Credit to Mom. She's the one who raised you to be the good man you are." The grief was audible.

"I miss her too." Helen had fully adopted Smith as her own, legally and emotionally. She was an amazing woman. "And I forgive you. You are a great father to me and to Tommy. Let the past go. Stop carrying any guilt." He chuckled. "And we both know I don't want to start bringing up all the reasons I have to apologize back." Smith had not been the most obedient teenager. "We're at a good place now, you and I. And Tommy too. Let's focus on that."

"Thank you, son. I've got to go, but come by the house sometime. I feel like I haven't seen you in a while."

Smith was currently avoiding the entire Emerald Bay neighborhood. "Yeah. Okay. I'll see you soon."

"I love you." Dad clicked off.

Smith cleaned up breakfast. Those words from his father felt nice. They warmed his chest like hot chocolate when he was a child. He guessed he would never be too old for kindness from Dad.

He thought of the impending holidays. Who said you must have a fancy meal on Thanksgiving? They didn't need decorations and homemade pie. They could do it grunge style, in their sweats, with bags and bags of chips and nonstop football. It sounded perfect.

Chapter 20
BANKS

Banks lined up his shot and swung. The golf ball sliced to the right and disappeared into the trees.

"Mulligan." He pulled another ball from his pocket. He always came to the tee prepared.

Roger chuckled but didn't say anything. He was meticulous about his scorecard whereas Banks didn't fill his out.

He drove his next ball straight onto the fairway and pumped his fist. A lucky shot. He was getting more of those lately. They climbed into the cart. Roger drove.

"Did you hear they're going to build a new mall around here?" Roger asked.

"I haven't heard that." Banks usually had good intel on that stuff. His brows pulled together. "Where?"

Roger's lips twitched. "Somewhere between your ball and mine."

He scoffed. "Funny. You could use a trip to the mall. Your clothes need an update." It wasn't even a good comeback.

Roger gave him a smug smile; then he wiggled bushy brows. "How's it going with Clara?"

"It took you seven holes to gather the courage to ask me." He didn't want to talk about her. But he kind of did too. "It's Claire."

Roger's thick lips curved into a dangerous grin. "Raven told me that *Claire* had really nice things to say about you."

Banks's pulse rose. "She did? What did she say?"

Roger tossed back his head and roared out a laugh.

Banks scowled, horrified he'd sounded like a teenager. "I didn't mean it like that."

Roger laughed harder.

"Screw you." He climbed out and got his seven wood.

Roger stayed in the cart. "You know, it's okay to like her."

Banks swung and missed. He glowered at his friend. He breathed out, lined up, and hit it well, nearly to the green. That calmed his nerves. He walked with dignity to the cart. "So, do you and Raven have any Thanksgiving plans?"

Roger rolled his eyes. "Fine. Don't tell me what it's like to come home to her every day."

Banks's neck got hot despite the cool weather.

"But you're depriving me of some fun entertainment."

"I feel so bad for you. And there's nothing going on. Truly."

Roger looked him over. He frowned. "How disappointing."

"You're telling me."

Roger grinned. "There's my man."

Banks laughed. It felt so good to laugh. "I need to thank you for these Thursday mornings. You've saved me. Literally."

"Why do I feel like there's a but coming?"

"I can't do every week anymore. I've cranked up my workload at the office again, and things are good. Can we move to once a month?"

"Works for me. But don't tell Raven. I don't want her to suddenly think I'm available Thursday mornings."

Banks chuckled. He leaned back and let the sun dance over his face. There were some perks to being wifeless. Untethered.

They ended after nine holes, and Banks went back to his office. He'd meant to get home in time to put Tommy to bed, but in the end, he walked into his house after 10:00 p.m. The kitchen was clean, the family room picked up. Claire was in her favorite chair by the windows. The lamp was on, highlighting her beauty. She clicked off her phone.

"Sorry to be late tonight."

"Was it a good day?"

"It was. We acquired a company that I'm excited about. Lots of upside."

"Congratulations. That's great."

"Thanks." He dropped his jacket over the back of the couch. "How did everything go here?"

She stood. He wanted her to sit back down. Stay with him a while. "Great. We went to the park after school and got sandwiches together, so there's no dinner for you. Sorry about that."

"I ate at work."

"Tommy left that drawing on the counter for you. He fell at school and scratched up his knee, and he said Kyle was a 'poop-poop face.' So there's that."

"Oh, to be five again."

She smiled. He really didn't want her to leave. She took three steps toward the door.

"What are you doing for Thanksgiving?"

She stopped. "My college girls, Indi and Edith, are coming home, and Mona and Millie too. We'll just be here. Traditional meal and all that."

"That sounds really nice."

"What are you boys going to do?"

"Same."

She looked him over. Her eyes softened. "First holiday without Helen."

He nodded, his throat suddenly too tight to speak.

"I'm sorry, Banks. That's really hard."

He looked at the blackness outside the windows, the weight of his responsibility hitting him. "Halloween was my one holiday. Helen did such a good job with all the other ones. I haven't even tried to find her Thanksgiving box."

"You don't have to be her. It's okay to make new traditions."

He really wanted Claire to walk over and hug him. "I just don't want to disappoint Tommy."

Claire opened her mouth, closed it.

He held his breath, hope clutching him like a giant fist.

"Would you and Tommy like to join us?"

Yeeeesssss. A secret thrill ran down his spine.

"It's nothing fancy. I'm not festive—it sounds like Helen was—but it might be a nice distraction instead of being here without her. I can guarantee mashed potatoes and pie."

He didn't even pretend to say no at first. He looked her in the eyes, sure she could see his gratitude just by looking at his pitiful face. "Thank you. The three of us would love to."

She jolted a little when he said three.

"If Smith is welcome too."

"Yes, of course he is." Her face went tight. "That will be great." Her tone sounded off, but he wasn't about to probe further and mess up this invitation.

"I'll look forward to meeting Indi and Edith and seeing Mona and Millie again." He was meeting her children. This felt like a move in the right direction.

Her brows pinched together briefly before she smoothed them out. She strode over to her shoes and jacket. "I'll see you tomorrow."

"Good night, Claire."

After she'd left, he pulled out his phone and texted Smith. Great news. Problem solved. We're going to Thanksgiving dinner at Claire's house with her daughters.

Three little dots indicated that Smith was typing. Then the dots went away, and no reply ever came.

Chapter 21
CLAIRE

Claire rolled over and checked her phone: 5:32 a.m. Thanksgiving. She'd gone to sleep thinking about all the things she needed to do today and woken up still mentally ticking up and down the list. Indi and Edith were sleeping and would be for a while. The three of them had stayed up late last night, giggling and unfairly judging people on TV. One of their favorite activities.

Claire put on sweats and sneakers and went outside for a walk. She needed to clear her head and her heart. It was wonderful having the girls home. Claire loved the noise, the warmth. But it wasn't the same as before they'd moved out. It would never be the same. They'd grown up. And left. They returned now as visitors, not residents.

Indi had two new piercings on the ridge of her ear she hadn't bothered to tell Claire about. Apparently, she'd meant to send a picture and plum forgot. And Edith was no longer a virgin.

Claire had felt so betrayed hearing about it a month after the fact. Edith even used the L-word when talking about this Tyson boy. Claire took solace in the fact that Edith and Indi talked to each other every day. They had each other. They didn't need her; they were doing great.

The house was still silent when she returned. She made a pot of tea and started on meal prep for the dinner they'd be having at 3:00 p.m. She'd made the pies yesterday and put together bouquets of fall foliage as centerpieces. She looked at her oval table—a tight fit with seven chairs. If she added candles, would it look less rustic and simple? But she needed the space for the dishes. She pulled the brussels sprouts from the fridge. *Stop worrying about it.* It was just the Sextons. They'd be having takeout if she hadn't invited them.

After Claire had washed and sliced the mini cabbages and scrubbed the potatoes and assembled the stuffing, Indi waded into the kitchen.

She rubbed her eyes and yawned. Her hair, usually a rich brown but now dyed an ebony black, hung wildly around her narrow shoulders. She wore a tank top that was too see-through to skip the bra. "Smells good in here, Mom."

"Good morning, honey."

Indi slumped onto a counter stool, her big eyes droopy.

"There's tea in the kettle."

"Coffee?"

"I forgot you switched teams on me. You'll have to dig it out of the cupboard and make it."

"Edith will want some too."

Coffee reminded Claire of Stevie. He'd drink it all morning, until he switched to drinking something else in the afternoon . . . or late morning.

"What are we doing today?" Indi asked.

"I'm making Thanksgiving dinner. You remember the Sextons are coming over at three?"

Indi rattled around the cupboard. "Oh, yeah. Do you mind if I go surfing with some friends this morning?"

"No. That's fine."

When the rich scent of coffee permeated the small house, Edith appeared. She'd inherited Stevie's curly hair and his gray eyes. Edith was a beauty. Indi wordlessly handed her little sister a steaming mug.

"Why are we doing this so early?" Edith asked. "It's a holiday."

Claire looked over her shoulder at her youngest daughter. "It's nine thirty."

"Like I said."

Claire chuckled. "I only have five and a half hours until company will arrive expecting a feast worthy of this day."

"What's the big deal?" Indi blew over her cup. "Isn't this the kid you babysit all the time?"

"Yeah. You're right. It's not a big deal. I just want it to be good."

"You always make it good."

"Thanks, Indi."

"Can I have a piece of pumpkin pie for breakfast?" Edith asked, tugging the pie across the counter toward herself.

An immediate refusal popped to Claire's tongue, but she swallowed it away. Indi was right; she was making too big a deal out of this, and the last thing she wanted was for her daughters to get suspicious. "Sure."

Edith grinned.

Claire handed her a knife. "Happy Thanksgiving, baby."

Edith put her arm around her mother. Claire melted into the touch, the familiar smell of her little girl. "It is good to be home."

The sweetest thing she could have said. As far as Claire was concerned, Edith could have all four pies for breakfast if she wanted.

The girls lounged for a while before they left for the beach. Claire puttered around, setting the table, straightening the bookshelf, cooking, dusting. Mona and Millie showed up at one fifteen. Claire still hadn't showered.

Mona, however, was dressed for dinner with the president. She'd put a couple of tiny braids down the side of her dark hair and loosely curled the rest. She had on more makeup than usual and a flouncy midthigh-length floral dress.

She sent her daughter a knowing grin, but inside, Claire's guts had turned to scrambled eggs. "I see you got my message about Smith coming."

Mona set Millie down in her baby carrier by the couch. "Since you won't set me up with him, I'll have to do it myself."

Was it too late for Claire to cancel on the Sextons? Fake sick? Yes, it was. Banks had confirmed just ten minutes ago. But she could do her own hair and makeup. She didn't have to wear sweats like she had last year. "I was just going to hop in the shower. I'll be back in a few."

"Where are Indi and Edith?"

"The beach. They wanted to surf. They'll be back soon."

"Annoying," Mona said. It sounded like jealousy.

Claire knew how it felt to be stuck at home with a newborn while her friends were out playing. Mona huffed onto the couch while Claire slipped back to her room. She showered, blew out her hair, put on makeup, and dressed in tight black jeans and a burnt-orange blouse. She left the top two buttons undone. She eyed herself in the mirror and decided she looked very good for a widowed grandma.

All three girls were in the front room when she emerged.

"Whoa, Mama," Indi said. "Hot damn."

Claire flushed.

"Who is this guy again?"

Claire hated that an image of Smith hung in her mind, and she had the urge to gush about his attentive kindness and sexy smile.

Mona gave Indi a sideways grin. "He's handsome and rich and widowed. And he's totally into Mom."

"What?" Claire frowned at Mona. "How could you possibly know that?"

"Please," Mona said. "Look at you. The old man must be drooling all over himself."

"I'm going to take that as a compliment." But Mona's words did not sit well with Claire.

Mona turned to her younger sisters. "And his son is a total hottie. And I'm claiming him."

"You can't claim him." Indi said it, saving Claire from having to.

"Isn't he like thirty?" Edith asked. "That's so *old*."

And Smith had seemed so young to Claire. But he wasn't really, was he? He didn't act like her daughters with their changeable life plans and naivete. He was steady, observant, and responsible. There was maturity in his manner and fine lines around his eyes when he grinned.

"That's enough." Claire slashed her hand through the air. "There will be none of this talk when our guests are here. Banks is my employer, and I know you all like the paychecks I get, so I expect you to use your manners. Also, Tommy is five, and he listens to everything, so watch your words."

Indi grinned. The tiny piercing in her nose twinkled. "So, no talking about pricks and dicks."

"Or bleedings and needings?" Edith added with wicked delight.

Claire did not tell her daughters they were witty. They already knew too well. She pointed to Indi. "And you must wear a bra."

"Picky, picky."

"Go get showered."

Indi giggled as she disappeared down the hall. Claire marched into the kitchen. This dinner was a terrible idea.

The doorbell rang at 3:08.

"I'll get it." Mona set Millie on her blanket on the floor and dashed to the door. Before opening it, she smoothed out her dress and fluffed her hair. When she pulled it open, a cool breeze gusted in, making her dress dance. Mona beamed. "Hello."

Claire was coming up to the side of the door. She couldn't see the Sextons yet. Just Mona's bright face. Youth and vitality. She didn't want to follow that act.

"Hello, Mona. I'm Banks, and these are my sons, Smith and Tommy."

"I remember."

Claire came up behind Mona as her daughter stepped outside and gave them all hearty hugs. Smith's eyes caught hers over Mona's shoulder, and Claire felt a jolt down her core when he didn't look away. Dammit. "Come in." She stepped aside in case they thought she was going to hug them too. She was *not*.

"Smells divine in here." Banks held out a bottle of wine to her. "Thank you so much for having us."

"Yeah," Smith muttered. "It's really nice of you." His tawny hair was combed back from his angular face. He wore dark jeans and a cream sweater that made him look disturbingly dapper.

Tommy wrapped his arms around Claire's hips and inhaled the scent of her shirt.

"Hi, honey." She softened. She was suffering through this for Tommy. Her little boy. It would be worth it.

Edith and Indi appeared, and she made introductions, trying not to notice if Smith took any special notice of them. He was polite and charming. Impossible to tell.

"Come on in. Make yourselves at home. Dinner is almost ready. Give me five minutes. Mona, maybe you can take Tommy over to play with Millie."

"It's time for her nap," Mona said to Tommy. "You can help me put her down." He followed, full of interest.

Claire turned her back on her guests and strode to her kitchen.

"Can we help?" Banks asked, following.

"Cool house," Smith said, looking at it with the eyes of someone who knows.

"Thanks. It's small and old, but it's home."

"I love the design details." His gaze snagged on the tiled fireplace. "The floor plan of this main area is great. It's hard to find open family rooms in these older homes."

"Stop trying to sign her as a client," Banks said.

"I'm not." He frowned at his dad. "I was just saying it's a nice space."

"Thank you, Smith." Claire handed Banks a basket of rolls. "Would you please take this to the table?"

He took it and turned away. She might need to put on another layer of deodorant. They hadn't even sat down, and she was already overheating.

"If you have a corkscrew, I'll open this." Smith indicated the bottle Banks had brought.

"Ah. Yes." She started opening drawers. Hopefully she still had one somewhere. Aha. Her first lucky break of the day. She pulled the corkscrew out from the back of the utensil drawer. She handed it to Smith, careful not to touch his skin. Now she was going to have to get out some wineglasses too. Good thing she hadn't smashed *all* those.

She quietly told Edith to put wineglasses at Banks's, Smith's, and Mona's seats. Indi and Edith were surely drinking at college—Claire wasn't completely blind. But there would be no underage drinking in her home.

After another ten minutes of flurry, the food was on the table and everyone gathered round. Every face turned to her. She warmed under the attention. It had been a long, long time since she'd hosted anything like this.

"It's so fun to have the Sextons join us. Thank you for coming. Please, everyone, sit, and let's eat before this gets cold."

"Yay," Edith said. "Time to pig out."

"This is a serious feast." Banks scanned the platters of traditional comfort. "Thank you again."

Claire looked down, realizing that Mona had laid out index cards with names written in block letters. Mona had been making place cards for dinner since she'd learned to write. She loved telling people what to do. Claire and Banks were to sit at the two heads. Smith was on Claire's right, seated next to Mona. Tommy was on Claire's left, with Edith and then Indi. Banks didn't say anything about moving Tommy to sit at his side so he could help his young child. So she would be doing the work. Fine. They all sat.

Conversation was usurped by the passing of dishes and filling of plates. Claire was glad to help Tommy; it gave her something to focus her nervous energy on. Banks stood, walked to the kitchen, and picked up the wine that Smith had left there to air. He came to her side first and scanned her place setting.

"Where's your wineglass? Tell me where they are, and I'll get you one."

"No, thank you, for me."

Cutlery stopped clinking as the adults turned their attention on Claire and Banks.

"You've got to try it. It's one of my favorites. I import it from Italy," Banks said.

She stared up at the earnest-looking man, and no words came.

"She doesn't drink," Mona said.

Banks's blue eyes widened. "Ever?"

Claire mutely shook her head.

"Why?"

Claire's insides curled up into the fetal position.

"Dad was an alcoholic." Mona's voice was frank.

Banks's face turned stricken. "I'm so sorry."

"He was wasted when he mistook that streetlamp for the road." By the venom in her voice, Mona was still pissed about it.

Claire turned her attention on Mona. She couldn't stand the pity in Banks's eyes, and she forced herself not to see what Smith's reaction was. "This isn't polite dinner conversation."

"I'm just telling the truth. It's not like Dad deserves our respect." Mona's voice was cold and unapologetic. She was old enough to remember too much. She'd heard things a child should never hear their father say to their mother.

"You're right, Mona. But let's leave it there for now." Claire's words were a whispered warning.

Mona flicked her gaze away from her mother. Her nostrils flared. No one moved. Mona swallowed. She picked up her wineglass. "I think I'd like to try some of that about now."

Banks hesitated before walking around the table and pouring her a glass.

"Thank you." She took a sip. "It's very good."

Banks set the wine bottle back in the kitchen before going to his seat.

"Please." Claire's belly twisted. "You should have some too. I didn't mean to ruin it for you." She wanted him to enjoy this meal. She wanted the ghost of her late husband to stop haunting her home.

He smiled, and some of the clamps around her ribs loosened. "I decided I think this looks perfect." He lifted the pitcher of apple-cider soda and poured it into his tumbler.

Claire breathed again. Banks was a good man.

"It's yummy, Daddy," Tommy said, taking a big glug of his own bubbling drink.

"Shall we all go around and say something we're thankful for?" Edith asked. Her cheeks were flushed and her brows pinched tight. Claire's sweet, peace-loving girl did not like conflict.

Claire opened her mouth, but Banks's booming bass cut her off. "Wonderful idea. Shall I go first?" Then he looked to Claire for permission after the fact. What else could she do but nod?

He held up his pink juice. "I am grateful for Claire."

Claire's insides seized back into knots. At this rate she wasn't going to get a bite to eat.

"She is an amazing mother to my—" Banks cleared his throat. "I didn't mean mother, although clearly she is that." He looked to her daughters. "But she's been so good to nurture and take care of Tommy. We were in a bad place when she found us and picked us all up. We are so grateful to have her in our lives."

Mona looked at her mom with a wicked grin. At least she managed not to wiggle her eyebrows. Smith's face was remarkably blank.

Claire managed to spit out a raspy "Thanks."

"I'm grateful the surf was good this morning." Leave it to Indi to keep it light.

Edith went next. "I'm grateful the inland fires are under control now."

"That's a nice thought, Edith. Thank you," Banks said. "What about you, Tommy?"

Claire tried not to let it bother her that Banks was acting the host. This was her house.

"I'm grateful for superheroes."

Banks grimaced. "I bet you can guess what type of movie we watched last night."

Claire's pulse was unreasonably high. "I'm grateful to have my three girls and Millie home with me today. And Tommy here too." There—easy, simple, done.

Tommy beamed at her, and she gave his knee a little squeeze.

Smith glanced sidelong at Claire before he addressed the table. "I'm going to go with running water and electricity."

Banks frowned.

"And this meal." He looked back at her, his tone genuine. "It's really delicious. You're an incredible cook. It was very generous of you to include us. This must have been a mountain of work. Thank you."

She nodded, unable to speak as she melted into his gaze. That felt very nice.

After a heavy pause around the table, Mona forced a giggle. "I'm grateful I'm not breastfeeding anymore." She lifted her wineglass. "To having my boobs back."

"Mona." Claire's voice was stern.

"Sorry, Mom." She did not look sorry. "Did that fall into the forbidden-topics category?"

Smith raised an eyebrow at Claire. "There are topics forbidden at this table?"

She found her lips curving up of their own accord. "Clearly we aren't so good with the rules."

Mona laughed and put her hand on Smith's arm. "I can tell you about them later."

"Um." Smith blinked at her.

"So, Indi," Banks said. "What are you studying at Boise State?"

Thankfully, the conversation drifted into safer waters, and Claire even managed to eat some. She thought she was all in the clear when Tommy's high voice rang out.

"Ms. Claire taught me different ways to kiss."

Fire roared over Claire's face. Smith choked on his drink, spitting soda over his plate. Banks drained of color, and she could sense his thoughts spiraling into terrible places.

She lowered her fork. "It's not like that."

Her three daughters had matching looks of amusement.

"Talk about forbidden territory," Indi said with a snort.

"Let's show them." Tommy climbed out of his seat and came to Claire's elbow. He took her hot face in his hands. "Regular." He kissed her cheek. "Noses." He brushed his nose against hers. "And flutter bug." He blinked his thick lashes against her face. Then he strutted back to his seat like the reigning champion of the world.

Banks sagged in relief, and irritation flashed through Claire. How dare he even think for one second that she was capable of anything remotely inappropriate with his son? She blanched . . . at least with Tommy, she was perfectly proper. Smith was Banks's son too. And she'd considered doing plenty of inappropriate things with him.

"At least she didn't teach him French." Smith muttered it into his cup, but everyone heard it.

Claire pinched his thigh under the table, and then pulled her hand back quickly at the feel of hard muscle. He laughed.

"What's that?" Tommy asked.

Banks glared at Smith. "Nothing."

Mona giggled, her intense gaze on Smith. She looked ready to give a tonsil-hockey demonstration with him right now.

Claire should be okay with Mona coming on to Smith. She was not. And she was not okay that she was not okay with it.

Tommy stepped back up to the side of Claire's seat. "Ms. Claire, what's french kissing?"

She chuckled awkwardly and looked around the table. She wasn't getting any help here. "In French culture, instead of shaking hands or hugging their friends like we often do, they greet people by touching their cheeks together and kissing the air." She demonstrated with him. "Like that."

"That's funny," Tommy said.

"It's a different culture. It's normal to them."

Tommy's eyes sparkled. "Let's start doing it."

Her lips curved up. "Okay, boss."

He went back to his seat.

Smith leaned over and whispered, "Well played."

"I will get you back for that."

Smith didn't look like he would mind that at all. His ocean eyes had dropped to her mouth, as if imagining a different type of french kissing.

And now that was certainly what Claire was thinking about. He had beautiful lips.

Mona was watching Claire, and her daughter's narrowed gaze had Claire flipping her coy grin into a frown. She looked away from Smith and focused on her still-full plate.

Chapter 22
SMITH

A baby's cry sounded. To Smith's right, Mona stood. She excused herself, pressing into his side as she rose from the table. She flounced down the hall.

"This meal is fantastic," Dad said. His gaze flicked to the wine bottle on the kitchen counter again.

Dad wasn't a big drinker—not like Stevie, apparently. Smith felt awful for Claire. And her daughters. He wanted to know everything. He wanted to fix all the hurts. And he clearly cared way too much for her. She looked beautiful tonight. Those jeans. Yeah. He was looking. But her shoulders were rigid. Too bad he couldn't sit her in his lap on the couch while they watched TV together and he rubbed out her tension. Shit, where were these thoughts coming from? Those were deep-in-the-relationship moves.

He wanted to take care of her.

Dad looked at Mona's nearly full glass of his wine. And Smith almost handed it over to him. It was Dad's favorite vintage. At four hundred dollars a bottle, he didn't give that to just anyone.

Dad really liked Claire.

Smith didn't blame him. Claire would be quite the catch for the widowered man, but she wasn't the right woman for Dad. It wasn't solely because Smith revolted against the thought of his father touching her. Claire was laid back and quirky in a way that didn't suit his dad. She deserved a man who wanted to cherish her, tend to her with devotion, lift her up. That man wasn't his dad. But mostly, she could *never* become his stepmother.

He should burn the drawings of her when he returned home.

He wouldn't.

Mona came back with a baby in one arm and a high chair in the other. She maneuvered her chair toward Smith to make room. When she sat, they were thigh to thigh. Smith tried to give her more room, but his scooching ran him into Claire on the other side. With Mona's hip touching his, and his knee pressed into Claire's thigh, he stopped trying. That about summed up dinner.

"Would you pass me the mashed potatoes?" Mona asked.

He did, and Mona splatted a scoop in front of a bleary-eyed baby.

"Sorry Mom doesn't have cable," Edith said. "You boys are missing the football."

She looked so young. With her big gray eyes and silky curls, she might one day be nearly as beautiful as her mother, but she was years away from growing out of her baby face. He scanned the table. All these daughters seemed so young. Flighty and deep in the self-discovery stage. A world away from where he was in his life now. He remembered college—albeit not that well at this point. It was long ago.

He was old. He wanted a stable woman to share his life with. To give himself to. When would he find the right fit? He tried not to look at Claire.

"Basketball is more my thing," Dad said.

"And I'm big into Netflix." Indi toyed with the stack of necklaces at her throat.

Edith waved her fork in the air. "Aren't we all?"

"Its stock price would indicate so." Dad's tone was stodgy.

Edith eyed him like he was the biggest nerd—and not the good kind. Her phone rang. She looked at the screen, and her face lit up.

Claire frowned. "No phones at Thanksgiving dinner."

"It's Tyson."

"It's rude of him to call during dinner."

Edith stood, her chair scraping back. "I'll be fast."

"You know," Claire said, "absence makes the heart grow fonder."

"That's not true anymore."

"Those things don't change. You could make him miss you a little."

Smith 100 percent agreed, but Edith wasn't listening. She'd moved into the hall. "Oh, hey you."

Claire sighed as she surveyed the carnage of her Thanksgiving feast. She stood and reached for Smith's empty plate. He lifted it first. Together they gathered dishes and took them to the kitchen.

"Just leave them," she said. "I'll get them later."

"Let me do the dishes . . . please."

She looked at him, then back at the crowded table. The ghost of a grimace passed over her face. "Okay. Thank you."

He rolled up his left sleeve, then fumbled with the right button.

"Here, let me."

He turned to see Mona take his hand and gently unbutton his shirt at his wrist. She rolled up the sleeve, her fingers lingering on his forearms. He was so surprised he didn't think to stop her. He looked up and saw Claire watching. She turned abruptly away.

"There." Mona looked coyly up at him through fake lashes.

She was attractive. Another time, another place, he might have been interested. A younger Smith. He wasn't that anymore. Especially not when he couldn't stop thinking about another woman here. He picked up the scrub brush and turned on the water. How fast could they leave without being rude?

"Is it time for dessert?" Tommy asked.

Thank you, brother.

"Of course you can have your pie now." Claire's voice was sweet. "You've waited so patiently."

She danced around Smith as she got out ice cream, berries, and whipped cream. It was a small kitchen, but neat and pleasant. Garden flowers and greenery filled up the window view above the sink. She opened a tall cupboard to Smith's right.

"Would you please reach me down that stack of plates?"

He dried his hands and stepped up close to her. She pointed. Rolling onto his tiptoes, he got them down.

She took the dainty dishes. "Thanks. It's nice I didn't have to get the step stool." She seemed to be saying it more to herself, so Smith didn't reply, but he wondered. Did she miss having a man around to do the annoying little things for her? Or did Stevie not change light bulbs or check the engine oil? He sounded like he'd been a douche. Smith took ridiculous pleasure in helping her. What else would she let him do? Did her bike need a tune-up? Air filters replaced? He wanted to do it all.

The pies sat in a line on the counter. Each one had a slice cut out.

"Well." Claire chuckled awkwardly. "Looks like my girls couldn't wait as long as Tommy." She eyed Edith, who'd just walked back in. "When you asked for pumpkin pie for breakfast, I didn't realize you meant pumpkin and pecan and apple. And what have you done with the banana cream?" A third of it was gone, leaving a giant hole the rest of the pie was threatening to fall into.

Smith chuckled. His mom would have lost it if she'd gone to serve her pie and found a messy chunk forked out of it.

Edith grinned like a girl who was used to getting away with murder. "Just doing quality control. And they are all good. Except the pecan is a little too soft."

"No one asked you." There was no heat in Claire's voice, just tolerance. She exhaled, then turned toward the dining table with a smile. "What can I get you, Banks?"

"Apple pie à la mode." Smith said it at the same time and in the same tone as his father. He chuckled. "It's always his first choice."

Dad tossed Smith an annoyed look before facing their host. "Is this the famous apple pie Roger told me about?"

"He does really like it." Claire tried to look demure, but Smith could see the pleasure she took in the compliment.

And Roger wasn't wrong. The pie was incredible, with a flaky crust, tart apples, and just the right amount of cinnamon. When they'd eaten as much as they could stuff in, Dad finally stood and started helping clear the table. Smith kept handing Dad dishes and napkins in an effort to stop him from sitting down and getting comfortable again. The man could talk forever.

"Thank you for having us." Dad folded a dish towel on the counter. "I'm sorry if we intruded on your family day, but it was wonderful to meet your daughters. You have a lovely family."

Good boy, Dad. Time to leave.

Claire stopped her tidying. She picked up the bottle of wine and stuffed the cork a half inch in. "I'm sorry you felt you couldn't enjoy this with dinner. It was thoughtful of you to bring it."

He accepted the bottle. "We had a fantastic time. And the food was amazing."

"Thank you."

Her daughters trailed her as they walked to the door.

Tommy put on his loafers. "Everyone french kiss on the way out."

Dad and Claire both chuckled with the same nervous cadence.

Claire knelt and kissed the air against Tommy's cheeks. "I'll see you Monday, okay?"

Mona blocked Smith's view, filling his vision with her eager eyes and beaming smile. "Nice to see you again."

"Yeah. You too." He tried to keep his voice from giving her any expectations.

She gave him a hug. He loosely tapped her shoulder. Did she just touch his butt? He pulled back and frowned. She grinned. Hard to believe she was Claire's daughter. Their vibe was so different. Claire leaned against the door in the most uninviting stance. There would be no hugging or kissing with her. Bummer. But at least she smiled at him.

"See you later," she said.

He really hoped she meant it.

The Sextons climbed in Smith's car. Smith's back pocket crinkled. He reached and pulled out a folded piece of paper. It had a phone number and the words *Call me. Xoxo. M.*

He crumpled it and shoved it into his cupholder before Dad noticed. When they were out of sight of the house, Dad uncorked the bottle and took a swig.

"Whoa," Smith said.

"I could smell it the whole time and couldn't even take a sip."

"You could have had a glass. I don't think she cared." Although Smith hadn't been willing to have any himself. Not when she'd clearly been traumatized by her late husband's drinking.

"Did you know Stevie died drunk driving?" Dad asked, brow furrowed.

"Yes."

Dad looked at him sidelong. "You did? How?"

Smith forced a shrug. "I don't know. It came up once." He remembered the hot tub conversation vividly. He'd never felt the need to kill or to kiss so acutely and at the same time.

Dad exhaled. "That was heavy shi—" He looked over his shoulder at the little boy in the back seat. "Stuff."

"Yeah. Poor woman. No wonder she's never remarried."

Dad squinted at the ocean over the dash. "Do you think she'll *never* remarry?"

That was such a loaded question.

"I don't know, Dad. Probably not. But maybe if she found the right man. Someone who would treat her like she deserves to be treated. Like a queen."

Dad didn't notice that Smith had never talked about a woman like that before. Dad was nodding and smiling at his own internal thoughts. The hope in Dad's eyes was so raw and hungry it made Smith physically sick.

Chapter 23
BANKS

Banks lay on his bed with his laptop open. He flicked through emails on the personal account he only checked every few days. Scan. Delete. Scan. Delete. Man, Tommy's school sent a lot of emails. His blood turned cold as he read.

> No school Friday, December 11.

That was tomorrow.

He cursed. What? Why? He sounded like a whiny child in his head. Tomorrow wasn't a holiday. They weren't supposed to spring this on him. Not when he was floundering. This was the opposite of the support he needed right now. It had been a rough couple of weeks for him, starting with the Thanksgiving meal at Claire's. It had been a perfectly delicious and lovely afternoon with delightful people, but it hadn't been *home*. He'd missed Helen's cranberry-jelly salad. Every year he teased her about the obscene dish, and now he would have given anything to have a scoop of the jiggly red walnut-and-pineapple mush. And he'd missed so much the tradition of rubbing out her feet. After the meal—and a divine bottle of wine—he and Helen would curl up on the couch and watch the Cowboys together while he showed his appreciation for her cooking by digging his thumbs into her flat feet until her back arched in response.

Never again would he get to do that.

He cringed remembering how he'd drunk the wine straight from the bottle on the way home from Claire's. He'd apologized to his sons, but he was still embarrassed.

Grieving politely wasn't one of his talents. He was now at a low point where he felt society expected him to be 100 percent, but his heart was just starting to accept that Helen really was not coming back. The future without her looked bleak and endless. And dealing with no school tomorrow seemed impossibly hard. It was the little things that seemed to disable him the most.

He picked up his cell. It was 10:48. Too late to call Claire. But he had to do it.

"Hello?"

"Claire. I'm so sorry to call this late." His voice came out raspy.

"Are you okay?" Her voice was tender with concern. "What's wrong?"

My wife is fucking dead. "I'm fine, but I dropped the ball and just found out there's no school for Tommy tomorrow."

"At least you figured it out tonight. I've taken my kids to an empty school before. Every parent has been there."

Banks was sure this had never happened to Helen. Or if it had, it hadn't mattered because she was home to deal with it. He had to be at the office tomorrow. He had two client meetings scheduled before lunch.

"I hate to ask this last minute, but is there any way you could be here in the morning at eight?"

"I'm so sorry. I have an appointment. And I can't change it now."

He knew he didn't have any right to be mad at Claire. This was his fault. Dammit. He'd messed up, and now he was dealing with this stupid problem at the last minute. "What time could you come in?"

"I could be at your house by noon."

Banks scowled. He needed to be in the office earlier than that. "Okay. I appreciate you being willing to come in early. Let me see what I can figure out. Can I call you right back?"

"Of course."

"Thanks." He hung up and dialed Smith.

"Hey, Dad. Everything okay?"

"I've got a problem. Tommy doesn't have school tomorrow. I just found out, and Claire has an appointment in the morning, which is terrible timing. She can't get out of it."

"She shouldn't have to."

"I know. Obviously, I know that, but I'm still in a bind. It's late, and I don't know how to fix this, and I'm frustrated, and I miss your mother."

Smith's voice was soft. "It's okay, Dad. We'll figure it out."

Banks exhaled, some of the tension in his chest loosening. He wasn't alone. He felt a wave of love for his oldest son. "Thanks for letting me vent."

"Always."

"I just hate being a burden on you. I know you have work, but I wanted to ask what your morning looks like and if you could take Tommy for a couple hours?"

There was a pause. Banks held his breath and crossed his fingers.

"I can clear my morning schedule, but you must, *must* pick him up by one p.m. at the latest."

Relief flooded Banks. "Yes. Absolutely. No problem. Thank you. I'll drop him off in the morning about eight."

Banks called Claire back. She agreed to pick Tommy up from Smith's house by twelve forty-five.

He leaned against his pillows and sighed in relief. Problem solved. He stared at the photo of Helen on his nightstand. It was his favorite picture of her, a candid of her cheering at Smith's high school soccer game, a huge smile on her face as she pumped her fist.

His phone buzzed with a text from Claire. What's Smith's address and phone number?

He shared the contact, then went to sleep holding Helen's cold pillow tight to his chest.

Banks pulled up to Smith's house in Corona del Mar at eight fifteen the next morning. Tommy knocked on the door. They waited. And waited.

What would he do if Smith had forgotten? He'd have to take Tommy to the office. Tommy could watch a movie while Banks was in meetings. He hadn't brought the tablet, but he'd figure it out. In the light of day, the problem didn't seem so big as it had last night. Tommy would have fun with the snacks in the office kitchen. Banks could run him home at noon to meet Claire. He found he wasn't even annoyed with Smith for not being here. He and Tommy would have an adventure. Time to teach his youngest about the business world.

The door opened. Smith was in gym shorts only. He rubbed his wild hair. Sleepiness glazed his eyes.

"Still in bed," Banks teased. "Must be nice."

Sunlight glinted across Smith's green gaze. Beautiful eyes that looked so much like his birth mother's. Banks hadn't thought about her in decades. The vacuum Helen's absence left was sucking up all sorts of weird thoughts lately.

"I stayed up late working to free up my morning for you."

"And I really appreciate it." He knew Smith worked hard. Most days, the overachiever was up early at the gym or on his bike. A change from high school, when it had taken a forklift to get the boy out of bed. Smith had grown up. Would he settle down with a woman soon? Start a family? Banks could only hope.

On the other hand, something about his son's thick hair and strong body on display made Banks jealous this morning. Banks was a single man now, and it was disconcerting that males like his son were the competition. Banks didn't stand a chance. "Thank you. I owe you big time." He bent down and kissed Tommy's brow. "You boys have fun."

"Come on in, T-bone." Smith looked at Banks, squinting against the bright eastern sun. "I'll see you before one o'clock."

Chapter 24
CLAIRE

Claire held Millie on her lap while Mona freshened up her auburn highlights. She could have canceled on her daughter last minute, but she didn't want to. Mona was expecting her, and she needed her hair done. But the bigger issue was that she didn't want to set a precedent with Banks. She was the nanny—not the mom. Those lines of duty seemed to have been blurred of late.

After a trim, Mona styled Claire's hair with a well-done blowout and loose curls. "You do such a nice job," Claire said.

"You make me look good." Mona set down the brush. "Prettiest mom in town." She went to the kitchen and pulled sandwich fixings from the fridge. "Smith hasn't called me. It's been two weeks."

Claire jolted. "Does he have your number?" She did not like how her pulse had jumped. She now had Smith's number. She also had his address, email, and birthday—May 4. She even knew his blood type, O-, and the code to his garage, 7530. Banks's contact file for his son had been quite thorough. She hadn't meant to invade his privacy.

Mona did her wicked grin Claire knew all too well. "I snuck it into his pocket at Thanksgiving."

"You did not." Obviously Mona had, and Claire's shock was a cover for the churning in her guts. "Maybe he didn't get it."

"Of course he did. But whatever. I'm over it. He's super lame because I'm hot stuff and he sucks."

"Sorry, honey." Oh, the lies she told her kids. "You'll find someone way better." Claire didn't believe that either. The Sextons, all three, were some of the best men she'd ever met.

Claire helped clean up, paid her daughter for the cut and color, and kissed Millie. Then she drove to Smith's house, a cozy beach cottage one street up from the water. Craftsman style with great landscaping. Dammit, it was darling. She knocked on the front door at a quarter past twelve. Smith's voice yelling at her to come in penetrated through the wall. Pulse rising, she turned the knob and slid into a sitting room with one leather couch and two linen chairs.

"We're back here."

She followed the deep voice down a short hall and into a bedroom. Smith's bedroom. She froze on the threshold. What was she doing here? She inhaled cedar and citrus and faint cologne. She tried not to look at the massive king bed, made up in shades of gray.

"Careful. Keep it flat." Smith's voice came from the bathroom across the room. The door was open. Steam and light spilled out.

Curiosity had her gliding to the door. She froze. Smith was wearing a towel around his waist. Only. Unless she counted the shaving cream on his face as coverage. She didn't. Tommy was sitting on the counter. Smith stood in front of him, his big hand over Tommy's, guiding the razor up his cheek.

She melted at Smith's tenderness. He was going to make the best father someday. A drop of water beaded off the end of Smith's luscious hair and dripped down ridged back muscles. His smooth skin was begging to be touched. Tasted. She wanted to trace the faint freckles on his broad shoulders and memorize the canvas of his trim waist. She chewed on her tongue as her whole body tingled with attraction.

Smith caught sight of her in the mirror, and he twitched in surprise. He hissed, pulling the blade back. Red dribbled down his cheek.

Horror cut through her core. Should she help or flee? "I'll wait in the other room." She fled.

She tried to sit on the couch, but jitters had her up and pacing the small living space. She'd never get the image of Smith's body, warm from the shower and golden from the sun, out of her mind. And he was letting Tommy help him shave. That was the sweetest thing she'd ever seen. Swoon. She cursed for a while inside her head.

Then she saw the sketchbook on the end table.

She shouldn't pick it up. She did. She flipped it open. His style was slightly animated, but bold and engaging. She stopped on an image of a whale and her calf. He'd made it so the intense detail on their eyes and touching fins drew her focus exactly to those points. To the powerful emotion and bond between the two beautiful creatures. Claire was riveted. Smith was really good. She turned more pages. Lots of people illustrations. She recognized Tommy, Banks, and Helen, but mostly there were sketches of beautiful women. She tried not to be jealous. And then she saw her face.

Her body stilled as her heart went bonkers. Her hands quivered, and her breath turned shallow. He'd drawn her as a huntress. A *hot* huntress. He didn't really think she was that sexy, did he? It was part of his style. It was just art. She, an artist, knew better than to believe that.

She needed to put this book down. Smith would walk in any second and see how invasive she was being, how horny this made her. She turned the page. Another of her. And another. One was of just her face, her eyes like glowing embers. She hesitated on the one where she was standing in Banks's pool. Smith was with her. They stood close. He'd captured the moment before a kiss. The tingle before the lightning. Just looking at the image sent fire and want through her body. Why was he drawing these pictures? She heard footsteps and snapped the book shut. She shoved it onto the end table and jumped back. Her heart was a freight train. Her skin was a furnace. She heaved in air as Smith and Tommy appeared.

Smith wore work slacks and a button-down. She itched to take his clothes right back off. Those drawings . . .

He looked to her, to his sketchbook, back to her. Worry filled his aqua eyes.

"Tommy." Claire's voice came out too loud. "Nice job on Smith's face." She cringed inwardly. "You get your stuff? You ready to go?"

"I'm sorry," Smith said. "I thought my dad was coming to pick him up."

"Surprise." Why was her voice so weird right now?

"Your hair looks nice."

Her thank-you sounded mostly normal. Now if she would just stop blushing like a pubescent. But he'd noticed her. Now she knew just how observant he was. In that last drawing, he'd even included the tiny freckle under her left eye.

Tommy picked up his backpack.

"See you, Tommy." Smith gave his little brother a fist bump. "Thanks for hanging with me this morning."

Claire led the way outside. Smith followed. She unlocked her car.

"I need to go potty," Tommy said.

Claire took his backpack. Tommy ran back toward the open door. She and Smith both said, "Wash your hands."

Smith chuckled.

"Jinx. You owe me a chocolate bar," Claire said.

"It's a soda."

"I changed it."

"Good for you."

Claire opened the door to the back seat and set in Tommy's bag. She jerked her attention up at the squeal of car tires. Twenty feet down the road, a white sedan swerved, its break lights flaring. A flash of fur darted in front of the car. There was a thudding crunch. And then a woman screamed. Claire's veins turned to ice. She followed Smith as he sprinted to the scene.

On the asphalt in front of the car lay a small motionless dog. Blood leaked from its mouth and ears. The woman knelt, weeping and making a panicked keening sound that made Claire's ears throb. The woman checked for a pulse, muttering and pleading with the lifeless animal. And by the howl she let loose, Claire guessed she didn't find one. The driver was an older man, white as a sheet as he got out.

"Can we help?" Smith asked as he stepped into the street. "Or call for help?"

The woman whirled, her eyes maniacal. "He's dead!"

Smith spoke softly. "Let me carry him home for you."

She broke down into another wave of sobs and turned her hunched back on Smith. "Go away."

The driver came and knelt at the shocked woman's side. He didn't say the dog should have been on a leash. He apologized and brought forth compassionate tears. Impressive.

Tommy had come out of the house and looked down the street toward them. Smith strode back to usher him into Claire's car before he could see what had happened. Claire followed at a slower pace. She'd need to calm the hell down before she got behind the wheel. In her mind, as clearly as if it were five years ago, she saw Stevie in the hospital bed. He'd died before she got there. Before she could say goodbye. The strength of her grief, even after everything, had been a shock. She'd never forget the lines of blood over his ivory skin. The destruction of his nose and jaw. The stillness and finality. Her daughters' father was gone. The man who had caused her so much heartache and stress was gone. Just gone.

She thought of the time she'd gotten a flat on her beach cruiser. She had it on her list to take to the shop. When she'd finally gone to do it, it had already been fixed. She'd thanked Stevie, and he'd shrugged.

"You're welcome, babe. It was nothing compared to all you do for me. I'm so grateful to you. Thanks for taking care of me."

Over. Their whole life together, good and bad, was gone in an instant.

She shuddered, her body trying to curl in on itself like a dying frond.

"Come here."

She blinked at the deep, gentle voice, so close, drawing her back from that faraway place. Strong arms wrapped her shoulders, inviting her into a comforting chest. She melted against Smith. Her arms came up, and she clutched his back. He shifted his hands, one around her waist, the other her shoulders, welcoming her closer into the haven of his body. He smelled of fine aftershave, woodsy and enticing. She pressed deeper into his warmth. Heaven. Indescribable pleasure. Her whole soul seemed to sigh and loosen. When was the last time someone had enveloped her like a living blanket?

Stevie hadn't held her like this very often, with his whole body focused on cradling her, not for sex, but to sustain her and feed her love. And it'd been five years since she'd had one of his halfhearted hugs. Any touch from him at all. Her hands cupped the broad planes of Smith's back muscles. She wanted to sink forever into this embrace, this magic. She allowed herself another long delicious moment of pleasure before she regretfully pulled away.

"You okay?" Smith looked her in the eyes, his brows tight, as if he truly cared.

"Yes. Thanks. Thank you. It is really nice to be held by you."

His eyes darkened, bringing heat to her cheeks.

Maybe people didn't say things like that, but she was too old to act coy, and she was standing upright because of the strength he'd just breathed into her. "It's just . . . you know . . . I mean . . . because Stevie died in a car accident. And seeing that little dog like that . . . I guess I haven't fully healed from the trauma." As she said the words, she knew they were true. She'd closed off for five years, and in that time, the wounds had festered. At first Smith had caused her defenses to flare up. He was a threat to her freedom and peace. But that was wrong. Looking in his earnest face and feeling his compassionate energy, she felt her fears ebbing away. He was healing salve. She exhaled as another portion of the old pain finally left her. She inhaled, feeling lightness and optimism.

He nodded. "I'm sorry. It must bring back such grief."

"It did. Thanks for allowing me my little freak-out, but I'm okay now. I'm more than okay. You being here for me, truly seeing me." She swallowed. "Makes me . . ." She smiled, and his gaze dropped to her mouth. She chuckled. "I feel good. It's awful that dog died, but"—she put a hand over her steady heart—"it's got nothing to do with me. Thank you for helping me see that."

"I didn't do anything."

She focused on his ocean eyes, the feel of his low voice vibrating through her core. "You did. You listened to me, and you held me, and you helped me take another step out of the hole I've been hiding in."

He leaned closer, his chin tilted down. His eyes darkened. "That's . . . I . . ." His gaze slid over her face and hovered on her mouth. His fingers reached forward and touched the hand she lowered from her chest.

Her body came to full alert. He was so close. She wanted to feel exactly how smooth a shave he'd gotten. His wide lips parted slightly. If his hug was that potent, what would a kiss do?

"Ms. Claire." Tommy opened the car door. "You coming?"

She jolted. Tommy. Yikes. She'd completely forgotten about him.

Smith leaned back, his eyes widening.

"Yes." Feeling fuzzy, she stepped toward the car. "See you, Smith."

"Bye, Ms. Claire." Smith's grin was as wicked and seductive as sin.

She closed the car door a little too hard.

She drove slowly, the opposite of her racing pulse. She checked on Tommy constantly in the mirror. He was buckled. He was safe. He was smiling and humming to himself.

I'm okay too. I'm fine. But it wasn't Stevie's death that was bothering her anymore. It was Smith, the pleasure of his embrace and the crackle she'd felt when his face had tilted toward hers.

At the house, she played Go Fish with Tommy, but her mind was far away, thinking about Smith. And Banks. And Stevie. Thinking about the fluttering in her belly that was as foreign to her as the dark side of the moon.

Claire's mom had told her when she got married that she should give her husband sex whenever he wanted it. If she didn't, he'd get it elsewhere.

She'd followed that terrible advice.

And because Stevie got sex whenever he remotely felt like it, he didn't bother with romance. Why would he care to wine and dine her? Why court her when she was caught? Or even attempt to be attractive himself? He farted like a trumpet in bed and thought it was funny. He didn't bother brushing his teeth in the morning before wedging his tongue between her teeth. It had been years since Stevie had tried to be sexy and charming or flirt. And forget about foreplay—he certainly had.

Claire hadn't accepted until today, with Smith's worried, tender gaze on her, his body flush against hers, that she craved romance. Affection. But lasting love stories were for novels—that's why they were called fiction. She'd never felt the epic sparks so poetically described in books. But today with Smith, a chaste hug had lit her up like a beacon.

By the time Banks got home from work at nine thirty that evening, she had disciplined her mind and reclaimed her cool, calm, collected poise. No dating. No men. No problem.

She insisted that she'd closed her heart back up and thrown away the key. Now she just needed Smith to stop rattling the cage.

"You look nice tonight, Claire," Banks said after he'd set down his suit jacket and briefcase. He eyed her hair and face; then his gaze slid down her body.

She stiffened, afraid to enjoy the compliment. Afraid to even move, lest her equanimity crumble.

"Thanks for picking up Tommy from Smith's. Did everything go okay?"

A touch of fire licked under her collar as she pictured the half-naked man in a tight towel, remembered the sexy images he'd drawn of her. "Yes. Fine." She moved toward the door.

"I know it's late. But do you have a minute?"

Dread crept down her spine. She nodded.

"Come to my office."

What had she done wrong? He didn't seem angry, but she felt like she'd been summoned to the principal's office. He sat in his chair and motioned her to sit across the desk from him. She perched nervously on the seat.

"We've loved having you here these last three months. You have been a miracle worker for Tommy. I'm grateful to have you. You're flexible and kind. I want to make sure you're happy here."

She breathed easier. This was a very nice turn of conversation. "It's been an ideal position for me. Tommy is wonderful. He's a credit to you and Helen."

"Thank you. But please be honest. Is there anything you want to see change?"

She could see why he had risen so high in his company. He was a good boss with a generous, thoughtful heart. "No. What about you? Do you have any complaints?"

He got a crooked smile. "We could do with more of your pecan-cinnamon bread."

She chuckled, the tension in her belly unspooling completely. "I'll take it under consideration."

"I'm kidding . . . mostly." He chuckled. He picked up a fountain pen and twisted it in his fingers.

She waited, nerves rising again. Clearly this meeting wasn't over.

"Every January we take a company trip to Hawaii. It's a perk of working for the firm, and everyone needs a break after the end-of-year rush. The employees bring their families. It's mostly relaxing and beaching, but we have a couple company meetings scheduled throughout the week."

Claire's mind whirled. She'd never been to Hawaii. Of course she wanted to go. But could she say yes when Banks was looking at her like that, full of hope and desire?

"It's a lot of fun. We do a big luau. There's sailing, surfing, swimming, snorkeling." He chuckled at himself. "Whatever *S* activities you want."

Sex.

Had Claire seriously just thought that?

Sex.

There it was again.

Seduce Smith. Quite the S *activity.*

Shit.

Also S.

Banks inhaled. "Would you come with us? I'd want you to help with Tommy while I'm in the meetings, but you'd have plenty of time to enjoy yourself too."

"Yes." Better not to think too much about these things. And obviously Smith wouldn't be going since Banks needed Claire to come babysit. Adult children were probably not invited on company trips. "I'd love to come. I've never been to Hawaii."

Banks beamed, his blue eyes filling with satisfaction. "Well, great. It's settled. You're going to love it. There's not a more beautiful place. I'll show you all around."

Claire wanted to be excited, but Banks's buoyant tone had her suddenly fearing she'd given him the wrong impression.

Chapter 25
SMITH

Smith stood in his dad's kitchen with Aunt Ivy. She and her husband and son had come into town from Vegas this morning, in time for Tommy's birthday party and to stay through Christmas. Smith and Ivy stood side by side, picking at the cheese tray.

"I've missed this view." Ivy stared starry eyed at the ocean out the window.

Smith followed her gaze, but his focus snagged on Claire, as it had been doing since he got here an hour ago. She wore a loose knee-length dress and her hair in a youthful ponytail. She stood at the edge of the pool, watching ten kindergarteners flounder around. She wasn't outfitted for a pool rescue, but Smith wouldn't mind seeing that dress get wet.

"Claire seems wonderful," Ivy said.

He dropped his gaze and picked up an olive. "She's great for Tommy."

"And for Banks."

They watched his dad walk over to Claire, touch her elbow, and lean close to tell her something. Claire pointed to the party-adorned table.

"How long until he asks her to marry him?"

Smith choked on the olive.

Ivy pursed her lips as she looked at him. "Oh, come on. You know you're thinking the same thing."

"I was not."

"Banks sure is."

Smith's insides curdled.

"I just can't figure out why he's slow playing. It's not like she wouldn't be all over it. He's a rare catch. Money, looks, charm, and the cutest six-year-old ever."

He frowned. "That doesn't automatically mean he can get any woman he wants."

"Yes, it does."

He forced his face out of a scowl and into indifference.

Dad opened the glass door and stepped inside.

"I approve of the babysitter," Ivy said. "I think you should keep her around for a *long* time."

Dad's cheeks flushed slightly. Caught. His grin went from embarrassed to calculating.

Shit.

Ivy giggled.

Double shit. Smith couldn't handle this anymore. Would he ever be able to handle Claire going *there* with his dad? He couldn't focus on it without his mind tripping. Triple shit. "Hey, I'm going to take off."

"Hold up. We're about to do the cake. At least stay for that," Dad said. "It's one of those good ones Franny Bell makes."

"Fine." Only because leaving now might hurt Tommy's feelings.

"I'm just looking for the candles." He opened and closed a bunch of drawers, then stuck his head out the door. "Claire. Where are the birthday candles?"

She walked over and came inside. "I bought them yesterday and thought I set them on the counter."

"Well, I'm not seeing them." His voice held frustration.

Smith bit his tongue to keep from telling his father to be nice.

Claire's face cringed with worry as she frantically began looking. She moved the fruit bowl. "Here they are. Phew."

"Ah, perfect. Thank you." Banks took them and grabbed the lighter. "Bring the ice cream, and then have the kids get out of the pool."

Smith didn't love his dad bossing her around. But Dad was her boss, and Smith should not care.

Claire went to the freezer, but Smith beat her there.

"I'll get it," he said.

She looked him in the eyes. His heart reacted with a leap. "Thanks." It was a whispered, intimate word. She hesitated for a breath, then turned away.

Smith cheered so loudly after the birthday song that Tommy scowled at him. "Happy Birthday, old man!"

His belly was too unsteady for cake, and Franny Bell used too much sugar. Merely thinking that made him feel grizzly and overly responsible. He got into a conversation with his uncle about race cars, and by the time he looked up, the party was over. The kids were filing out, and Claire had her purse in hand. Ivy insisted on doing cleanup and sending Claire home. Claire didn't argue. She looked tired as she kissed Tommy and wished them all a merry Christmas and left.

A piece of Smith went with her. He'd been here two hours and said exactly three words to the woman: *I'll get it.* What a wasted opportunity. Opportunity for what? *Stop being daft.* He helped Ivy clean up. He showed Tommy how to use the remote control truck his awesome older brother had bought him. He said goodbye with a promise to come back next week for Christmas Eve.

At the door he noticed Claire's cream sweater on the entry table. No big deal, she'd be here Monday and could get it then. But next week was Tommy's winter break. Ivy was here. Claire wouldn't be back until January. Trying not to think about it too much, Smith picked up the sweater and walked out. He drove slowly up to her house, the sweater puddled on his lap. It was soft. He lifted it to his face. It smelled faintly of orange blossoms and laundry soap. Feeling odd and fluttery, he pulled up to her house. He climbed out, smoothing out his golf shorts and T-shirt.

The snap of branches and a curse sounded from the side of the house. Grinning, he stalked around the corner. He found her deep in the tangles of an overgrown tree. Vines and branches crept over the bricks, and honeysuckle dangled from the pergola. Cut tree branches littered the ground. Claire had changed into a white tank top and yoga pants, which hugged her willowy form. Beautiful. From her narrow calves to her square shoulders. Olive skin and long messy hair. Attraction rose through him like a wildfire.

"You okay?"

She whirled, her sheers coming into an attack position. A vine whacked her face.

He couldn't stop his bark of laughter.

"Oh. Smith." She lowered her trimmers and dropped them on top of her cuttings. "What are you doing here?" She seemed more flustered than accusatory. She swatted at the hanging vine that smacked her right back again.

He stepped forward and lifted the offending honeysuckle away from her stunning face. The sweet scent of blossoms tickled his nose. "You left your sweater, so I thought I'd drop it by on my way out."

She took it, holding it against her chest as if it were a security blanket. "That was nice of you."

Well, he'd done what he came to do. Time to go. But he wasn't ready to leave. He was here with her. In this charming tangle of trees, no Dad, no Tommy. She was the huntress he'd drawn. But real. Here. Vibrant and magnetic, eclipsing the living beauty of her garden. He was a starving man lost in the woods, hungry for her. He couldn't stop himself from imagining having a taste.

His hand lifted to her face, and he brushed at a smudge of dirt on her cheek. She jolted at his touch. The current zapped up his arm. She turned huge vulnerable eyes up at him. His fingers slid below her chin, her skin satin against the roughness of his hand. Her makeup was sultry, with dark eyeliner and copper shimmering on her lids, making her irises pop. She looked down. Away. Every particle of him reached for her. Tenderly, his palm slid to cup her cheek. Her skin was impossibly soft. When she didn't move away, he tilted her face up. Her focus caught on his lips, and her pupils went inky as midnight. Then she looked him in the eyes. Fire roared through his core.

"You are glorious," he whispered.

Her breath caught. The sweater slipped from her fingers and brushed his shins as it fell. The garden faded, leaving only her. She was his world.

He hesitated, giving her a chance to step back before he closed the gap. With aching slowness, he lowered his mouth to hers.

Sparks shot through him. She shifted closer, her hands finding his waist. As her lips parted, she let out a soft sound of desire that had him drawing her body tight against his. Sticks cracked beneath their feet, like kindling for a fire. Her tongue found his. Her eagerness stoked the flames. She tasted of apples and salt. She felt like a dream. His hands roamed her back, moving lower. He could not remember a kiss so full of magic. He could not remember anything. His touch slid over smooth spandex and round curves. Her hand cupped his neck and raked into his hair, sending currents over his scalp. She drew him deeper into her mouth, her embrace.

He was a goner.

Abruptly she pulled back, her eyes wide and frightened. She pushed out of his embrace.

"No." Her lips were flushed red as rose petals. "We can't do this."

"No. We can." The words came out in a breathy pant. The thought of stopping was agony. His whole body thrummed with want. He reached for her.

She shook her head, her eyes as big as a startled horse's. "I'm sorry." She turned and darted toward the back of the house.

"Claire. Please. Wait. I'm sorry." He was taut as a bowstring, his veins fire and ice.

She didn't reply. She was already gone.

Chapter 26
CLAIRE

The tears had come before Claire even made it inside. She rushed through her back door and engaged the lock behind her. She half wanted Smith to follow her, half feared he would try to come in. That kiss. That was . . . she felt bewitched. His soft lips on hers. The heat of his body pressed against her, wanting her. His hands had turned her to molten jelly. Her lips throbbed, and her skin tingled. She ran to her room as if she could outrun the fear that roared through her mind, outrun the beast, awake now and hungry. Ravenous.

Brine dripping off her cheeks. She hadn't cried since Stevie's funeral—since the last man she'd let into her life. She sank to her bathroom floor as emotions overwhelmed her, and the flood raged unchecked. As much as she wanted to rush back to Smith and see where that unbelievable kiss would lead, feel his hands on her again, satisfy her overwhelming want, revel in his attention and rugged sexiness, she told herself *this* was why she didn't want a man.

They all made her fucking cry.

When she'd purged every last drop of sorrow and confusion and desire from her body, she peeled herself off the ground, washed her face, and went back to attacking the ill-mannered tree on the side of her house.

That night she went into her garage studio. She picked up her paintbrush, and this time when she approached the blank canvas, she didn't stop at the edge. She hurled herself into it, drowned herself in a world of color and creation. She started with a blue so inky it was nearly black. A jagged thrash of it that carried the pigment up the backs of her hands and arms. A dark beginning. Panting, she stepped back. It was already beautiful, stark and harsh, but it wasn't what she wanted it to be. She didn't want to leave it there. In pain. She found a smaller brush, and out of the angry mess, she layered on a million lights in golds and pinks and yellows. All tiny, but together, they made a shimmering tapestry of fire.

One ember at a time, she transferred the burning from her heart to the canvas. Her ragged breathing slowed. She sagged.

It was near dawn when she slumped in her chair. Her arms, paint splattered over them like a starry sky, hung limp in her lap.

She lifted heavy-lidded eyes to her work. It was new, different from anything she'd done before. In her earlier works, she'd used a lot of watery textures and flowing lines. This was fragmented and intoxicating. One word whispered through her mind in his low voice, *glorious.*

That's what he'd called her.

This is what it felt like.

She hauled herself up, brushing wisps of hair off her face, and circled her easel. On the back she inked the title.

GLORIOUS

She dragged her heavy body to bed and slept until Indi and Edith came home the next day.

She delighted in the distraction of her daughters. Over the next few days, they did all the traditional things: cookies, ice-skating, movies, shopping. In the busyness and fun, Claire almost convinced herself that she wasn't thinking about the Sextons, wasn't waking in the night in a hot flush, imagining what might have happened if she hadn't run from Smith.

Her daughters were thriving. Edith had finally memorized her PIN. Months away from home had matured her. Successfully raising independent daughters had been Claire's goal. Now that she'd attained it, the question rolled around in her mind. What next?

As she vacuumed up the fragments of an ornament that had fallen off the tree and shattered, she realized she wasn't done living. The ornament was painted with the Swiss Alps. Stevie had given it to her one Christmas with a promise to take her there one day. He hadn't taken her, and she hadn't taken herself, and she still wanted to go. She had the rest of her life ahead of her. She wanted to dance and sing and love and cry and feel many more rounds of magic. She wasn't sure what it all meant, but the bubbling optimism inside felt like a good sign.

Christmas Eve came. She lined up her neighbor gifts on the table. Like every year, she'd baked orange rolls for her closest friends. The croissant dough took her two days to make, but it was worth it to hear Roger gush about them all year. At the end of the row sat Tommy's and Banks's gifts. After five days, she missed Tommy. She just wasn't ready to face the other two Sextons. Banks with his hope and Smith with his temptation.

"Who's doing deliveries with me?" She looked over at her three daughters sitting together on the couch.

Mona groaned and patted her belly. "I ate too much dinner."

Edith bounced Millie on her knee and cooed at the baby. Not even listening.

Indi stood. "I'll come with you."

"Thank you, darling."

Together they loaded the car. She hit her closest neighbors first, sharing smiles and well-wishes. There were Dorian and Fran, the sweet couple at the end of the street who'd always been willing to watch her girls when she was in a bind. George and Hattie were next to them, chatty, chatty. The young Campbell family, who always left skateboards in the street. Lily Hewes, Claire's hiking partner and listening ear. Lily had helped Claire through a lot of sadness on those long walks. And she didn't forget Sam, the teenage boy who mowed her lawn. The Wittings had liked Stevie better than Claire, and she didn't talk much with them anymore, but she still dropped off a bag of chocolates and a card to them.

With her neighbors done, she and Indi headed south to Roger and Raven Char's. When they arrived, Indi carried the six pastries for Roger, and Claire had a tin of Raven's favorite tea.

When Roger opened the door, the women said, "Merry Christmas."

"Mylanta! You like to stress me out by waiting until the last minute." Roger lifted the plate from Indi's hands, peeled back the plastic, grabbed a roll, and took a huge bite. Sugar dusted his wide grin. He leaned forward and kissed Claire's forehead. She wiped away the wet granules he'd marked her with. "*Now* it's a merry Christmas."

Indi laughed. "You're a little nuts."

She'd learned that phrase from her father. Stevie had constantly said that about Claire. It wasn't so endearing back then, back when he'd blamed her for every discontent.

Roger winked at Indi. "Best way to live." He shoved the rest of the orange croissant into his mouth and picked up the next one.

"You've convinced me." Indi's face was alight with amusement and interest.

He looked behind them. "Where's Edith? Too shy to show her face around here? Well, Jimmy's not here anyway. But I'm still hoping we can get those two back together. Come in. Come in." He swallowed and hollered behind his shoulder. "Raven. Clara Bear is here."

Indi giggled, bringing her hand up to cover her mouth.

"Seriously, get inside already," Roger said.

"I can't. I have a gift for Tommy, and I want to catch him before he goes to bed."

"It's Christmas Eve. He'll be up for hours."

Claire and Indi let themselves be led into the warm, vibrant house.

"How's it going with those Sexton boys?"

For the billionth time, she pushed away the thought of kissing Smith, the fullness of his lips on hers. Salt and male and life. She thought she was pretty good at denying it by now. "It's great. Thanks for setting us up."

Roger got a wicked grin at her choice of words. Claire held up her hand to stop him right there.

Raven appeared and swept Claire into a tight hug. She gushed over the tea and handed Claire a gift wrapped in blue and gold. Claire opened it and exclaimed at the three high-end paintbrushes. Her favorite brand too.

"For when you're ready to start again," Raven said.

Warmth washed over Claire. She didn't tell Raven she'd spent the last five mornings in her garage. The creative streak still felt vulnerable and fickle. Raven—wise, discerning Raven—would ask what had brought about this change. Stupid Smith messing with her Zen was what. Claire needed to cover up the cause before Raven went digging around. Claire cradled the gift to her heart. "These are perfect."

"How nice of us," Roger said.

"Thank you too." Claire grinned at him.

He lifted a roll from the plate and held it out to Raven. "Here, honey. You can have this one. It's the smallest, but you'd better take it before I change my mind."

"That's the Christmas spirit." She took it.

"You can be grateful I shared any of them with you." He started on his third one.

"You can be grateful I share my bed with you."

He licked his fingers. "I am, dear. You know I am."

When the pastries were long gone and they'd enjoyed a cup of Raven's tea, Claire and Indi said goodbye.

"I like them," Indi said as Claire pulled her car onto PCH.

"Me too."

"I'd like to marry someone like Roger."

Claire stared out at the road, at the stoplights that flashed in Christmas colors. "I hope you do."

"He runs happy," Indi said.

What a poetic way to put it. Indi watched the world, and Claire loved when she got to see glimpses into her daughter's deep thoughts. "It's a good trait."

"Dad wasn't exuberant. Ever."

Claire sighed. "No. He wasn't." She pictured Roger shoving her croissants into his mouth as if they were the best thing in the universe. It made her feel like gold. Roger's love wrapped her like a bear hug, bold and undeniable.

Stevie had liked her cooking. He didn't let a meal pass without saying, "It's good, babe." But after hearing that a thousand times in the same flat voice, it didn't mean anything anymore. No variance, no thrill when she went to the extra effort of a layer cake or homemade Bolognese. It was the same with his *I love you*s. Rote. Habit. Nice, but boring as reading computer code. It wasn't her language.

Stevie had insisted her complaints stemmed from her being needy, asking for too much. He'd provided her a great life. He said she needed to cheer up and be grateful. That would solve her problems. She was responsible for her own happiness. Not him.

Even years later, his words got under her skin, made her wonder if it really had been all her fault. If she'd demanded too much in wanting an attentive, caring husband. Maybe she really had driven him to drink. If she got with Smith, she'd eventually screw it up with him too.

She exhaled. *No.* That was her trauma talking again. On their hikes, whenever Stevie came up, Lily would insist, "He emotionally manipulated and abused you, Claire."

She was not responsible for Stevie's actions or deserving of his contempt. She was not toxic. She was not crazy. She inhaled. *I am good and worthy of love.*

Feeling strength and peace, she reached for Indi's hand. "I am so proud of you."

Indi looked at her sidelong, interest in her kohl-lined eyes.

Claire stopped at a red light and focused fully on her middle child. Indi was creative and smart and funny, but sadness sometimes clung to her narrow shoulders. She had a melancholy side that gifted her insight and compassion. She was sensitive and passionate but often used humor or bold fashions to protect herself. "You are amazing. I'm in awe of your kind energy, brilliant creativity, and deep goodness. You deserve every great thing in life, including a man who treats you like the goddess you are."

Her daughter squeezed her hand with warm fingers. Indi's voice was achingly tender. "You know the same is true for you. Don't you?"

Claire's throat tightened against the sudden threat of tears. Good tears, healing tears.

Indi's bold brows pinched in concern. "Don't you?" Her tone sharpened.

Claire's chest swelled with love. She nodded.

"Say it, Mom. Say out loud: I am amazing. I'm kind and beautiful and genius. And even quite funny at times. Any man would be so lucky as to lick my feet or suck on my toes. I am fucking awesome."

"Indi!" Claire let out a cross between a snort and a cough and a chuckle.

Her daughter grinned, her hand still clasping her mother's.

"When did you get to be so wise?"

"Say the words, Mom."

Claire did. Word for disturbing word. And with her daughter's bright gaze on her, she believed it.

Heart warm and happy, she pulled up to Banks's house, now nearly as familiar as her own. She picked up the last two gifts from the back of her car, conscious that it was past 9:00 p.m. She prayed Tommy was still awake.

Smith answered the door. He wore fitted jeans and an ugly sweater with a tuxedoed snowman holding hands with Mrs. Claus. He was the last person she wanted to see. And the first. His gaze paralyzed her. He was more handsome than she remembered, his jaw sharp and his hair curling under his ears. She thought of the words she declared to Indi in the car. And she allowed herself to wonder. To want. Every feeling she'd suppressed flooded back. Her heart reached for him. Her skin awakened with the memory of that brief embrace. She ached to close the gap.

It was a solid four seconds of silence before Indi said, "Um, merry Christmas."

With robot arms, Claire held up her packages. "I just have something to drop off for Tommy. Is he awake?" She didn't have anything for Smith. Why would she?

He stepped back. "Course he is. That little Tasmanian is so hyped up it'll take a horse tranquilizer to put him down tonight."

"Ms. Claire!" Tommy's shriek echoed through the entry hall as he tore across the rug. Claire knelt, set down the gifts, and held out her arms. He flung himself against her and held tight. All the awkward tension in her chest dissolved. Tommy. That's who she was here for. When had she gotten so attached? She held on a moment extra, suffering a flash of regret that she'd never had her own son. She couldn't lose Tommy. And she needed to be more careful not to mess up her good gig. She gave him her gift, and he sat with her on the floor to open it.

Banks came up as Tommy was exclaiming over the toy construction trucks he'd unearthed. "That was nice of you, Claire."

Banks had already given Claire a gift—a cushy check folded into a holiday card with a lovely winter watercolor on the front. Good for him to still send out a card. Claire hadn't done any since the accident. Maybe next year she'd do cards. If Banks could do it, so could she. She'd been resentful of a dead man for far too long.

Indi helped Tommy untie the trucks from the packaging while he gave her a lesson in their make and model. Claire stood and held out the slim package to Banks. He opened it and held up a mahogany pen. She'd had his name engraved on the gold section.

"It's beautiful, Claire. Thank you." His voice was soft in appreciation.

Claire suffered a moment of discomfort. She'd thought a pen was a pretty generic, safe way to go for an employer gift. Why was he being difficult and acting all touched? It was all sorts of uncomfortable having Smith watching. She forced herself to be mature and look at him. "I should have something for you. I'm sorry." The apology wasn't for the gift. She willed him to understand.

He held her gaze and opened his mouth.

"Won't you come in?" Banks asked.

She shook her head. "I left the others at home. I didn't want to bother your evening, just wanted to wish you a merry Christmas."

"One minute," Banks said. "I have something for you."

He disappeared around the corner. Indi and Tommy played on the floor. Smith and Claire sized each other up. The three feet separating them turned taut and heavy.

"I'm sorry, Claire." Her name in his bass tones reverberated through her core. "Forgive me for overstepping." His voice was low, but she glanced at Indi, who was rolling a truck along the edge of the blue rug.

She nodded mutely, afraid of what she might confess. This wasn't the place. She breathed easier when Banks returned. Until she saw the light-blue box. What the hell was that?

"Merry Christmas, Claire."

"But you already got me something?"

"That was an end-of-the-year bonus. This is a Christmas gift."

From the most romantic jewelry store on the planet? She didn't want to open it. Smith stood like a statue as Claire lifted the lid. She pulled out a small crystal bowl. She chuckled and sighed. It was adorable and so *not* jewelry. She was so relieved she didn't even worry that it was heart shaped. "Thank you, Banks. I love it."

Indi stood and turned it over in her hands. The fifteen rings she had stacked on her fingers clinked against the crystal. "Don't be surprised if this mysteriously disappears when I go back to Boise."

Claire chuckled as she settled the heart back in its box. She said her goodbyes and well-wishes. Tommy gave her a hug. And then Banks did. She stiffened and leaned in awkwardly, but by the size of his smile, he didn't seem to notice.

And then Smith was in front of her again. She couldn't hug him right now. She was still suffering the shock waves from the explosion last week. She held out a hand. He raised an eyebrow, the expression in his gaze unreadable as he wrapped her palm in his. The warmth of his touch traveled up her arm and down her legs. She retracted her hand quickly. Apparently kissing palms was even too much right now.

Claire led her daughter out the door. "See you gentleman next year." It would be too soon.

Chapter 27
BANKS

Today was the day. Hawaii. The trip was finally here. Banks had been giddy about it since Claire had agreed to go. Five days in paradise with her. His heart danced as he shuffled down the stairs to Tommy's room.

"All set?"

Claire looked up from where she zipped Tommy's suitcase closed. "I think so. I packed a long-sleeve rash guard, but do you think he'll want a wet suit?"

"No. The water is warm."

She turned to Tommy, who was scanning the bookshelf. "Did you pick your two paperbacks for the plane?"

"Three?" Tommy held up four books.

She gave him the stink eye, but it wasn't very effective when combined with her smile. "Let's see if they all fit in your backpack."

"We can't forget the snack bag."

She bopped his nose lightly with her index finger. "Good remembering."

Banks had seen the zip-top bags in the fridge. One with his name on it with clementines, nuts, and fine chocolate, and one with Tommy's name that had crackers, string cheese, grapes, and mini lollipops—to help equalize his ears on takeoff and landing, Claire had said.

The woman was perfection. She thought of everything. He looked forward to coming home to her after work. He dreaded the weekends when he wouldn't see her. He would have been devastated if she hadn't come to Hawaii with them.

It was time to take this relationship out of the nanny zone and into the dating zone.

He just needed to figure out how to do that.

Together they loaded their bags into Helen's old Porsche Cayenne.

"Did you get the iPad charger?" he asked Claire.

"Yes. It's in my bag. We charged it last night. Tommy picked a movie to download. I hope that's okay."

He wanted to kiss her, but instead he said, "Thank you."

And as they drove away from his house, Claire in the front seat next to him, it felt as if they were already a family, going on vacation together. It felt like the sunrise after months of night.

Banks drove the familiar route to Smith's house, thinking about a life with Claire as his wife. He barely resisted the urge to reach over and hold her hand. It seemed so natural to do so.

"Are we making a stop on the way to the airport?"

He glanced over at Claire as he turned onto his son's street. "Smith is going to ride with us."

Her face drained of color.

What was that about? "Is everything okay?"

She forced a smile. "Yes, of course." Her voice came out raspy.

Had Smith said something rude to her? He could be a little too arrogant and outspoken at times, but he was a good kid. Banks parked the car. "I'll get him." Suffering waves of stress, he jumped out and ran to the door, but Smith was already coming out, his duffle slung over his back.

Smith locked his front door and strode toward the car. He stopped short when he saw Claire in the front seat. He swiveled toward Banks, turning his back to the car. "Why didn't you tell me she was coming?"

"I just assumed . . ."

"What? That when you invite the nanny on our family vacation you don't have to tell me?"

Banks balked at Smith's tone, then his face hardened. "I'm paying for this trip. She's my guest, and you will be nice to her."

Smith's jaw rippled, but he bit his tongue. He whirled and stalked toward the car.

Sure, Banks knew that Smith would have been happy to help with Tommy in Hawaii. Banks didn't *need* Claire to babysit on this trip. He'd invited her because he wanted her there. With him. He had a real problem if Smith and Claire weren't going to get along. He added their relationship to the list of issues he needed to fix.

Claire hopped out of the car and opened the back seat door. Smith put his hand on the door and loomed over her. She flinched when she looked up at his angry eyes.

"You sit up front," she said, voice meek.

"No. *You* sit up front." His tone was cold.

She slunk back to the front, and Smith thrust his body into the back seat. He closed the door too hard.

Yes, this was definitely a problem. Was Smith sullen because he didn't want Claire to replace Mom? Whatever the problem, that kid needed to get over it fast because Claire was here for the long haul.

"Aloha," Banks said as he pulled away from the curb. "Who's excited?"

"Me!" Tommy yelled.

Banks glared at Smith in the rearview mirror, but his son was staring out the window.

"Do you think we'll see turtles?" Claire asked.

Banks grinned at her, once again stopping himself from holding her hand. It was just resting there on her thigh. Waiting. "I'll sign us up for a snorkel at this place where there are always a ton of turtles."

"Is Tommy big enough to do it?" Claire asked.

"Yeah. Of course. We'll all go."

"No, thanks," Smith said.

Banks almost stopped and made him get out of the car. No one spoke for long minutes. It was a relief when the airport came into view. After they checked in and went through security, Smith announced he and Tommy were going on a fry hunt and they'd meet Banks and Claire at the gate. And then they were gone.

Banks looked at Claire. It was just the two of them for a few precious minutes. He didn't want to squander this. "Want to go to the lounge and get a drink? Er. I mean, they have sodas and coffee."

"You go ahead without me. I'll head over to the gate and make sure everything's fine."

"I'll come with you." Like he'd leave her. Although the lounge was his favorite part of flying. He swallowed away his disappointment.

At the gate, Claire stood by the window and watched the tarmac. How often had she flown? He'd gotten the impression it wasn't much. Banks visited with his firm's employees who were booked on his same flight and currently scattered around the waiting area.

Smith and Tommy appeared just as Banks was starting to stress about them being late for priority boarding. Tommy held up a massive box of fries.

"Want some?" Tommy asked between bites.

Banks lifted a few. "Offer them to Claire."

Tommy wandered over, and within seconds he was pointing out the different vehicles outside to Claire. Banks smiled at the two of them together. Picture perfect.

Smith slumped down next to Banks and pulled out his phone. He didn't look up until they were called to board.

They had four first-class seats, two and two.

"I'm sitting with Smith," Tommy said. "I already called it."

Well, thank you, Tommy. Banks looked over at Claire as his sons settled into the row behind. "Aisle or window?"

"Either is great with me," she said.

"You want to look out the window, don't you?"

She smiled, the first genuine one of the day. She nodded.

He ushered her in, touching his fingers to her lower back. He tried to wrangle his grin and failed. Claire buckled her seat belt and went straight to looking out the window like a curious child. He was struck by how different she was from Helen. Helen always had a huge purse, stuffed full of everything. Claire brought a small bag, neatly organized with the basics—he'd seen her open it. Helen fussed when she got on a plane. Fussed with her seat, her stuff, her husband, Tommy. Claire was as calm as still water, and as peaceful to be around. Helen wore loungewear on a plane for comfort. Claire had on fitted jeans and wedges.

"Banks."

He turned toward the voice and greeted the coworker who'd appeared in the aisle. He'd hoped Claire would notice how familiar and magnanimous he was with the employees as they passed his seat, but her focus remained elsewhere. When the attendant asked if Claire would like a drink, she declined. Banks stood to get an extra pillow from the stash he'd noticed in the overhead.

"Look what Ms. Claire made me," Tommy said to Smith.

Claire's attention snapped to the row behind them. She leaned over to look between the seats.

Smith took Tommy's snack bag. "How nice of Ms. Claire." His tone was slightly off.

"She made Dad one, too, but with old-person stuff."

"Not that old," Banks muttered. He leaned over, his forearms on the back of his seat so he faced his sons. "Did you tell Claire thank you?"

Smith chuckled. "She didn't make me one."

Banks obviously hadn't been talking to Smith.

"I didn't know you were coming," Claire interrupted.

"Excuses are like buttholes." Smith's voice was serious, but his eyes danced. "Everyone has one, and they all stink."

"Smith!" Banks frowned at his son, horrified. Truly horrified.

"Charming," Claire said, her voice deadpan. But as she turned away from the boys, Banks caught her chewing on her lip to suppress a smile.

Helen would not have been so forgiving of his rotten mouth.

Tommy laughed. "That was funny."

"That was gross," Banks said. "We don't say *butthole*."

"You just said it!" Tommy laughed so hard half-chewed bits of peanuts spewed over Smith.

"Whoa. Turbo Tommy. Ms. Claire might think you don't like her snacks." Smith's laughter was like low thunder rolling through first class.

Banks gave up. He turned around, snapped his seat belt on, and scowled. Claire looked over at him, and he softened his face. "I'm sorry. Your daughters probably were never ill mannered like this."

Claire snorted. "Girls are just like boys. Maybe with a touch more nuance."

"They seem so sweet."

"Sweet and sour."

He chuckled, hoping she'd say more, tell him personal things. She didn't. As a voice came on the PA giving takeoff instructions, it occurred to Banks that maybe he should ask her. But what questions would be good? Why was he being such a child right now? "Helen and I went to Hawaii on our honeymoon." He could punch himself in the face. Why had he said that?

Her face fell. "I'm so sorry." His arm rested on the center console, and she laid her hand over his. The touch felt so good. "This must be really hard. I'm sorry."

"No, I didn't mean to bring that up."

"You can talk about her."

"Where did you go on your honeymoon?"

She lifted her hand off his and leaned back in her chair. "We didn't. We got married right after high school. And then Mona was born. My parents cut me off financially." A pause. Her voice lowered. "And socially. We couldn't afford vacations for a long time. And then we just never got to it. Kids and all that."

No words came to Banks's mind or mouth. She'd never been on a romantic getaway?

She gave him an understanding half smile and turned back to the window.

The plane rolled away from the gate. Banks inwardly cursed himself, then gave himself a pep talk. His first swing was a miss. *It's okay.* He'd step it up with his next shot. But he was too cowardly to ask any more questions, and Claire seemed content to watch the world from her bird's-eye view. Banks took out his computer and worked.

Claire's body twitched. He glanced up as her head snapped back and then slowly began to roll down again. She'd fallen asleep. One fourteen in the afternoon and she was zonked. Adorable. He stacked the pillows on the armrest and gently guided her down, enjoying the fall of silky hair over his hands. He nested her head on the pillow, his palm cupping her neck for one second. She relaxed. Her hair fell into his lap.

He was in love.

Chapter 28
SMITH

As they touched down in Maui, Smith and Tommy finished off the annoyingly good bag of snacks Claire had packed. He should have known Dad would bring her on the trip. But he hadn't thought of it. Maybe because he'd banned all thoughts of her after she'd given him blue balls for three days.

Clearly she regretted the kiss. Big time. She didn't want Smith, but he shouldn't have been so rude to her and Dad. It was the shock of seeing her, of still wanting her with everything, that had set his teeth grinding and his temper flaring.

It wasn't obvious that this was a babysitter-type vacation. Smith and Dad could handle Tommy just fine on their own. And it's not like Claire had done anything helpful yet—snack bag not included. Smith was the one who'd played one thousand games of iPad Uno and taken Tommy to the nasty bathroom three times in the last five hours. He was happy to do it, truly anything for Tommy. He was just pissed she'd rejected him. He was determined to be sour.

"We're here," Dad said, standing as the seat belt sign dinged off. "Paradise awaits."

Smith wouldn't have to see her much. He was a grown man, and with her here to babysit, he could do his own thing. Lots of solo surfing. Maybe he'd rent a bike tomorrow morning, disappear until dinner.

Outside the airport, vans lined up to take the entire company party to the hotel. Smith sat up front with one of the drivers, leaving Claire to do her job and sit with Tommy in the back seat.

At the hotel, Claire and Tommy stopped at the koi pond by the entrance. She seemed as enthralled by the fish as Tommy was. She was going to love snorkeling. He wished he could be there to watch her. But, nope, snorkeling with Claire was on his bad-idea list. Everything with Claire was off limits until he stopped wanting to lasso her the moon.

Dad appeared with keys. "We've got a suite with two rooms for us boys." He handed Smith a card. "And here, Claire. You take Tommy's key. And your room should be right next door."

She took the two cards. "Thank you, Banks. This is so nice." She looked around at the vista of marble lobby and glittering ocean. She inhaled fresh blossoms and clean oxygen. Nowhere smelled better than Hawaii. "This place is incredible." She looked so pleased she might cry.

And just like that Smith repented of his earlier spite. He was happy that she could be here to enjoy this. She deserved a little spectacular in her life. He'd heard what she'd said earlier about her dick husband never taking her on a romantic trip.

If Stevie was her entire experience with men, no wonder she didn't want to try again. If only Smith could prove to her that Stevie was a rotten apple and Smith was, well, a juicy, crisp apple? That metaphor needed some work. As did his plan.

"They'll bring the bags up, but I told them we could find the rooms ourselves," Dad said.

They had better be able to. It was only the fifteenth time they had been to this resort. It was good every time. Smith smiled as a woman placed a lei around his neck.

They stopped at Claire's room first. All three of them walked her in. She had a king bed and an ocean view. She set her purse on the desk. Smith wanted to set his backpack down in here too.

"Will this be okay?" Dad asked.

"This is too nice. Thank you, Banks."

Dad beamed.

They left as the attendant brought in Claire's bag. Dad slipped him a tip.

"Can we go to the pool now?" Tommy asked.

"Yes, sir. Just as fast as we can get changed." Dad turned to Claire. "Would you like to join us? You don't have to."

"Of course I do. Just give me a couple minutes."

The boys trailed out. Dad unlocked their door, one down from Claire's. Two bedrooms and a sitting area. One bedroom had a king, and the other had two doubles.

As Smith and Tommy set their bags down in the room they would share, Smith felt like a little child again. He didn't like the feeling. And Claire was just on the other side of this wall in that big king bed. He was in the wrong room.

Dad strode in, wearing his swimsuit and T-shirt. "Ready?"

"I think I'm going to check out the surf instead."

Dad's face fell. His jaw hardened. He looked to Tommy, then back up at Smith. "Come with me for a minute, son."

Son. At what point would he grow out of the lectures? Smith followed his dad into the living/kitchen space, out of earshot of Tommy.

Dad spoke in a harsh whisper. "Is this about Claire?"

Smith tightened his lips, his pulse spiking with worry. Dad couldn't know about the kiss, could he? He was sure Claire wouldn't have mentioned it.

"I don't know what you did."

Dad would never know.

"But you need to fix this. She's a wonderful woman. If you give her a chance, you'll see that. I know you're angry that she's not Mom, but it's *important* to me that you try to get along."

Dread pooled like liquid nitrogen in his guts as Dad's intentions with Claire became clear. Hell no. "Don't do anything stupid, Dad."

He twitched. "What does that mean?"

Smith's stomach churned, but he softened his voice. "It's obvious you want more from her than a babysitter, but I'm not so sure she feels the same way."

Dad glared, looking hurt and angry at the same time. Smith mirrored the emotions.

"I'm ready," Tommy announced as he came into the room.

"Great," Dad said, voice too high. He turned to Smith. "Get your suit on. You're coming with us."

Smith could say no, but instead he sighed and nodded. He didn't want to fight with Dad.

Two minutes later they met up with Claire in the hall. She wore her white long-sleeve cover-up and had a wide-brimmed hat in her hand. Tommy held Claire's other hand. No one spoke on the walk down. Smith relaxed as they settled into loungers at the pool. This was paradise. Nothing was going to stop him from enjoying it.

With the time change, it was past dinnertime in California, and Tommy complained of hunger after ten minutes of swimming. They enjoyed the luxury of eating burgers poolside. As the sun set, Tommy curled up in Claire's lap with a towel as a blanket.

"He's almost out," Claire said to Dad.

"I'll take him up."

"Want my help?"

Dad looked to Claire and then two chairs over at Smith. "I've got it tonight. Smith's going to take you for ice cream."

Smith jolted to an upright sitting position.

"There's a little place next door with the best pineapple ice cream ever. You've got to try it."

Claire opened her mouth. Closed it.

Dad leaned over and lifted Tommy out of her lap. Tommy laid his head on Dad's shoulder. Smith stood as Dad walked by him.

"This is your chance to make friends," Dad whispered, tone sharp. "I expect you to be nice." He walked away, leaving Smith and Claire staring at each other in stunned silence.

After a long moment, she said, "You don't have to take me. Obviously you hate that I'm here."

He walked over and sat on the lounger Dad had just vacated next to Claire. He sat on it sideways, so he faced her. "Two things. First and most important, the ice cream is that good. You will be getting some."

The worry on her face melted into a tentative smile that pricked his heart. Her cover-up lay in a heap on the end table. He kept his gaze on her face, ignoring the long lean legs, the narrow waist, the tightness of her red swimsuit over her curves. Although he did appreciate how often her gaze dropped to his bare chest.

"And two. I don't hate that you're here. I hate that you dropped me faster than a spam call when I kissed you, and yet, I still want to do it again."

Big hazel eyes turned soft and watery.

Really, really wanted to do it again.

"I didn't mean to hurt you or lead you on." Her voice was soft and intimate, drawing him closer.

"I'm the one that started it."

"I don't want a relationship." The dark dreaminess in her eyes belied her words. He knew she liked him back. Her determination to deny them both the pleasure of being together was, unfortunately, her stupid choice to make.

"I will respect that." But he hated it. "Whatever you want." It scared him how much he meant it. He wanted only the best of everything for her.

Her bottom lip quivered. He wanted to suck it between his teeth. Torture. "Thank you, Smith."

He also hated that his dad was angling to make a move on Claire, but he didn't say that part. Instead he laughed. "All right, then. That's settled. Let's get the queen some ice cream." He stood, walked back to his chair, and put on his shirt and sandals.

He led her down to the beach path. In the aftermath of the sunset, streaks of pink and gold painted the sky. Soft music wafted from speakers set along the path. It was the epitome of romantic settings. Cosmic torture.

"Look." She pointed to the dark water and let out a happy coo. "Dolphins."

Their fins reflected the glittering sky as they breached. *Now* it was as romantic as it gets.

"Hawaii is as amazing as everyone says, isn't it?" Her dress fluttered in the wind blowing in from the ocean.

He didn't tell her that she was the most amazing thing here. "Wait until tomorrow when you're sunburned all over. You'll see the dark side of the island then." He scanned her up and down. "Maybe not, since you're wearing an entire curtain."

She burst out laughing. "Make fun of me all you want."

Teasing felt like a good way to move into the friend zone. Die. "You really took the term *cover-up* to the next level."

She pulled a face.

"The circus called; they want their tent back."

"Okay. Stop." She poked his arm. "I take back what I said about all the teasing you want. I underestimated you."

"Something you should never do."

She got serious. Her gaze dropped to his mouth. "Yes. I'm learning that."

A spark zinged down his core. "And I'm kidding about your dress. You have great style. You always look beautiful."

"Thank you." Her tone came out heavy with sincerity.

So much for keeping it light.

She turned away from the glorious view and continued along the path. He took a few highly oxygenated breaths before following. At the ice cream hut, they got in line behind some teenagers.

"I'd ask you what you want," Smith said. "But you want the pineapple whip."

"I want to try the mango."

"You want wrong." He leveled a stare at her that made her giggle. "I see you're keeping up the theme of being difficult. But for four dollars and fifty cents, I'll allow it."

"You might want to get an extra-big pineapple in case I decide I'd rather eat yours."

He chuckled. Was he going to keep smiling like a smitten buffoon all night? When they got to the window of the grass-and-sticks hut, he ordered a child's mango and a monster pineapple. While they waited, they watched the teenagers. The kids yelled and laughed and touched at every chance they got. And they were having fun doing it. Living fully. Vibrant. Smith wanted a little more of that in his life. He'd been so serious these last few years, everything planned and scheduled. Working hard in his career, never missing a gym session, going to bed at a decent hour. Eating his vegetables. Acting grown up.

Their order came up, and they carried their treats to a secluded bench with an ocean view. The sky was a deep-blue color now, the stars beginning to peek through.

Claire took a bite of her mango ice cream. She took a second bite.

"Don't tell me I should have gotten you the big one." He sat on the bench next to her.

She held out her cup.

He reluctantly took a bite. "It's good," he admitted.

"It's great," she said.

"No. *This* is great." He held out his pineapple whip.

She spooned up a bite and slid it between her lips. A seductive grin spread over her face. "Yours is better than mine."

Delight rushed through him. "Oh. The validation." She reached for another scoop of his, but he pulled it out of reach. She scooted closer to try and get it. Her dress had hiked up, and her bare thigh pressed against him. "Say it."

Her gaze went from the treat to his face. Her lips were within inches of him. Now was the time to kiss her, when her mouth would taste cold and sweet and with the stars as witness.

"Say it."

She pursed her lips.

It took everything in him not to close the gap. He'd done that before. It hadn't gone well. It was her move now. And she didn't want to play.

"You were right, Smith."

He nodded like a badass and passed over the ice cream. He leaned back with a satisfied sigh.

"You're acting like it's the first time it's ever happened."

He coughed out a laugh. "Well played, Big C."

"Big C?"

"I'm trying it out."

"And?"

"Could be better."

She passed him the pineapple whip, their fingers brushing. It was like he was thirteen, noting every touch and glance.

"So, are you painting again?"

She looked out at the ocean. "Yes."

"The inspiration came back. That's great."

She glanced sidelong at him. "Yeah. You could definitely say the inspiration came back."

By the heaviness of her words, he wasn't sure if that was a good thing or a bad thing.

"Thanks for asking," she said. "It was nice of you to remember."

"Of course. It's super cool that you're an artist."

She looked out at the water. "Stevie didn't think so. He liked the sales, obviously, but he didn't like that I took over the garage with my mess. He wasn't interested in seeing my work. At first, I'd ask him for feedback, but when it was clearly a chore for him to come to the garage and try to find nice things to say, I stopped asking. We were walking downtown once. I stopped in front of the gallery window that had my painting on display. I asked him what he thought of it. He said it was fine if you were into that sort of thing, but he wouldn't spend money on it. I didn't tell him it was mine." She sighed. "Honestly his ambivalence made me angry and resentful, which made me paint more. So I guess he was supportive in his own way."

Smith silently cursed the dead dickhead. His hand fisted, snapping the plastic spoon. He passed Claire the ice cream. "I'll get a new one."

She handed him her spoon. "We can share."

He took a deep breath, trying to conquer the fury he felt on her behalf. "You didn't deserve that. I've seen your artwork online. It's beautiful and powerful and unique. I know art is subjective, but it sucks that he wasn't supportive of you. I wish I could take away the hurt he caused you."

"When you say things like that, I wonder what the catch is. I can't help thinking that you're working an angle."

His head tilted back, offended. "I am not. It was not okay for him to belittle you." His voice was full of emotion.

She put a hand on his leg, her fingers cold from the ice cream, yet his thigh went hot. "I'm sorry. I believe you. At least I'm trying to believe you. I know that you're right. I didn't mean to doubt you—it's more that I'm still working on not doubting myself."

He softened. "Good." He gave her a half smile. "Keep working on it until you realize all the way through your soul that you are top notch."

She grinned. "Top notch?"

He chuckled. "The toppest." It seemed like the safest adjective to go with at the moment—considering she didn't want the relationship he ached for.

"Thanks, Smith." His name was honey on her tongue. She settled back against the bench and took another bite. "So, how's work? Houses selling well in Newport?"

"They always are."

Passing the spoon back and forth, they talked and talked. About work, restaurants, hobbies, books.

"Do you want any more?" Smith held out the last of the melty mound.

She shook her head. "I'm getting too cold to eat it." Goose bumps carpeted her skin, and she'd folded her arms against her body.

He tossed the ice creams in the trash, then slid close to her. He wrapped an arm around her shoulders, holding her against the warmth of his side. She rested her head on his shoulder. A long moment of silence passed, but it was a comfortable quiet of companionship. She felt so good, so right tucked under his wing.

She spoke in a whisper. "I am sorry about the other day, Smith. I should not have let that happen."

"It's my fault. I kissed you."

"I kissed you back."

He chuckled, low and gravelly. "Yes, you did."

"I couldn't stop myself."

His body warmed, felt every point of contact down his side. "You seemed to stop yourself just fine."

"You're angry." She glanced up at him. Seemed to realize how close they were and turned her face back to the nightscape.

"I'm not mad. I'm just having a harder time moving on than you." His arm tightened around her, as if he could keep her from slipping away. Make her want him back, yet knowing he was powerless.

"I don't mean to keep bringing Stevie up, but I owe you an explanation, and I'm trying to explain why I'm so screwed up."

"You're not screwed up. You've been through a lot. I'll be your safe space. You can tell me anything. I want to know."

She softened deeper against his side. His heart throbbed for her—it wasn't the only organ.

"I loved my husband, but . . ."

Smith barely stopped himself from saying rude things about a dead man he'd never met.

"It did not always feel good to be loved by him."

The air seemed to wither in his lungs as the pain of her words settled over him. "He was a fool for not realizing what a treasure he had with you." His heart cracked for her. "He was one man. I'm not him." *It did not always feel good to be loved by him.* What a terrible truth. He was honored she'd shared her sorrow with him even if it made him feel sick.

Beneath her cool exterior there was a vulnerable, broken woman who was very, very afraid. He wanted to fix it, but he felt powerless. All he could do was sit here and hold her close. Clearly she wasn't willing to find out what it would feel like to be loved by Smith. Although, he swore if she ever gave him the slightest chance, he'd make damn sure that she'd never be able to say the same about his love.

Finally, she spoke again. "Why have you never married?"

He exhaled. "I saw my parents' marriage. They married when I was four, so I was there for their entire relationship."

"Literally."

His lip quirked up. "Before Helen, my nana mostly raised me. Dad was working long hours to build his career. I used to watch out the front window of Nana's house in Connecticut, waiting for my mother to appear. When Dad married Helen, I stopped watching because my mom had come."

"That's really beautiful." Claire's voice was soft.

"Dad and Mom were good to each other. They had their fights, but nothing big or scary or cruel. Dad was a bit bossy. He thought he outranked her sometimes, but Mom never seemed to mind. I think she liked being taken care of in that way and treated like a prize. I want more of a partnership."

Claire mumbled a noise of agreement and nestled closer.

"But they made it work well. I hadn't found a woman who was worth it, who I was willing to put the work in to make the relationship succeed." He shrugged, embarrassed he'd said *hadn't* instead of *haven't*. "Maybe it's my fault. I know that I've changed these last two years with Mom's health troubles and her passing. Life feels shorter and more valuable. I always wanted to have a family sometime in the future, but now I feel the clock ticking." He sighed. "But I don't look back at past girlfriends and wish I were still with them. I can't see myself growing old with any of them. I want a real partner. A best friend who wants to share her life with me because she likes me and my company. I haven't found that yet, but I need to do a better job looking for it. Sure, I've been in love. At least there are three women I've said it to, but I'm not sure that was *real* love. It wasn't the deep, abiding kind that I hear people talk about. The all-consuming, sacrifice-everything kind." He stopped talking as he realized he'd never felt before what he was feeling now. For *her*.

"You're a good man, Smith." She was looking at the stars, not him. "I'm sure you'll find a woman who truly deserves you."

The kindness in her rejection didn't soften the blow. His chest felt as if a giant hand were squeezing his heart like a lemon. The juice burned down his core like acid. He grappled toward safer waters. "I mostly feel bad for Tommy. Mom was a good woman, doting and patient and didn't take herself too seriously. Selfless." He paused, realizing how that might have sounded offensive. "Of course, he's lucky to have you in his life now."

She waved a hand, dismissing his worries. "You'll make a fabulous father someday."

He looked out at the inky waves. "I hope so. If I get to be so fortunate."

"I've seen how tender you are with Tommy. Your child will be the luckiest kid in the world to have you loving them."

Warmth encircled his heart. He looked down at her, couldn't bear it, focused on the ocean. "A little girl, I think. We don't have enough of those in our family." He could picture her in his mind, with big eyes and unruly curls, holding tight to his thumb with her tiny hand. He yearned for her.

"I can't wait to meet her."

If Claire didn't have such a compassionate look on her face, he'd think she was deliberately torturing him. She leaned closer. His arm tightened around her back, and his palm cupped the narrow muscles of her upper arm. He had to force himself not to explore. The conversation faltered, and silence wrapped them together. The waves caressed the beach in a soothing, endless rhythm. Stars painted the sky in brilliance. Sweet pineapple and bitter brine danced in his nose.

"Tommy . . . he makes me . . . I love that little boy."

He had to tilt closer to hear her whispered words before the wind stole them and carried them away to the place of secrets and dreams.

"He makes me wish for a son." She stared at the vast expanse of water as she made her confession. "After Edith, I swore I would never, ever again. I was exhausted. Overwhelmed. Defeated. Stevie even got a vasectomy. Things got rough." Her voice caught. She pulled her knees up and hugged them to her chest. Like a child herself. He resisted the urge to cradle her on his lap. "But these last months with Tommy, I've felt the fear and the resentment slip away. He's reminded me of the joy and satisfaction that come from creating your own little human and helping them find their way. He's softened me again." She looked at Smith, her eyes reflecting the glittering heavens. The depth of her gaze sapped the breath from his body.

His chest filled with want and sorrow and inadequacy. "I've seen how sweet you are to Tommy too. Would you ever consider having another child?" It scared him how much he wanted her to say yes.

She shrugged. "Six months ago, I would have said no, but now, with Tommy reminding me how much I love tending to a new life, seeing again the way children view the world with curiosity and open hearts, it helps me to be more open and hopeful and exuberant too. I think just maybe I would love to have another child. I'm still fertile. At least I'm healthy and have regular periods and all that." She grimaced. "TMI, sorry."

He didn't mind. He shouldn't hope, but he was thrilled, and he enjoyed the intimacy, the feeling that she was sharing things with him that she'd kept private for years.

"I just don't think it will be in the cards for me." She lightened her tone. "I've already played my hand. And I've got a whole lot to be grateful for."

He stayed quiet, listening without giving in to the urge telling him to demand she stop being stubborn and give love another chance. He'd be happy to knock her up right now. *Classy, Smith.*

Before he could think of some clever bit of optimistic wisdom, she gave him a half smile, and with a squeeze of his thigh, she slipped out of his arm, leaving him cold.

Dad could give her Tommy as her son, truly. Dad wanted Claire. Claire wanted Tommy. Would she agree? *Please, no.* The thought made Smith nearly as sick as the notion of how much he wanted to give her a son—the traditional way.

She picked up her beach bag. "Thank you for tonight. I'd better get back. Tommy's going to be up early tomorrow."

Smith walked by her side with his hands in his pockets. She seemed as subdued as he. Weighty matters of the heart hung heavy. She'd basically admitted to never wanting another man again. And he'd just fallen a little more in love.

Chapter 29
BANKS

Banks, Tommy, and Claire waited on the beach with a handful of others from their work group. Banks was glad Smith had gone surfing this morning. It had been a tad disconcerting how late Smith had gotten home last night after taking Claire for ice cream. Smith had assured him that all was well. He and Claire were friends now. It was the way his son had said it, the unreadable emotion in Smith's eyes that had put Banks on edge.

"Have you been snorkeling before?" Banks asked Claire.

She rubbed sunscreen over Tommy's face and neck. "Yes."

"It's my first time," Tommy said, his brows tight.

"It's going to be your favorite thing." Claire took Tommy's hand and squeezed.

A young man with long blond hair, sun-browned skin, and faded tattoos approached with a big box of gear. "Rules: You may *not* touch the turtles. They are federally protected, and you could be fined a massive amount. I'm not kidding—class C felony with fines up to $50,000. But the truth is, it's dangerous for the turtles. You can make them sick. Don't do it. Don't touch anything. Respect the wildlife. Enjoy the beautiful view without destroying it. Can you manage that?"

No one spoke. Tommy squeezed his hands together at his waist.

"Good. Pick out a mask that fits. Fins are over there." He pointed to the lineup in the sand. "I'll be out in the water if you need me for anything or have questions. I'll see if I can find some cool stuff to point out if you want to follow me. Sometimes we get lucky with a reef shark, eel, or octopus. You're welcome to get out of the water whenever you want. There are cold drinks in that cooler. Help yourself."

Tommy turned big worried eyes up at Banks.

"I'll stay right by you," Banks said. He should have brought a life jacket for Tommy. Too late now. "You'll be perfectly safe."

Tommy nodded, setting his chin, but the stress never left his face.

Claire pulled a life jacket from her bag. "I know you're a very good swimmer, but it's much easier to snorkel with a jacket on. Will you try it for me?" She helped Tommy into it.

"You brought that for him?" Banks's heart was wobbly with gratitude.

"Of course. It really makes a big difference. Especially for a child."

Was now a good time to tell her he loved her? "Thank you. That was incredibly thoughtful."

"Come on." Claire gave Tommy an encouraging grin. "Let's go check out those fish." She fit a small mask over Tommy's face and had him test out the snorkel. She taught him a hand sign for *okay* and *go up*, and then they made up a wiggly-finger sign for when they saw something cool.

Banks stood and watched. Why interfere when she was perfect? It healed the broken edges of his heart to see her and Tommy together. He still thought of Helen with every breath, but it didn't hurt so much.

With their fins on, Claire, Tommy, and Banks waddled out to the water and into a whole new world. Tommy pointed out everything. His giggle resonated through the waves. They stayed together, like a three-link chain, like a new family. When Tommy got cold and tired, Banks took him up to the beach so that Claire could keep swimming with the turtles. She'd lit up when she'd seen her first one. Banks liked to think he had a little part in bringing that glorious vibrancy to her soul.

They had a taxi take them to a fish-taco stand on their way back to the hotel; then they washed off at the pool. As Claire and Tommy shared a lounger under the shade of an umbrella at his side, happiness flooded through him. Claire was easygoing, kind, patient, gorgeous. It was almost too good to be true. He didn't feel like he had to work or pretend with her. He was himself. And when she smiled at him, he believed she felt the rightness of this too.

"You said the luau is tonight, right?" Claire asked.

Banks opened his eyes, half expecting to wake from a fantasy, but Claire was still here, looking at him, holding Tommy. "Yes. It starts at five thirty, but I need to be there at five. You and Tommy please be there by five thirty. Remind Smith, will you? And it's beachy business casual." He chuckled. "Whatever that means."

"It means you want us to look nice."

"Yes."

She nodded. "Will do."

Banks stood. "I'm going to head up now. I've got some things to do. You've got a key to my room for Tommy?"

"Yes."

"I'll see you later, then."

Banks had a skip in his step as he went to his room. He fired off emails and checked in with his secretary about the awards for tonight. Then he showered and changed into linen pants and a button up before heading to the back lawn where his party was being set up.

Like every year, the luau was a success. The highlight of the trip for many. Claire, Smith, and Tommy sat at his table, but Banks was rarely with them. He bounced around, visiting with each guest. His happiness suffusing the entire party. He was extra funny when announcing this year's awards, the pig was extra smoky and juicy, and Claire looked extra beautiful in her summer dress.

He took his seat next to Tommy when the fire dancer came out. He ate pineapple cake while watching the reflection of the flames play over Claire's eyes and face. As the program ended, Banks took the mic again. He thanked everyone, talked up the firm's recent successes, and then invited them all to stay, drink, and dance the night away. To the sound of applause, he returned to his table eager to invite Claire onto the grass turned dance floor. Tommy had moved to her lap, his face on her shoulder.

"Are we going to dance tonight?" The question was vague, posed to the entire table, but intended only for her.

"Tommy is about to pass out." Claire brushed the boy's hair off his brow.

Banks frowned in disappointment. "Well, okay. I'd appreciate it if you'd take him on up to bed."

"Of course." She set Tommy onto wobbly feet. "Come on, honey. It's time to go up."

"I'll take him," Smith said to Claire. "You don't want to miss the fireworks."

"No," Banks said. "There's someone here I want to introduce you to. Shannon's husband has a real estate deal he wants to talk to you about."

Smith looked to Claire.

She smiled. "I'm happy to take him up. That's why I'm here."

"Good night, son." Banks kissed Tommy's forehead. The kid's eyes drooped and glassed over. "You'd better go."

Claire gently turned Tommy, and together they shuffled away. Smith watched them with a furrow in his brow.

"Come on." Banks took Smith's elbow and steered him away.

Chapter 30
CLAIRE

Claire let herself into the Sextons' suite. Tommy stumbled to his room and flopped onto his bed. He acted the rag doll as she changed him into an oversized T-shirt and brushed his teeth. Smith's toiletries lay on the counter. Toothbrush, razor, deodorant. All the regular things every man had, but they felt intimate, and she felt like a creeper. Smith's swimsuit hung on the towel rod to dry. She turned away, mind and body.

She had to prod Tommy in the back to get him to pee. He crawled into bed, and she pulled the sheet up to his chin. She kissed his nose.

"I love you." He didn't open his eyes as he whispered it.

"I love you too."

He rolled over, and his breathing evened out. She glided past Smith's bed, where Smith would sleep tonight, a mere wall's width away from her. She left the bedroom door cracked open and sat on the couch in the sitting room. She kicked off her sandals and put her feet on the coffee table while she flipped through the photos she'd taken today. All were of Tommy or tropical vistas. She texted her daughters, sending them the photo of a flock of green-and-red birds in a tree.

Looks like fun, Mom, Edith replied.

Looks like the start of a horror film, Indi texted.

Mona didn't respond. She was probably already asleep. That was motherhood.

The door hissed and opened. She expected Banks, but Smith strode in alone.

"If you go right now, you should be able to catch the fireworks." He set his key on the table and folded his arms over his short-sleeve linen button up.

He'd left the party early, for her. No words came over the fluttering in her belly.

He chuckled when he looked at her stunned face.

"Where's Banks?"

"Still talking. He might be there a for a while."

"You should go enjoy the night," she said. "I'm fine here with Tommy."

"Go," Smith said. "Get out of here."

She gushed out her thanks.

He smiled and opened the door for her. And suddenly she didn't want to leave. She wanted to curl into him and make their own fireworks. She forced herself past him, out the door, and back outside. She ducked into the shadows of a wide tree as the popping and crackles started. As she watched the explosion of heat and color splatter the sky, she wished she had a paintbrush and canvas. The ocean was a glittering mirror, reflecting the churning of her heart. The longer she watched the fireworks, the more agitated she became. When the last of the dynamite faded into darkness, she trembled with emotion.

She made herself go to her room, wash off the day, brush her teeth, and change into pajamas. She sat on her bed. She stood. She paced. Banks wasn't treating her like an employee. She'd seen tonight how he treated his payroll, distant and magnanimous. He was treating her with familiarity and a bit of presumption. He was treating her like a wife.

She knew it like she recognized the dread clinging to her bones. The worst part was, she'd be dumb to turn him down when he made his move. She thought of the hefty tuition bill that sat on her kitchen table back at home. Banks wouldn't even blink at the amount. He could make all the worries go away. He could give her a plush life. With vacations like this. She huffed out an ironic laugh. She was loving it here. He could give her Tommy. She bit her lips, remembering Tommy's tenderness, his vulnerability, his cherubic face. And then that face morphed into an older version. Smith. Smith. Smith.

Smith.

Last night, sitting on that bench together under the stars had felt like coming home after a long, hard journey. He listened, coaxed her into being herself, her best self. She felt safe with him like she'd never felt with Stevie.

Tears pricked at her eyes. She needed to get out of here. Out of her mind. Away from the Sextons. She needed to find her way back to that quiet place of six months ago, when her life was placid as a stormless lake. And just as boring.

Not caring that she was braless, wearing only a thin camisole, silk shorts, and flip-flops—Indi would have been proud of the outfit—Claire left her room. She skirted the hotel, careful to avoid the remains of Banks's party. She walked the beach, ignoring the looks she got. She imagined she was a sea spirit, wild and mysterious. And free.

Many minutes later, and not at all calmer, she prowled up a narrow path that wound through a dense garden. She inhaled tropical blossoms. It was getting cold, but she welcomed it; may it freeze her frustrations. She turned the corner where the path bumped up against the wall of a building. A figure appeared ahead. He was almost to her by the time the dim path lights reached his face.

"Claire?"

Her heart picked up speed. Smith had changed into a cotton T-shirt that clung to his chest and arms. “What are you doing here?” Her tone was accusing.

“I needed some air.”

She inhaled, practically panting now, her body revving up. But for what? To fight or . . . or that other thing that starts with an *f* . . . maybe? *Stop it, Claire.* “Me too.”

He stepped closer to study her better in the dim light. “Are you okay?”

“No.” The truth came out before she could stop it.

He looked down, noticing her shirt, or lack of one. Her nipples were hard, demanding attention. His gaze darkened as he focused back on her eyes. “What’s wrong?”

She melted at the genuine concern in his voice, and the huskiness.

He brought a hand up to her elbow. Her nerves went haywire at the touch. “Tell me.”

Her tongue didn’t wait for permission from her brain to say, “I want to kiss you and pretend it didn’t happen.”

Smith went still. Her body awakened with a crackle. She was not nearly as shriveled and old as she’d thought.

One hand slid up her arm. The other wrapped her neck. She let out a soft gasp of anticipation as he lifted her mouth to his. *Yes.*

His lips parted, welcoming her. He tasted of salt and male, delicious in a way that had her questioning if she’d ever truly been kissed before. Back arching into him, she pushed him against the brick wall. She needed closer, wanted to crush every sliver of space separating her from his heavy male-scented warmth.

He wanted her. She felt it in every electrified cell in her body, heard his desire in his barely audible moan. His eagerness, focused entirely on her, tasted like a quick high. She melted at his touch. His hands roamed and slid under her shirt. Skin brushed against skin. His breath sent bliss down her body as he kissed her jaw, her neck, lower.

She dug her fingers into his silky hair and fisted her hands tight, as if she could fight this off. He gasped, a reaction that only sent her spiraling deeper. She was a supernova, an exploding dam after so many years of silently building tension. He ravished her mouth with his, a promise of what he was going to do to the rest of her. She wanted it all. She pulled his fat bottom lip between her teeth. No one had the right to taste this good, like spice and fire. Both his big hands tightened over her shorts. Shit. Those hands. She had not lived before this moment.

Smith whispered into her lips. "We shouldn't be doing this out here." Her insides clenched at the sounds of his ragged voice.

She let out a deep, gravelly laugh as she kissed him. Pleasure rolled through her body. She felt down his warm neck, his broad shoulders, his heavy chest. She didn't want to stop, didn't want to start *thinking*. He put his hands on her ribs and lifted her off his muscled body. He stood and took her hand. Dim light caressed the angled planes of his face. His lips were flushed, his eyes melted sky. The picture of fantasies. He led her to the elevator and kissed her as it rose. He grinned. As they stepped out, he sucked on his lip where her mouth had claimed his. It was the sexiest thing she'd ever seen.

But as they approached her door, the door right next to Tommy's, her feet slowed. What about tomorrow? She knew *exactly* how sex could irrevocably change a life. It had been one time in high school with Stevie. One stupid time.

Had she learned nothing? Was she so weak, ruled by her appetites yet again?

She took her hand out of Smith's. He turned, dread staining his features.

She didn't say anything, but hoped her eyes told him just how sorry she was.

He sighed, his shoulders drooping. "You told me the deal. Kiss and pretend it didn't happen. Straight up." He set his forehead against hers, and she almost gave in. Her body was one giant throb of desire. She leaned in as he stepped back. "Good night, Claire." He pulled out his key and stepped away. He turned and sent her a wicked grin. "I hope you sleep as poorly as I'm going to tonight." He went in and closed the door, leaving her as stunned and vulnerable as one newly born to this world.

Chapter 31
SMITH

Smith did not sleep. He lay in bed, listening to his small brother's soft breathing and thinking about Claire. Was she seriously okay with this kiss-and-cut-it-off thing? She was a forty-year-old tease, and he was the schmuck falling for her anyway. He wanted to go knock on her door, but he wouldn't let himself. He would not. But he spent the rest of the night imagining what would go down if he did. If she let him all the way in.

"Good morning!"

Smith winced as Dad's overly cheerful voice cut through his lucid, X-rated dreams. Dad pulled back the drapes, the light like knives attacking the darkness.

"If you want breakfast before boating, it's time to get up."

Oh yeah, the boat. Smith had arranged it for Claire to see the whales and dolphins. And despite last night, he was still excited to take her out on it. He wanted to see her smile. He wanted to be near her, kissing or not.

Tommy skipped in from the other room, looking disturbingly awake and vibrant. Smith felt like a raccoon pelt.

"Thanks for waking me." Smith felt like a teenager being dragged out of bed. "I didn't sleep well last night." He looked over at his little brother. "T-bone snored like a train."

"I did not!"

Smith threw a pillow at him. Tommy ran, leaped onto the bed, and crashed into Smith. Smith rolled onto his stomach and let the little man do his worst. The fists, knees, and elbows digging into his back were like a cheap massage.

A knock at the main door halted the beating.

"That'll be Claire," Dad said.

Smith's body reacted at the sound of her name. He curled into the fetal position.

"Put a shirt on before you join us," Dad said.

And just because he'd said that, Smith didn't want to. He took a quick cold shower, brushed his teeth, and put on swim shorts. He let them hang lower than was appropriate for breakfast—or anytime—and walked into the sitting room. Claire sat with his family around a four-top table. She looked up. He took *immense* satisfaction in the slackening of her jaw and the warmth of her gaze as it traveled down the long length of his torso . . . below his belly button. Her eyes had liquefied by the time she focused on his face.

He grinned. Point Smith. She'd started it, but he wasn't surrendering that easily.

She coughed and took a sip of water.

Dad looked up at Smith and pursed his lips.

"You said *don't* put a shirt on before you join us, right?"

"Very funny." Dad was not amused. "No nipples at breakfast."

"We have that rule at my house too," Claire said. "It's surprisingly hard to enforce."

Smith laughed, a genuine thing that had his abs rolling. He'd left his shirt on the couch yesterday—how convenient that was. He picked it up and slid it over his head. Claire exhaled. Dad wasn't watching, so he winked at her.

She raised a brow, and a hint of a challenge rose to her eyes.

He held back a cowardly flinch. Her next move might kill him.

He sat down and turned his attention to his omelet. But he wasn't hungry for food.

After breakfast, they migrated to the lobby. A car was waiting. Dad sat up front with the driver. Tommy sat between Smith and Claire in the back seat. It was an apt placement. Tommy wasn't the only thing keeping them apart, but he was a big thing.

Smith caught Claire's eye above Tommy's curly head. "How was your night last night?"

Her cheeks reddened.

His lips curved up.

"I slept like a baby."

"Liar—"

Dad's voice cut in. "Good. Smith said he didn't sleep well."

Smith wanted to kiss that smug grin right off her face. Another point for Claire. Keeping score would not be good for his self-confidence.

At the docks, a friendly captain welcomed them onto his cabin cruiser. They moved to the bow. Smith wasn't sure if he appreciated that Claire had skipped her muumuu today or not. This cover-up barely veiled her butt and plunged lower than her swimsuit in front.

Truly the death of him.

She adjusted her wide-brimmed hat and helped Tommy into the life jacket she'd brought for him. How thoughtful. He didn't like being reminded that, yes, she was smart, considerate, and selfless as well as sexy.

Tommy and Claire sat together. Holding hands. Dad smiled at them, a tender, loving smile that sent Smith stumbling toward the stern of the boat.

But when they saw the first whale, he was drawn back to the bow by the sheer force of her exuberance.

"Look! Do you see that?" Her voice was high and vibrant. She pointed out the obvious giant of a humpback cresting off the starboard.

Dad beamed—as if he were the one responsible for her miracle.

The captain turned the boat and edged closer to the whale.

"There are two," Claire cried. She'd gotten to her knees and now leaned partly over the side. Her hat lay forgotten on the bench. A whale breached. She let out a soft exclamation. She looked over her shoulder as Smith came to stand nearby. "They are right there. Right there!" Her smile was brighter than the sun. "They're magnificent."

So was she.

They watched the two humpbacks until their unturned flukes indicated deep dives. Claire sighed. She lowered onto her heels. "That was incredible." She looked up at Smith. "Thank you for arranging this."

His belly went warm, and his heart melted.

Claire sat when the boat picked up speed again. Wind danced with the hair that had fallen out of her braid as she turned her face to the breeze. The boat suddenly slowed, jerking them in their seats. Smith looked to the captain. The old man pointed straight ahead as he brought the craft into idle. Claire stood, her hands still on Tommy, always aware of the boy. And then they saw it.

"A baby!" Claire sounded like she might cry.

They stood and crowded around the bow as the little giant twisted and frolicked in the water around its mother.

Claire brought a hand to her mouth, her eyes glittering as she watched, unblinking. Another moment Smith would have to draw before he could rest.

When the whales glided away, Claire turned to Smith. He stood right behind her.

"Thank you." Her eyes glowed. Tears coated her lashes. "That was the most amazing thing I've ever seen." She reached up and threw her arms around his shoulders. He wanted to wrap her up and hold her like a lover would; instead he stood like a statue.

She pulled away, too elated to notice Dad's furrowed brow or care that Smith hadn't hugged her back. She settled into the seat with Tommy again and shone brighter than the sun the entire way back to the hotel.

Chapter 32
CLAIRE

Claire kept seeing those impressive whales in her mind. The fluidity, the elegance. The feeling of flying in her breast as she watched them. They felt like a sign from the universe just for her. A message of hope and daring. She wanted to be strong like that mother whale. She wanted to take up space and be bold.

She wasn't sure yet how to do that, but "mother whale" was her new mantra. She welcomed the graceful, unapologetic energy into her soul. Her body hummed with life as she waltzed into the hotel amid tropical blossoms and bubbling fountains.

"Can we go to the pool?" Tommy asked as he sipped the passion fruit–juice cocktail a woman in the lobby had given them.

"I'm happy to take him," Claire said to Banks as she sipped her own divine nectar. "You have a meeting this afternoon, right?"

"It's not until four, but you can't take him to the pool now."

Smith looked at his father as a simpering smile spread over Banks's face.

"You have an appointment in thirty minutes."

"What?" Had she forgotten something?

"For a massage. At the spa."

She stared at Banks, not really getting it. It wasn't her birthday. Stevie had never booked her anything just to be nice. And Stevie had loved her for seventeen years. He'd been a pretty decent husband for most of them. But he'd never done anything so romantic.

"It's just a little thank-you for all you do." Banks brushed his gray hair back, looking a bit timid. "This was supposed to be a vacation for you, too, and you've been taking care of us the whole time. I want you to go relax and enjoy yourself."

"This is the nicest vacation I've ever enjoyed. I don't deserve more. And you are already too generous to me."

Banks basked in her words. "We'll see you later."

The three boys left her standing in a puddle of luxury. This was paradise. This was how Banks Sexton lived. And she knew that if she wanted, he was willing to share it all with her.

At the spa before her service, she wallowed in mud baths, scalding tubs, and cold plunges. She drank cucumber water and inhaled essential oils. Then a woman with massive hands worked out every kink from top to bottom. When Claire stumbled out of the spa, she felt looser than a belly dancer's hips. She found Banks and Tommy sitting by the pool eating nachos. She plunked down at the foot of Tommy's lounger.

"Thank you, Banks. That was amazing." Between the whales and the massage, she was flying high.

"You are welcome, my dear."

She let the endearment slide, too blissed out for worries.

"Tommy's worn out," Banks said. "I think he'd like to rest while I have my meeting this afternoon. Then we can all meet up after for dinner. I made a reservation at a fun hibachi place down the road."

"Sounds perfect." Her smile was starting to hurt her cheeks.

She helped Tommy stand. His cheeks were red, the skin dry and cracking, his eyes bloodshot. They left Banks relaxing in the shade.

"Straight into the shower," Claire said as she opened the door to the suite.

"I don't want to," Tommy said.

"You can have screen time after you shower and lotion and drink one glass of water."

"Fine," he grumbled as he tugged at his shirt.

She followed him into his room and stopped short when she saw Smith sitting at the desk. "Oh, I'm so sorry. I didn't think you'd be here." This was his room. "I shouldn't have assumed that, though."

"Good thing I wasn't naked."

Heat flamed up her core and over her face as she imagined it.

He grinned.

She looked away and noticed the sketchbook on the table. Closed. But he still held the pencil. "You were drawing."

"Yes."

"Can I see?"

"No."

Remembering the sketches she'd seen earlier, her face heated. She lowered her chin, unable to hide her blush from him.

His eyes narrowed. "You looked through my sketchbook before. At my house."

"Yes." She could practically feel steam rising from her skin.

"Did you see—"

"Yes."

"Did you like—"

"Yes."

His teal gaze nearly swallowed her whole. His breathing turned shallow.

"Ms. Claire." She jolted at the sound of Tommy's voice. "How do you turn on the hot?"

She rushed into the bathroom as if she could flee the feelings blossoming in her heart, as if she could escape the look on Smith's face.

When they emerged after Tommy was clean and lotioned, Smith was gone.

Claire hated that she was disappointed. She hated that she cared at all.

He'd left his sketchbook. It sat on the desk, the lamp shining down on it like a spotlight. As if willing her to look. A temptation and a trap. She would ignore it. She got Tommy his water and set him up on the couch with the iPad. She sat with him, but it was ten seconds into his game when she was up again and in the bedroom, staring at the little book. Heart singing, she picked it up and flipped to the last pages.

She was on the boat, her face radiant, pointing out to sea, laughing. In the next one, she was hugging Smith, and this time he held her back, in an embrace that melded their bodies into one graceful shape.

Her heart flipped and flailed. She marveled at her emotional reaction, taking pleasure in the thrill and, at the same time, feeling horrified by her lack of self-control.

She knew she shouldn't have opened the sketchbook.

Because as she looked at her face reflected in his eyes, she didn't see Claire Rosalie Williams Kehoe, an untrusting, broken, tired, widowed granny. She saw a fantasy. He'd drawn her, *her* as a ray of freaking starlight. She wanted to be that woman.

Chapter 33
BANKS

Banks whistled in the shower. This trip was going so well. He'd feared it, coming here without Helen. But Claire had softened the sting of her absence. This vacation was new to Claire, which made it feel new to him too. She enjoyed everything, even the simple things like the passion fruit nectar and leis, with a childlike wonder that drew Banks in like a gnat to honey. He'd seen a hundred whales, but today he saw them differently. Claire turned humpback whales into magical creatures. She made him feel as if his whole world were fresh and remade. He stepped out of the shower and toweled off. Looking in the mirror, he didn't see his wrinkles or sunspots. He felt young and alive. He pulled a seductive face. "Hello, Claire."

He jumped and covered himself with the towel when he heard Smith's voice through the door.

"That was the front. The car is here."

"Okay." His voice came out a little unsteady. "Give me five minutes."

"I'm taking Tommy to look at the koi."

"I'll meet you down there." Banks leaned over the counter, panting, his skin hot. He splashed cold water over his face and cleared his throat.

He politely folded the towel and hung it up. He did not look in the mirror again.

Dressed and pulse back to normal, he strode to the lobby. He stopped when he saw them. His new family. Claire wore a floral dress and her hair in loose, dark waves. She was crouched next to Tommy, smiling that radiant smile. Smith stood next to her. He leaned down, put a hand on her shoulder, and said something as he pointed to the fish. She laughed. Yes. Picture perfect.

He floated forward and took his place among them. "Who's hungry?"

"I am," Tommy said. He looked up at Claire. "Hibachi is my favorite."

She chuckled. "You've got it pretty good, kid." She took his hand, and together they walked out of the hotel.

Banks thought tonight he might offer to have Smith sit up front so he could sit back with Claire, but no. He liked to make sure the driver was going the right way. He liked an unobstructed view. The three young ones had already climbed into the back seat together anyway, Claire in the middle seat this time.

The driver was a chatty one, but Banks liked to hear strangers' stories. Claire and Smith were visiting quietly together. It was gratifying to see them getting along. He needed Smith on his side with this.

At dinner, he arranged it so he sat by Claire, with Smith and Tommy on the adjacent side. Parents and children.

They looked over the menu.

"Have you had hibachi before?" Banks asked Claire.

She giggled as if he'd said something funny.

"Dad!" Smith's brows were tight in disapproval.

"What? Was that rude?"

"It was fine. I haven't done much compared to you, but I have been to a teppan grill before."

"Of course," Banks said, seeing exactly how his comment had sounded condescending. "I'm so sorry. Please forgive me. And . . . well . . . if you're interested to know, I really like the filet."

Smith rolled his eyes.

"Thank you, but I was looking at the ono. It says it's fresh caught this morning."

"That will be good too."

Her soft smile let him know that she was not unhappy with him.

Smith ordered sushi rolls. When the server left, Banks said, "That's no fun. The point is to get your dinner cooked in front of you."

"Tommy and Claire aren't going to eat half their food. I'll have plenty of that too. Good thing I'm between them."

Claire and Smith shared the table corner, and now that they were sitting, it seemed she was closer to his son than to him. Not how he'd wanted it to turn out. "You're not allowed to eat Claire's food," Banks said.

"Why's that?" Smith asked. He shared a look with Claire that Banks couldn't interpret.

Banks shifted in his seat. Why was Smith being so annoying? "She gets to eat her dinner."

"Okay, Dad."

Claire bit her lip to hold back her amusement.

Banks frowned. He should have let Smith stay at the hotel like he'd asked to instead of insisting he come tonight. But Banks had wanted a true *family* dinner. Was it too late to send both his sons home and turn this into a romantic date? That was exactly what he should have done. It seemed so obvious now. They couldn't be part of every facet of his relationship with Claire if he was going to make this work.

"So." Banks leaned forward on his elbows. "What's everyone's favorite part of the trip so far?"

"You're going to say 'being together.'" Smith snapped his chopsticks between his fingers.

Banks's temper flared. "You are making me rethink that."

Smith sobered. "Sorry. It is nice to be together."

Banks nodded in acquiescence, but his face was still hard. He looked away from his punk of a son.

"I liked snorkeling and seeing the eel." Tommy's peppy voice washed over the tension.

"That was really cool." Claire smiled. "We've done so many amazing things, I don't think I can name just one."

"You have to." Smith's tone was teasing. "It's the rule. It's not meant to be fun. View the question more like a pop quiz."

"Stop it." Banks's voice was cold. "Just let her talk."

Smith leaned back as if Banks had flicked his nose.

Banks needed to rein in his annoyance. He was trying to impress Claire, not show her how impatient he could be.

"Please, Claire," Smith said in a fake-serious voice. "What has been your *favorite* thing you've done in Hawaii?" One side of his mouth quirked up.

She looked at him sidelong a lingering moment. Her cheeks heightened in color. "I did love the sea turtles, and Tommy pointing out all the fish while snorkeling. He held my hand and made me feel safe."

Tommy beamed.

She was perfection.

"But those whales this morning might have stolen my heart." She paused and looked to Banks. "And I loved that massage, thank you." She sighed. "This has been the best day of my life."

Banks's whole body went warm at her statement, until Smith said, "Is that a twenty-four-hour clock you're using?" He winked at her.

Her face flamed.

"What?" Banks's pulse rose. "What happened last night?" Last night was the party; he'd sent her home early with Tommy. She'd missed the fireworks, and Smith had been bugged with him about it. "I'm so sorry about the fireworks. I should have taken Tommy to bed."

Claire cleared her throat. Cleared it again. "It's fine—"

"I made sure she still got fireworks." The arrogant drawl in Smith's voice sent alarm bells ringing through Banks.

Claire turned toward Banks, her face alluringly flushed. "Yeah. He, um, came back early so that I could go down. I ended up enjoying them after all."

Banks sighed in relief, not even sure what he'd been worried about. "How nice of you, Smith."

"It was my pleasure."

Claire looked down at her plate. And again, that weirdness returned to Banks's gut.

The server set the sushi between Claire and Smith before refilling their drinks. No alcohol. Smith had ordered a soda, so Banks followed suit. He would have liked to relax with a sake. Was he never going to drink again? He guessed not at family dinners. He'd still have beers with his buddies and drinks at business dinners. A small sacrifice for this woman.

Last year here with Helen, they'd left their sons sleeping and snuck down to the bar together. She'd worn a tiny dress and downed her shots as fast as she could, the sooner to get on with the dancing. Drinking and dancing made Helen horny. When they'd finally stumbled into their suite in the middle of the night, Smith had woken. He'd cracked his bedroom door open and given them the stink eye.

"Get a room," he'd said.

Helen had giggled uncontrollably. "Precisely what I'm trying to do." She'd wrapped herself around Banks, her spaghetti straps falling off her shoulders as she kissed him so hard he'd nearly fallen over. He'd held her tight to himself in one arm and groped around for their bed with the other.

"Taste it." Smith's voice drew Banks back to the present. The post-Helen era. Smith held a slice of sushi roll in the air with his chopsticks.

"That's a big piece." Claire eyed it with distrust. "And a lot of wasabi."

"Open wide."

"I don't think she wants it," Banks said.

A flicker of annoyance flashed over Smith's face when he glanced at his father.

Claire opened her mouth, and Smith stuffed the piece in. Her cheeks bulged as she chewed. Her eyes misted. Smith chuckled as she fanned her face. She swallowed and took a long pull from her water.

"You loved it," Smith said.

"You hated it," Banks said.

She looked from one man to the other. "Spicy."

"But good." Smith's brows rose.

"Yes."

Why did Banks find that so irritating?

A man with a two-foot-tall paper hat appeared with his cart. "Ready for some good eating?"

Tommy clapped.

Banks relaxed as everyone's attention turned to the show.

With the meat and veggies on the heat, the chef cut up shrimp. "Here we go. Around the table. You first, young man." The chef pointed to Tommy as he balanced the half shrimp on his spatula.

Tommy tilted his chin up and opened his mouth. The shrimp landed on Tommy's plate. The man leaned over the griddle, picked up the piece with chopsticks, told Tommy to open again, and dropped the shrimp into Tommy's mouth. They all cheered.

Smith caught his piece out of the air and talked the chef into tossing him a second.

"You ready, lady?" The chef motioned to Claire.

Claire nodded, but her brows furrowed. She leaned forward and opened her mouth. The shot was a little short. She snapped for it, but the shrimp hit her neck and dropped down her dress between her breasts. The chef's face slackened, his eyes worried. The whole table went quiet until Smith burst out laughing.

Claire chuckled as she looked down.

"I'm so sorry," the chef said as he piled reparation shrimp onto her plate.

"It's fine." Claire's neck rolled up as she tried to see down her dress.

Smith snapped his chopsticks. "Need some help? I'm very good with these."

"Smith!" Banks was appalled. Truly disturbed. To speak to his would-be stepmom in such a manner.

"What? You'd rather I use my fingers?"

Heat rushed to Banks's face. He'd been imagining himself doing just that. His cheeks got hotter as he watched Claire stick her hand between her cleavage and rummage around.

Smith really needed to stop laughing at her.

Claire pulled the shrimp out between two fingers. There was a twinkle in her eyes above her beautiful blush as she slipped it in her mouth.

Banks's jaw loosened as he watched. Helen would have excused herself to go to the bathroom and take care of it. She would not have felt herself up at the dinner table. It was improper . . . and arousing.

Smith wiped tears off his face with his napkin. "This. This is my favorite part of the trip."

"That is inappropriate," Banks said, talking to Smith, but hoping Claire got the message too.

Smith started laughing all over again. He was laughing so hard he'd moved into the keening-animal zone. It infected Claire, and then she was laughing too.

Banks scowled. It wasn't *that* funny.

"Can I have your shrimp?" Tommy asked Claire.

Banks was going to tell his sons to leave the woman alone, but he bit his tongue. Talking hadn't done him any favors tonight.

Claire choked back her giggles enough to pass over her plate.

The chef went back to work preparing their meal. With each dish, he gave Claire an extra-large portion. She set the plate between herself and Smith. They ate it together.

Banks tamped down his jealousy, reminding himself that this was a very good thing. Smith had finished Helen's food at nearly every meal. It was a gift to see Smith developing the same sort of relationship with Claire.

Chapter 34
CLAIRE

Claire brushed her teeth on their last night in Hawaii, thinking about what a lovely time she'd had. Everything had been easy and sunny. She liked the Sextons. She fit in with them and wanted to remain firmly in their inner circle. Their easy banter and generous hearts lifted her soul. A soft, tentative knock sounded at her door. Smith. Her pulse skittered, betraying how much she wanted to see him, invite him in. She was glad she hadn't washed off her makeup or changed out of her dress yet.

She forced a calming breath but couldn't stop her smile as she opened the door. Then she frowned. "Banks?"

He wore the same slacks and linen shirt he'd worn to dinner—a casual place that specialized in poke bowls. He twisted his hands in front of his belly.

"Is everything all right? Tommy?" She stepped forward in worry.

Banks's smile looked nervous and forced. "He's fine. Passed out already. I just thought there's a lovely mermaid statue at the edge of the resort, and I wanted to make sure you got to see it before we leave. It's close by. Walk with me?"

She hesitated. Just the two of them on an evening walk? She shrugged off her worries. He was her friend, and he was being thoughtful. She'd rather visit with him than sit here wanting Smith. Not to mention the mermaid sounded cool. She stepped into the hall. "I'd love to see it."

He beamed for a moment before his face slipped back into an uncomfortable grin.

"Is everything all right?"

He turned, and she walked at his side. "I'm sorry about the hibachi dinner last night. If Smith was disrespectful or overstepped . . . I don't ever want you to be uncomfortable with us."

Claire chuckled at the irony. "Kind of you to worry, but please don't. I really enjoy the company of all of you. I can handle a bit of teasing. My girls can be ruthless."

"Maybe they'd like to join us here next year."

"Oh." She pulled back in surprise. That felt odd. Generous, but not quite right. *Hmm?*

"Or not," he said quickly. "We can revisit that idea another day."

They rode the elevator in awkward silence. It got better outside, with the space and the beauty and the breeze. "I love the smell. The flowers here are divine. I wish I could bottle them up and take them home."

"I think you can buy that in the gift shop."

She huffed a short laugh. "It's not quite the same."

"No." He looked at the stars and inhaled. "It's not. Helen used to say how the wind carries stories. You smell them and feel them instead of read them. The air in each place has something different to share."

"What a lovely thought." She inhaled brine and blossoms. "I like that a lot and am going to have to think about that more. The wind whispers stories. Delightful."

Banks's face drooped in sadness, and she could almost see his grief tightening around him like a net of cinching ropes.

Claire touched him gently on the forearm. "She sounds truly amazing. I bet it's really hard to be here this year without her."

He shook his shoulders as if he could shimmy free of the uninvited emotions.

Claire knew better. He couldn't shoo the suffering away like a pesky rat. It would claim its due time one way or another. Her heart went out to him.

His face perked up. "It would have been, but you're here. You've made all the difference. You're amazing too."

Claire felt a touch of self-consciousness. She didn't want flattery right now. She didn't want to be compared to Helen ever. As much as he might wish it, she couldn't be a bandage covering his wounds.

They rounded a corner of the gravelly ocean path, and the statue came into view, a young woman with ebony skin and a bronze fish tail. Long curly hair covered her naked chest. She gazed out at the ocean with a look of longing that punched Claire right through the heart. Claire felt for her. Claire was her.

Her breath caught. "Oh. Oh, wow. She's stunning."

Banks watched Claire watching the mermaid. She tried to ignore him as she drank in the art, the emotion, the connection she felt to this female. This woman who wanted what was just beyond her reach. Claire brought a hand to her empty womb and another to her yearning heart. It pounded against her fingers, healthy and strong. There was still time for living yet. She wanted fiercely and with sudden clarity to leave the safe harbor she'd built for herself these last few years. She'd needed time at the dry dock to heal, but now she was ready to set sail again. And her heart was charting a course toward Smith.

Finally she turned to Banks. She couldn't look him in the eyes. Didn't want to see the expression there or share her soul with him. She was eager to find his son. "Thank you for bringing me here." Formal tone. "This is the most incredible trip I've ever been on." She turned to walk back toward the hotel.

He stepped up and put fingers on her forearm. "Wait. I want to ask you something."

An icy snake coiled around her chest as she faced him.

Hope and anxiety sprouted over his face as he held out trembling hands to her.

She hesitantly set her hands in his, worried about where this might be going. Her brow furrowed.

"You are amazing, Claire. Gorgeous, smart, kind, funny."

She didn't say thank you. Her thoughts darkened as dread rose through her.

"You have been a blessing to this family. Tommy loves you." He swallowed. "I love you."

She puffed out a shock of air as her body suffered the attack of a million tiny needles. *No.* She lifted her hands from his. Bless his broken heart. But no.

He stuck his hand into his pocket and pulled out a jewelry box.

Curse words went off like bombs in her brain. She couldn't think straight. The blood drained from her entire body as he opened the box to reveal a stunning diamond solitaire.

He knelt in the gravelly path. The wind toyed with his hair. What would Helen say the breeze was thinking now? It sounded mocking in her ears. He tilted his handsome, hopeful face up to her. "Will you marry me?"

She couldn't breathe. She felt like a suffocating stone corpse. Her jaw came unhinged.

"I don't expect you to replace Helen."

Yes, he did. Of course, he did. He wanted her to make all the hurt and discomfort disappear. It was total foolishness, but she understood it. "Is that her ring?"

His expression faltered when he looked at the ring, a powerful symbol of his years and devotion to Helen. His eyes clouded, like maybe he hadn't let himself focus on what he was doing, the quick fix he was trying to force. Claire got the impression he hadn't dared look at the ring since stealing it from his closet, a hostage on his mad mission. He swallowed, and the uncertainty in his features smoothed into a charming smile.

"We can get you something else if you want. I thought this was a good placeholder until then."

Stunned back into speechlessness.

"You're already part of the family. It feels so natural to have you here. You're such a good mother to Tommy." His brow furrowed. "And Smith too."

Oh, holy hell. Smith. This was going to hurt him. Did he already know about this proposal tonight? Did he give Banks his blessing? No. No.

"Tommy needs you."

"Tommy has me." Her voice came out dry and crackly.

"I need you."

"You need to give yourself a bit more time to heal. What you need me for is what you have me for, a nanny and friend. Besides, we've never been on a date. Or even kissed."

Banks rose to stand. Claire watched, paralyzed, as he leaned forward and pressed his mouth to hers. His lips were softer than she'd expected. Baby soft. Her vision went cross eyed as she tried to focus on his face. The future seemed as blurry as he was. He was a handsome man. He offered her so very much. Did she need to give this a try? The kiss wasn't unpleasant. It wasn't magic like . . . *oh, shit.*

When he brought his fingers to her waist and shifted his lips to deepen the kiss, she knocked his hand off and stepped back.

"No. Nope. No." She was panting. Her heart pinched in pain. "No. I'm sorry. No. My answer is no."

"No?" He looked confused.

She softened her tone. "You don't love me. You're grieving and alone, and I'm here. I'm nice and good with Tommy and pretty. I'm an easy answer, but I'm not the right one. I am confident that, with time, you will find a better woman for you. I am not she."

He opened his mouth, but no words came. Hurt and humiliation darkened his face.

"You are amazing in so many ways. But we are not the right fit as husband and wife. Nanny and employer, yeah, we're perfection together." She silently begged him not to get angry. She could picture Stevie's reaction. He would manipulate her, turn his pain into a weapon. He couldn't stand to be miserable alone. She would be devastated if Banks fired her for this. He couldn't. "You are a wonderful man, Banks. I am so happy with Tommy. This job you've given me has not only saved me from debt but brought me so much joy. I'm truly heartbroken for your loss, but please don't ask this of me. Please understand that we shouldn't get married." Her voice turned pleading.

He closed the ring box and stuffed it back into his pocket. He stared at the ocean. She crossed her fingers and hunched against an impending blow. Finally he turned to her. "You're right. Of course, you're exactly right. I'm sorry."

She held her breath.

"I put you in an uncomfortable position. Which you handled with grace. I'm embarrassed. Please forgive me. Can we pretend it never happened and move forward as before?"

Pretend it never happened. She exhaled pure relief even as she registered it was the same impossible thing she'd asked of Smith. She felt sick. "Yes. Of course."

"I think I'll just head up to bed now." He looked so sad and broken she had to resist the urge to try and comfort him.

She nodded. "I'll stay with our mermaid for a bit longer if that's all right."

He looked relieved. "I'll see you in the morning."

"It will be a fresh new day." She sent him an encouraging look. "Good night, Banks."

He strode off. As his footsteps faded, her body sagged. She sat down at the base of the statue, her body trembling. She shook like a leaflet in a tornado. She cursed for long seconds. Let the wind take that story and share it.

Who the hell did Banks think he was dropping that bomb on her, treating marriage, *her*, like a company to merge with? She could get over the idiotic proposal. The bullshit declaration of love. He didn't love her. He loved what she did for him. He'd thought elevating her to wife status was a promotion. He was grieving and seeking any comfort. All forgivable. She did understand, and she did forgive him, the poor sap. But then he'd kissed her. Her lips were her own business.

And she'd given them to Smith.

Smith.

And she'd given her heart to Tommy. She'd fallen for that golden boy just like she'd fallen for her daughters. She'd suffer anything for them. She'd beg and plead to keep her place with Tommy.

She whimpered. Stevie couldn't have taken her daughters from her, but Banks had all the power over Tommy. Would she have to marry him to keep Tommy? She pinched her eyes shut. She couldn't do that. But part of her truly wished she could have done it for Tommy. Banks would give her a beautiful life, adventures, and luxuries she'd never afford on her own. He was a good man, so good she believed he would move forward from tonight with no hard feelings. It was going to be okay. They were okay. He'd made a mistake, but he was man enough to accept it. Comfort sprouted in her chest, only to be squashed again by the real problem. Smith.

She couldn't keep this from Smith. It would eat her up inside.

That's what her anger was really about. She was pissed at Banks for putting her in this position with Smith. She must tell Smith the truth because she actually, fully, deep down, adult-style, honest-all-the-way-through cared a fuck-ton lot about Smith.

Before she lost courage, she pulled out her phone and forced her fluttery fingers to text. One last ice cream before we go?

She waited. No reply.

In what twisted world could a man and his father develop feelings for the same woman? No, that wasn't true. Banks missed Helen; he didn't love Claire. Smith was young, but she couldn't write him off anymore. Or her own feelings. No more pretending. Spending time with him here had been as smooth and easy as honey. And just as sweet.

Meet in the hall in two minutes?

Her heart surged. She wanted him to kiss her better, use those hands to fix her up nicely. I'm already outside. I'll meet you at our bench instead.

She was not interested in being Banks's wife, but as she said goodbye to the stranded statue, she let herself imagine what it would be like to be loved by Smith.

Chapter 35
SMITH

Smith strode eagerly down the path toward Claire, stunned and thrilled she'd texted. She was coming around. He knew she liked him back; finally she was starting to accept it. Today had been mellow: surfing, swimming, and snacking. No drama. He felt Claire loosening up around him. Last night at the hibachi dinner, she'd laughed without reserve. She'd left her leg pressed against his. He sensed her shields coming down. He had hope. He burned with it.

He didn't want to go home tomorrow. He didn't want this dream vacation to end. When she went home to that house she'd shared with Stevie, would she remember her fear and close up again? Was he kidding himself that she'd ever let herself be vulnerable?

He found her on the bench at the top of a small rise overlooking sea and stars. She held out a mini pineapple ice cream. Her face looked pale and somber. His stomach tightened in dread. He accepted the treat and sat down at her side. "Putting me on a diet, I see. Probably good after the week we had." He took a bite. "Where's yours?"

"I don't have an appetite." Her voice came out weak.

Was she breaking up with him? He almost laughed out loud. There wasn't anything here to break. Except his heart.

He wanted to pry, but instead waited patiently, eating the ice cream he no longer wanted, watching the ocean that seemed to bode bad news. A *bewitching sea*, as Mom would have called it.

"I feel like I need to tell you what happened tonight. You should know."

The cream and sugar in his stomach curdled. He set the bowl on the bench.

"Banks asked me to marry him."

"What?" It was the only word he could find to say. He'd sort of known Dad might try something—the poor, heartbroken asshole—but a marriage proposal?! He didn't think Dad was stupid enough to actually pop the question. Unless . . . "What did you say?"

Her head snapped toward him. Her eyes turned to hellfire.

It was incredibly reassuring. Although he still felt sick.

"He even had Helen's ring. It was gorgeous."

His gaze dropped to her bare left finger. He knew the 4.2-carat, cushion-cut pink diamond well. He'd hoped to inherit it for his wife someday. He glanced at the only woman in the world he could have imagined giving it to. And his father had just tried. Acid roared up his throat.

"Offering her ring just shows how much he wasn't thinking straight." A lock of hair blew across Claire's flushed cheeks. "He wasn't wanting me; he was missing her. He knows deep down he can't replace her, but I can't be too angry at him for wanting to try."

Smith was angry enough for the both of them.

She sagged. "I need to admit that he kissed me."

"He." Smith gagged. "Did what?"

Her shoulders curved in. "It wasn't a big thing. There was nothing there."

"Did you kiss him back?" He didn't want to know. He had to know. He couldn't possibly hurt more than he already did.

"Not exactly."

"What the hell does that mean?"

Her voice lowered as he rose to his feet. "It means I should have pulled back sooner. I sort of froze up for a second."

He lurched forward, stumbled over to the bushes, and leaned on his knees. Pineapple-flavored bile rose to the back of his throat. He swallowed hard and forced deep breaths. He gave himself long seconds to get a grip before he turned around.

Claire was white as a sheet, her wide eyes full of terror. He had no idea how to rescue her from this. Or himself. At least she hadn't asked him if he was okay.

He was not.

Smith clutched the back of the bench. This sucked so bad. At least he knew how much he really cared about her. A giant fucking lot.

Nothing but love hurt this much.

"I'm so sorry. I need you to know that there is nothing there. Nothing between me and Banks."

He didn't sit down. He wanted to punch his father. Dad's attempt to win her had blown up in his face. Was this a warning to Smith? That pursuing this path would only bring him to the same painful end?

A tear dribbled down her face. It tugged at his chest. He sat next to her and brushed it away with a thumb. His voice was soft. "Hey. It's okay. It's not your fault." She leaned into his hand, and he thought he might die.

"He caught me off guard. I hesitated. I thought of Tommy."

Tommy. He was the one she loved. He leaned back. "So what happens now?" His voice was bitter.

"We're going to pretend it never happened."

Pretend it never happened. This was one situation where he was on board with that plan.

"He knows it was a mistake. He's still grieving, and he wanted a quick fix. I think he realizes now how very much I'm not the right fit for him." Her eyes glittered as she held his gaze. "I'll keep taking care of Tommy. We'll all move forward as usual."

There was his answer. His rejection too. She was here for Tommy. Smith wasn't going to be the one to ruin that for his little brother. He must step back, leave her alone. Tommy needed her most.

He almost willed himself to believe it.

Chapter 36
CLAIRE

The walk back to the hotel felt a mile long and at the same time, mere heartbeats. She trudged to her doom, to goodbye.

After hearing about the proposal and the kiss, Smith was out. She'd expected him to be unhappy but not so angry and unforgiving. It hadn't been her fault, but he barely looked at her as they parted to their separate rooms, separate lives.

As she stepped into her empty room, the grief at losing him nearly knocked her to the floor. She crumpled to her bed, shocked by the waves of sorrow. Yet she still wanted Smith in her future. A revelation she wasn't ready to unpack.

Banks had dropped the nuke, but she'd been the one to make sure Smith took the hit with her.

She wasn't being fair to herself. She couldn't regret her honesty with him. She'd done right by cleaning the wound.

But the sadness.

It was overwhelming. As strong as had been the earlier pleasure he'd stoked to life within her. How had she let herself feel so much for Smith?

This was why she had her rules about men. This soul-shredding pain. All her past hurts seemed to rise up inside her like a vicious mob. *Yes, I know. I wasn't supposed to let this happen again. I was supposed to be smarter. I was supposed to have learned, protected myself.*

She didn't wallow in self-pity as long as she'd expected to. Tonight's disaster wasn't her fault. She was pretty badass to have drawn the interest of two great men. As much as she tried, she couldn't bring herself to regret kissing Smith. It had been that good.

She washed off all her unhealthy thoughts in the shower and stepped out feeling quite proud of her maturity. Dripping wet and skin steaming, she stood in front of the mirror. She looked herself in the eye. *You are everything you need. You are okay.*

Despite all her positive self-talk, she was still anxious and torn up inside. She did not sleep well.

In the morning, Banks and Smith looked as destroyed as she. Dark circles ringed their eyes. She caught Banks popping back aspirin while she helped Tommy pack up. Had he gone out drinking? She couldn't blame him if he did. He wasn't Stevie. It was none of her business. People drank; not everyone turned into mean alcoholics. At least Tommy seemed okay, blissful in his ignorance. During the silent ride to the airport, she was deeply grateful Banks had ruined the trip on the last night, not the first.

"I want to sit by Smith again," Tommy said as they walked up to the gate.

"No," Banks said, his voice stern. When everyone looked at him, he did an awkward tweak of his lip and said in a fake-excited voice, "You get to sit by me this time. I downloaded a superhero movie for us to watch together."

Tommy grinned, and Claire exhaled in relief. Only a few hours and all the adults could be not together, and all would be fine.

Smith gave Claire the window seat in the row behind Banks and Tommy. She sat. He sat. They both stared at the seat backs in front of them. She almost wished they were crammed in coach so she wouldn't feel so far away from him.

They didn't talk. And didn't talk. The plane took off and headed east. She expected him to take out headphones and turn on a movie. But he just sat there, looking at nothing. And she just sat there, pretending like she wasn't watching him. She couldn't take it anymore. From her purse, she pulled out a small notepad and flipped to a blank page.

She wrote *Are you okay?* She slid the pen and pad onto his tray by his open bag of peanuts.

Still not looking at her, he read the note. Her pulse rose when he picked up the pen. He handed back the note. He'd written in a hasty all-caps script *I'M DONE FEELING LIKE I MIGHT VOMIT.*

She didn't want him to be done with her too. She took the paper and wrote *I'm sorry.* One of her girlfriends always said to never apologize for things that weren't your fault. It made people blame you. It was self-sabotaging. Claire hadn't been good at it with Stevie. And that man never apologized. Claire crossed out the words and wrote *I think Banks is sorry.*

Smith finally looked at her, and it was like dawn broke through the clouds. He scanned her face with sad eyes for a long moment; then his lips curved up. Her belly flipped.

He passed the paper back, and Claire read *HE'S SORRY YOU HARD-CORE REJECTED HIM.*

She laughed. Smith's enchanting eyes twinkled, and his shoulders softened.

She wanted to take his hand. Touch him. Really, she wanted to crawl into his freaking lap. Her pen seemed to gain a will of its own. *Are you going to disappear from my life?* It was easier to write the words than to say them out loud. After passing the note, she looked out the window, too cowardly to watch his reaction.

He sighed before writing in his bold font: *I CAN'T STOP IMAGINING MY DAD KISSING YOU AND TELLING YOU HE LOVES YOU AND TRYING TO PAWN MOM'S RING OFF ON YOU.*

Her heart cracked as she took the paper, folded it up, and put it in her purse. So that was that. He wasn't going to change his mind. Good thing she hadn't had sex with him and accidentally gotten pregnant or more attached. Damn good thing. She shriveled farther into her seat as she realized that wasn't true at all. She would love to have Smith's baby growing in her belly. She held her arms tight around herself. It wasn't much comfort.

She did not bother Smith again for the rest of the flight. He seemed to appreciate that, which tore her further apart inside. But it was her own fault. She knew better. She was suffering the natural consequence of breaking her rule. This was what always happened when she let someone in. They left her gutted.

When Banks pulled his car up to her curb, her house looked like heaven.

"Thanks for an amazing trip," Claire said. She tugged her bag from the back. "I'll see you on Monday at the bus stop, Tommy. Enjoy the rest of your weekend." She strode up her walkway and let the familiar smells of home envelop her. She inhaled quiet and serenity.

She didn't unpack, or shower, or call her daughters. She dropped her bag and went straight to her garage. She pulled out her biggest canvas, a seven-foot-by-five-foot monster. She'd been feeling this painting for days, composing it in her mind. She often worked to music, but not today. Today she painted in rhythm with the song of her heart.

She picked up her brush. And she painted. And painted.

She stopped only to pee and guzzle water. It was late the next morning when she finally stepped back, spent in body and mind. Not really at peace. But the beast was satiated—for now.

The painting was mesmerizing. One of her best. Maybe the best. The expression of intense desire and discouragement. Curving lines gave the shape of embracing torsos. Sienna, pink, cream, brown, gold, the colors of *him* were overlaid in a storm of inky blues. A quiet stillness lay at the center. The painting moved on its own, with just enough of a feeling of being off balance to be completely intriguing, a song in a minor key. She titled it **PRETENDING** and wrote the date of January 27—the day of the kiss that killed her.

She'd overheard someone at an art show once look at her paintings and say, "She paints so beautifully; her soul must be a terrible place."

She understood that now. She embraced it.

After lacquering and the final dry, Claire took her masterpiece to Main Street Gallery and left it with a very happy Sheila Rivers.

"Wow, Claire. Just. Wow."

Claire smiled with pride.

"I was worried about you when you picked up that unsold series last fall, but each one you bring in now seems to be better than the last. Whatever has happened these last couple months has been magic on your art."

And tragic on her heart.

"I have a buyer who's looking for something like this. I've been searching for ages. I'll call him today. This is going to be a big sale."

Claire walked out of the gallery grinning. She didn't need Banks's money. She was back in business.

It was all good until the next day, when she saw her painting hanging in Banks Sexton's front hall.

Bloody nightmare, it was.

Every day, when those rusty pinks and soft curves slapped her in the face, she relived all the wanting and fire and dissatisfaction.

Chapter 37
BANKS

Banks went through his front door with a skip in his step. He'd taken Margo out on a second date tonight, and he was looking forward to a third—already scheduled for Friday. After Hawaii he'd escaped into the stack of phone numbers on his dresser. Five dates in less than three weeks. Spending time with new people had taken his mind off both his embarrassing moment with Claire and his loneliness. When he was chatting with an interesting woman, it was easier to pretend he was doing okay. He enjoyed the laughter and flirting and distraction. He was trying not to feel guilty about it.

He nodded to the new painting on his wall as he waltzed past. Helen never would have bought a piece so bold. It was only shapes and colors—but wasn't everything? This composition, though. There was something provocative about it. It made him feel alive and strong. Sexy. He'd never heard of the artist, not that he knew the art scene at all, but apparently she was local, which was cool.

Claire strode up, purse already in hand. Her rejection still chafed his ego a bit, but she'd been right. He was relieved he wasn't engaged to her. That would have been a disaster. Now that he was pulling off the blinders of denial, he was horrified he'd offered her his wife's ring.

He'd been in the depths of avoidance when he'd snatched the box from Helen's drawer and taken it to Hawaii. He and Claire weren't a great fit for marriage. She had an exotic energy and quick wit that he couldn't match. He wanted to relax, more quiet evenings and pampering. And he was still neck deep in grief. He wasn't close to being ready to consider remarrying yet. All truths he hadn't wanted to acknowledge but was starting to.

He appreciated that it seemed she hadn't told anyone about his humiliation. Roger hadn't brought it up, which meant Roger didn't know. He respected Claire for that. These last couple of weeks had been smooth sailing. He treated her now as he probably always should have, with friendly civility. He didn't try to invite her to family events or visit with her after work, except to talk about Tommy.

"How did it go tonight?" he asked.

She glanced quickly at the painting and away. So, she was in Helen's camp, not an abstract lover. She couldn't handle the raw power of this art, the feelings it stirred up.

"Great," she said. "Tommy's runny nose seems to have dried up. I left his schoolwork on the counter. He's especially proud of the valentine that Harper gave him."

Banks raised an eyebrow. Yesterday was the holiday of love. Banks did not ask Claire how she'd spent it.

She chuckled. "There's a permission slip for you to sign. And if you can remember to put an ice pack in his lunch in the morning, it will help keep his sandwich fresh."

"Great. And thanks for staying late tonight."

"Happy to." She slid her purse strap over her shoulder and walked out.

Banks hummed as he undressed and got ready for bed. He texted Smith: Can Tommy sleep over at your house Friday night?

Why?

I want to have my own sleepover here. Would Smith get what he was implying?

I'm going to vomit.

Yep, he got the message. So I'm never allowed to move on? A strike of grief hit at the same time he pressed send. He didn't want to move on from Helen. He wanted to move right on back to his wife.

Smith didn't reply.

But Helen wasn't here. He didn't want to be sad and lonely anymore. He was done, dammit. Her name is Margo. She's 49. Divorced. No children. She's an attorney. Smart and pretty. Nice eyes. You'll like her.

I'll take Tommy if I don't have to hear any more about it.

Banks chuckled.

On Friday he came home from work early. Claire and Tommy were eating dinner together. He joined them at the table.

"Would you like some?" Claire asked.

He looked over their bowls of broccoli-cheddar soup. It looked good, but his stomach had twisted into a knot. He hadn't had sex with anyone but Helen for twenty-seven years.

What if he did it wrong tonight? What if Margo didn't like his moves? Did he have any moves? What if he didn't like her moves? What if it was awkward?

"Are you okay?" Claire asked.

He shook his head. "Yeah. Sorry." He really wanted to talk to her, ask her about how to set the mood tonight. What would Margo like? Man, he felt creepy. He cleared his throat. "You can go."

She looked taken aback but set her spoon next to her full bowl.

"No. Sorry. Crap. I didn't mean that. Please eat. I've just got something on my mind."

She shifted to stand.

"Please eat with Tommy. There are a couple emails I'd like to send if you can give me a few minutes." Total lie.

"Of course." She settled back in her seat.

He rushed from the room. He sat in his office chair. He pulled up his email. Nothing urgent. He couldn't focus anyway. Instead he did an internet search for foreplay ideas. It was not helpful. Now he had a boner and was even more nervous. He closed all the tabs and shut down his computer. He made himself calm the crap down. He did not want to see Claire right now. Not at all. Finally, he went back to the main room. Claire was cleaning up dinner, wearing that damn kiss-the-cook apron. He was going to throw that away when she left. Which would hopefully be very soon. He wanted her out. *Out.*

"I'll finish up in here," he said.

She turned, looking about to object. But she seemed to read his face like an open book, then nodded. She took off the apron. "Have a great weekend." She kissed Tommy and left.

Banks sagged in relief. He stuffed the apron in the trash. He got Tommy's overnight bag packed up, since Claire hadn't done it because he hadn't told Claire about it. Tommy played on his iPad while Banks took his time showering, shaving, and dressing. He worried he was already sweating by the time they were in the car, which made him sweat more.

"A sleepover with Smith," Banks said. "That's going to be fun."

"Yeah." Tommy didn't look too happy. He looked tired. Was his cold coming back? Was Banks being a terrible father? Was it wrong of him to invite another woman home tonight without Tommy knowing? Should he cancel? Then he could spend the evening alone, pining for a dead woman.

He sighed sadly and pulled up to Smith's. They let themselves in. Smith was sitting on his couch watching TV. He flicked it off when he saw them.

"Thanks for watching Tommy."

"Happy to. I've missed my main Trombone."

They hadn't seen Smith for a while. How long had it been? Maybe since Hawaii? Things had been busy, but he'd need to remember to invite Smith over soon. "He's tired tonight. Will you put him right to bed?"

"It's seven thirty."

"He's tired."

Smith nodded and took Tommy's bag. "Got it."

"I'll pick him up in the morning. But not too early." Cockiness entered Banks's tone, a lie if ever there was one. He felt awkward and unsure.

Smith frowned. "Nope. None of that."

Banks forced a grin.

"And I'll bring him over in the morning," Smith said. "I want to check out a house that just listed down the street."

"I'll let you know when the coast is clear."

Not even a flicker of amusement on Smith's face. His son shook his head as he walked Banks back to the door. Smith glanced over his shoulder. Tommy was looking through the pantry cupboard far across the room. Smith lowered his voice. "Please wear a condom."

Banks's heart stopped. Panic thudded through his body. He sent an imploring look at his son.

Smith's eyes went wide; then his features hardened. "No. Absolutely not. Stop at a pharmacy. Bye." He closed the door in his face.

At the store, Banks felt like a teenage pervert. There were so many kinds, and they were all boxed like adult candies. That was Helen's department. Of course, they hadn't used any contraceptive for the twenty-one years leading up to Tommy's birth. Banks was going to be inexcusably late if he didn't leave now. He grabbed one that said **Classic**. That seemed like an appropriate label for him—hopefully in a good way. At the checkout, he kept his chin on his sternum.

"Are you going to want a bag for this?" There was definite mocking in that young man's voice.

"Yes." Chin still on chest.

"Have a *great* night."

Face hot, Banks took the bag and made off like a bandit. *I am fifty years old. Fifty, Banks. Get a grip.* In the car he fumbled with the box, opened it, and put one of the slim packages in his wallet. That's where people put them, right?

He stuffed the rest under the seat. Deep breath.

Now for the date.

Margo looked lovely. She wore a tight black dress around her voluptuous body. Her smile relaxed his nerves. Dinner went well. He didn't rush. They talked business and travel. She was sharp as a tack and would keep him on his toes. He liked that. He thought he liked it. It was a bit intimidating. He tried not to worry about anything else, just enjoying this present moment with this pleasant woman. And he did enjoy it. They shared a Tuscan wine while talking about their experiences in that lush foreign region. The date was going very well. But as he pulled out his wallet to pay the check, his pulse rose again. He slid his credit card from the slot, and the condom flopped out onto the table.

Margo's thick brows rose.

His face flamed.

She picked it up with bold red fingernails. "Are you going to invite me back to your place, Mr. *Sex*ton?"

He swallowed. *Sorry, Helen. I love you; I miss you. I'm going to take this woman home and do her in your bed.*

Margo waited.

"Yes." It came out squeakier than a rubber mouse.

"Then let's go."

Frick, that was hot. He stuffed his card back in his wallet, dropped a wad of cash, and stood. She kept the condom as he took her other hand.

Turned out, he remembered his way around a female body just fine. Better than fine.

Chapter 38
SMITH

You can bring Tommy home now.

Smith cringed as he read the text from his dad. It was 11:00 a.m., grossly late in the morning, but it was the smiley face emoji at the end that was the most disturbing.

So Dad had gotten laid last night. First time since Mom. He'd waited longer than Smith had expected him to. It was bizarre, but at least it wasn't Claire. Dad could do anyone as long as he stayed the hell away from her. If Smith couldn't have her, he didn't want anyone else to either. He wondered again, as he had every day for the past three weeks, what was she doing? *How* was she doing? He was still hung up on her. It was literally the worst.

Smith walked Tommy into the front entry of his dad's house a half hour later. He proceeded with caution, afraid if he inhaled too deeply he'd smell what had happened here. He'd be contaminated. Who was being immature now?

When had Dad gotten a new painting? Smith stopped as Tommy ran off. A heaviness settled in Smith's belly as he looked over the art. He squinted at the tiny signature at the bottom. *C. Williams.* Holy shit. This was Claire's. He stepped back, heart hammering.

"Incredible, right?"

Smith jumped out of his skin at the sound of Dad's voice. "When did you get this?"

"A couple weeks ago. A woman at a gallery downtown has been keeping her eye out for a piece for me since Mom died and Jennifer took off with the horse. The gallery finally found one I like." Dad frowned as he studied Smith's face. "Don't you like it?"

Smith glanced at the painting, at the weaving curves and wantonness. The earthy color spread pulled at his insides. "It's incredible." His voice came out rough and guttural. Images of Claire filled his mind. He could almost still feel her lean muscles and soft lips.

Dad grinned, which was an unpleasant intrusion on the intimate thoughts.

Smith cleared his throat, trying to drive away the desires. "Do you know who painted it?"

Dad squinted in thought.

He had no idea. Unbelievable. Smith chuckled darkly. The universe was screwing with him.

Dad got a silly grin. "I'll remember. Just give me a minute." He tilted the bottom of the painting off the wall a couple of inches to look.

Smith went to the other side and read the label on the backing. His focus slid over *Claire Williams* and homed in on the title, **PRETENDING**. She'd dated it January 27, of *this* year. His body turned to burning ice. That was the date of their kiss in Hawaii. This was brand new. This was about them—him.

He stepped back as his belly turned inside out. He saw the painting with new eyes. *Pretending.* The title was pure irony because this was Claire's truth right here on this canvas. And she was burning inside. He felt her fear and wanting. Emotion seared across the swirl of colors. Hopeful agony exploded through his body like shooting stars. She had hidden all this from him. His pulse rose.

He couldn't keep pretending.

"Could you see a name?" Dad asked.

Smith jolted at the deep voice. He turned away from the roaring painting on the wall and the sputtering in his chest. He faced his father. "So, how did it go on your date last night?"

Dad's grin said it all. Smith could see the fun and vibrancy of new love and potential written all over his bright face.

"Good," Smith said. "I'm glad for you."

"Margo was nothing like Helen."

Smith held up two hands. "Nope. I'm sorry I asked. No. *No.*"

"Sorry," Dad said, not seeming sorry. "It's just I didn't expect to be excited about a woman again. She was so energetic."

Smith frowned. "I will barf. And I will aim for your face." But he wasn't disgusted with his father. He was sick with jealousy. His father had plowed forward, making decisions and going for them. Mistakes be damned; he was a fighter. Smith felt like the biggest wimp. He glanced over at Claire's bold painting, hanging on the wall like a declaration of her desire and genius.

"Want to stay for lunch? Claire left a pot of broccoli-cheese soup and garlic bread. It's good."

Just hearing her name on Dad's tongue sent an uncomfortable spark down Smith's spine. He really needed to man up. "No, I've got to run. I'll see you later."

"Sooner rather than later this time?"

Smith nodded and was out the door.

He drove by her house three times before stopping. He stuffed his hands in his pockets as he walked to the door.

"Smith." She blinked at him in surprise; then a deep smile split her face. "Nice to see you." Her voice was low with sincerity. She sounded like she meant it.

His pulse fluttered. He'd missed her so much. She wore an oversized T-shirt and leggings, both splattered with paint. He was still crazy attracted to her. More now than before, if that was possible. "Are you painting?"

"Yes."

What was she creating now? He wanted to see. He wanted it all. "I saw your piece at my dad's."

Blood rushed to her face.

Damn, she was beautiful.

And he'd been right. Those feelings were for him. His heart threatened to explode.

Could he kiss her right now? Of course the last two times hadn't ended well. He didn't want her to bolt this time. Or leave him ever again. He fisted his hands in his pockets, holding himself back. *Tread carefully.*

"He doesn't know it's mine."

"I didn't tell him."

"Thank you. I should tell him, but the thought makes me feel exposed. I painted that for you. About you. And I don't want to talk about it with him. I don't want to make it weird with him again."

Smith's whole body seemed to sigh. That little bit of fear that had wormed its way into his mind, constantly pestering him that maybe Claire and his dad had something between them or could develop feelings, that dread shriveled up and died. He felt dizzy with hope. "The painting is incredible. Truly captivating."

Hazel eyes speared him.

He dropped his voice. "Just like that *pretend* kiss."

She glanced down at her painting clothes, and then back up at him. "Yeah." She took a fortifying breath. "I was pretty torn up after Hawaii. I guess I'm not so good at pretending when it comes to you. Painting has always helped me work through things." She forced a chuckle. "Turns out your kisses make for really good art."

Smith could barely breathe over the want threatening to choke him. "I'll take that as a compliment."

"You should." Her eyes glittered with longing as she looked at him, an openness there that he hadn't dared dream of finding.

He felt like bursting, but he kept his voice as steady as he could. "I have some friends going out tonight on a boat to try and see the phytoplankton. The bioluminescence is supposed to be really vibrant." He'd thought of her the minute he'd gotten the text three days ago. The bioluminescence was a rare treat in this part of the ocean. He wanted to share it with her. "I thought you might like to see it."

Her bold smile was sexy as hell. "Yes, Smith. I'd love to go with you."

He grinned back. He couldn't contain his happiness. Pleasure flared through his veins. "The boat leaves the dock at eight. I was going to grab a bite on the way . . ." He raised a brow in invitation.

She nodded.

"I'll pick you up at six."

"Okay."

"Okay."

"See you soon." She hesitated a moment, then sent him an adorably coy look before she shut the door.

His body hummed, but he forced a demure walk to his car. He drove around the corner before he pulled over and had his little freak-out. He speed jabbed the air and made the most unmanly squeal. Then he laughed. His whole body relaxed into a pleasant puddle.

He had a date with Ms. Claire.

Chapter 39
CLAIRE

Claire stared at the back of her front door, at the piece of wood between her and Smith. *Smith.* Had that really happened? Was it a lucid dream, or was he coming back for her in a few hours? To go on a *date*? That was against her rules. Well, it was just the one rule she had. And she was more than ready to break it. She certainly wasn't going to cancel on Smith. She was too fluttery and excited to even consider it. Her heart had hurt for three weeks straight, and with a snap of his fingers, she felt whole again.

She knew it was trouble. He was trouble. Just the kind of trouble she was aching for.

Her insides churned and bubbled as she padded back to her garage art studio. She'd been struggling with this painting all morning. It was too dark and depressing. She hadn't been able to fix it. Looking at it now, she knew just how to counter that sucking silvery hole. She channeled the skipping in her belly, and she added bright, dancing strokes of blue and green hope.

An hour later she stepped back. The painting had been transformed into a story of optimism and dreams. The darkness was there, but it wasn't winning anymore. She exhaled, not wanting to look away. She drank in the feelings of the piece, reveling in the warmth of possibility, reliving the scene on her doorstep. Smith had come to her home, looking nervous and adorable, and wanting *her*.

"So this is what you do, Smith." She sat back on her stool, gaze glued to the swirl of color over gray. Smith was the sun breaking through a storm. She was ready to step into this new, happy space he'd created in her life and revel in the pleasure of his company.

She sucked on her bottom lip as she got to work cleaning her brushes. With hours to go before he would come back for her, she turned her nervous energy to cleaning her house. With the sheets washed, bed remade, dust removed, surfaces gleaming, she finally turned to herself. She shaved everywhere, exfoliated, and lotioned. By the time the clock struck six, she was a new woman. She wanted to be new. Leave Claire Rosalie Williams Kehoe, widowed grandmother, behind and just be a girl going out with a boy. Being open and vulnerable might not be easy, but she was determined to try.

A knock sounded at the door. She checked herself in the mirror once more. Blue jeans, white sneakers, soft V-neck shirt, hair blown out in loose waves, simple makeup. She allowed herself a smile. She looked pretty dang good for all her miles. She grabbed her coat and opened the door. She swooned a little inside at the sight of his thick blond hair, high cheekbones, and fitted jeans. Twenty-two years ago, Stevie had shown up at her door to take her to the high school dance. She'd thought he was the best thing ever. She'd been so stupid and naive. But all these years and sorrows later, she found herself thinking the same thing about this man. Fool me once, shame on you. Fool me twice, shame on me. For shame, Claire. But she was smitten.

And it felt so damn good.

Felt even better for what she'd learned and been through. Teenage Claire hadn't experienced enough to have earned the deep satisfaction now swirling in her chest.

The look Smith gave her, bold and fiery, made her nerves buzz, but he didn't tell her she was beautiful. He didn't hug her. Didn't even take his hands out of his pockets. "You ready?"

That seemed like a loaded question. Ready to break her rule and go on a date? Ready to risk another broken heart? Ready to live? "Yes."

He gave her half a smile, but it was plenty potent.

He didn't open the car door for her. Good. This wasn't Victorian London. She preferred to do it herself. She slid into the leather seat.

"You like bibimbap?" Smith asked.

"It sounds weird and fun."

He chuckled. "Just like you."

"I set you up for that."

"And I knocked it out of the park."

He rested his hand on the console. Not on her thigh. Didn't try to hold her hand. Maybe this was just a friendly I-know-you-liked-seeing-the-animals-and-so-I'm-being-nice-and-inviting-you deal. It wasn't a *date*. She hated the disappointment that snaked through her body. Hated her desire to be touched. Hated feeling weak and needy. Was it too late to have him take her home? The plankton weren't worth this torture.

Smith pulled up to Happy Hot Bowls, a tiny, hidden place in Corona del Mar. Not touching, they walked across the parking lot. He pulled the restaurant front door open and held it for her. The smell of soy and spice made her mouth water.

"Ah, Smith!" The middle-aged man fist-bumped Smith. "Welcome back. And today you bring a pretty lady. Nice work."

"Thanks, Sung-ho. She's never had bibimbap before."

The thin man turned to her. "You will like it."

"I'm glad to hear that," she said.

Sung-ho turned back to Smith. "I like her." He motioned them to come. "I will give you the best table."

Sung-ho strode forward. Smith reached out to Claire, putting his fingers on her lower back. Sparks shot down her spine. He removed his fingers just as quickly. Dammit!

He spoke over her shoulder. "He's never given me the best table before."

"I find that hard to believe."

Nestled in the corner by the window, the two-top had a peekaboo view of the ocean and a poky plant next to it.

"You've been hiding this spot from me," Smith said.

"You were not ready for it."

Claire let out a delighted chuckle.

He started to sit.

"No, Smith. No." Sung-ho's frown made his whole face wrinkle.

Smith stood straight back up.

"The lady will sit on that side."

"Yes, sir." Chewing back amusement, Smith bowed to Claire and gestured for her to take her place as if it were a throne, not a stained wooden chair.

When they'd both sat, Sung-ho nodded. "Now the power of the salang table can work its magic."

"What's salang?" Claire asked.

"I don't think we want to know," Smith said.

Sung-ho gave him a stink eye that Claire was glad wasn't directed at her. "You laugh, but I expect to be invited to the wedding." With that he walked away.

Smith's brows rose to his hairline.

"Just like I expected," Claire said. "Weird and fun."

He burst out laughing.

She bit her lip as she picked up the laminated menu. "So I want to get one of these hot bowls? It actually says on here that it's guaranteed to make me happy. That's a recklessly bold statement."

Smith opened his mouth, closed it. Stared at her. She imagined him saying that he could guarantee making her happy. He didn't. He said, "They haven't failed to deliver yet."

She wished he'd been recklessly bold enough to tell her what she wanted to hear. But that was the thing. It wouldn't have been a guarantee. It would have been bullshit.

He looked down. "I like the short ribs best, but the bulgogi is good too."

"How annoyed will you be if I do the vegetarian bowl?"

He looked to the side as if deeply contemplating. "I'm at a level zero on that one."

Her lips curved. How was he not married? How had one of the many impressive women in this world not snatched him up?

Sung-ho appeared. "I see that smile," he said to Claire.

Her face heated.

"The magic is working already."

Smith leaned back. "Where does the magic come from? It must be from that plant." He pointed to the thing that looked more like a spiked weapon than a botanical. "Otherwise why would you want that creeping on the customers?"

Sung-ho lifted his chin and turned away from Smith with a sniff. "What can I get you?" he asked Claire.

After they'd ordered and Sung-ho had moved out of earshot, Claire leaned forward. "I don't think he liked you offending his plant."

Smith leaned in. "Why are we whispering?" He glanced over at the greenish-yellow lance-shaped leaves. "Do you think it can hear us?"

Claire picked up her paper place mat and held it between their heads and the plant. "I think we're fine as long as it can't see us."

"Did that paper just make us invisible?"

She snorted out a laugh and sat back. He reminded her of Tommy. Or maybe Tommy reminded her of Smith. Either way, it was a good connection. "Who will be on the boat tonight?"

Smith went down the list. Two married couples—that surprised Claire. But why should it? "And then Chris," Smith said. "He's also supposed to be bringing a date."

Also. Just one little word, but it turned Claire's lips up. So this was a date. She laughed at herself inside. What did it matter what she named the night? She was here with Smith, at a magical table, feeling a lot of nonplatonic things. She couldn't label any of that away.

Sung-ho brought a smattering of tiny dishes of kimchi, gochujang, and cucumbers. Then he set down two sizzling bowls. Brown eyes speared Claire. "It's hot."

"Okay." She skipped the chopstick option and picked up her spoon. This food looked good. How had she missed this all her life? It's not like she'd gone out a ton with Stevie. And he'd liked what he'd liked. Burgers, chicken wings, beer, and . . . well, that was mostly it.

"No. I don't think you are listening to me," Sung-ho said. "It's hot."

She tried to appear serious and probably failed. It didn't help that Smith was chewing back amusement. "I promise, I'll be careful."

"Don't blame me when you burn yourself." He walked away.

"It's like I'm five." She spooned up some rice and put it in her mouth. Then dropped it back onto the spoon when it seared her tongue. "Ouch. That's hot."

Smith laughed so hard his hand shook as he handed her ice water.

She sipped, then squinted across the restaurant to where Sung-ho was typing into his computer. "Maybe he is magic."

Smith dumped toppings into his bowl and stirred. He hadn't tried to take a bite yet. "Nah, he just knows everyone burns their tongue the first time."

She rolled a piece of ice around her mouth. "Dang. I hate being an everyone."

He looked her in the eyes. "I don't think you need to worry about that."

Her chest tightened, and she accidentally swallowed the ice chunk. It didn't do much against the heat rising through her core.

She ate slowly, savoring the meal and the company. She may have laughed more in this one meal than she had all year. When she'd eaten all she wanted, she passed her last third to Smith. He finished it as if it were the most normal thing in the world.

When the check came, she reached for her wallet, but Smith shooed her off.

"I picked this place. I buy. Next time, it's on you."

Next time. Those words shot around her system like untethered helium balloons. She didn't trust herself to speak, but she nodded.

He popped a mint in his mouth and handed her the other. After he paid, she stood. As she reached for her coat, her elbow swung back and struck the plant. "Ouch." She rubbed the spot, and it hurt enough that she checked to make sure it wasn't bleeding. A drop of red bubbled below her elbow. "It got me."

Sung-ho appeared. "It's okay. It is a good omen." He gave them a knowing grin. "It is a very good sign." His brows wiggled like caterpillars.

Smith ignored the insinuation as he took her arm. His warm fingers wrapped the meat of her forearm. "Do you have a bandage?"

"I do. We keep a box for the cook." He rushed away.

Smith chuckled, his hand still a notable presence holding her. "That is not something I wanted to know."

"Good thing we already ate." Claire imagined some poor sap in the back of this sketchy place with bandages covering his bloody hands as he tried to chop carrots.

She was sorry when Smith finished doctoring her and took his hand away. He didn't put his arm around her. No one had held her hand for five years, and she'd insisted she hadn't missed it. She was missing it now with an ache that pressed into her chest.

"You really got beat up in there," Smith said as they walked into the parking lot. The sun had set, and chilly darkness had taken over. "It's going to get more dangerous from here. You going to be okay?"

She stopped and turned around to face him. They stood between two cars in a narrow alley of privacy. "You must have heard how that sounds."

He feigned innocence. "What? If you lose your footing on the boat, you might get more than a minor boo-boo."

"I didn't lose my footing."

He grinned.

"Or maybe I did. I sure don't feel like I'm in control of my footing. And for all your talk of danger, I still want to take the jump." There. Take that chunk of honesty and eat it. Her breathing deepened. She felt as if she'd thrown herself at his mercy.

He'd gone still.

"And no. I do not think I'm going to be okay."

In the dim light, his eyes glittered with blue flame as he stared. He didn't move to close the one-foot gap between them.

"Did you make a no-touching-me rule tonight or something?" Because she was *dying*.

"I did."

"Oh." Her body came alive as her thoughts flip-flopped. "It's driving me crazy."

An arrogant, seductive, sexy smile spread over his face. "Good."

Acid sharpened her tone. "I didn't take you for a mean streak."

His face fell.

She hadn't meant it, but the want in her body was so tight it hurt.

"I'm not pretending this date didn't happen, and I'm not kissing you again unless you mean it. That would drive me crazy."

Oh. With his broad shoulders and hard jaw, he looked so bold, so unbreakable. Her courage failed her. She looked down, not quite ready to tell him just how much she'd meant that last kiss. She'd never been good at pretending. "I'm sorry about that. I was the one being mean in Hawaii."

"I forgive you. And I've learned my lesson. Now get a move on so we don't miss your glowing sea bugs."

She smiled, the strain in her belly unspooling. It was easier to sit by him in the car while not touching, knowing that he was waiting for *her*.

They were the last of the group to arrive at the dock. A curly-haired man who looked to be in his late twenties greeted her with a grin and a can of sparkling coconut soda.

"Hello, Claire. I'm Chris. It's so nice to meet you."

He said it as if he meant it. As if he'd heard of her.

The others had beer, but he hadn't offered her or Smith one. Which meant Smith had told him not to. It was a thoughtful gesture. Smith had been thinking of her, of how he could make her comfortable. She looked over at Smith, the sea and sky behind him. He smiled at her as if he knew what she was thinking. But he couldn't know that she was thinking about how much she wanted to go all in with him. She could only hope love would be better the second time around.

"All aboard," said a tall, thin man with wiry glasses.

"It's not a train," a woman said.

"And we're already all aboard," another said.

"And you are no fun." The tall one started the engine.

Claire held Smith's drink while Smith untied the rope and pushed the boat away from the dock. And then they were off, the wind in her hair, the smell of salt and freedom filling her chest. It was too loud to visit, and Claire was glad. She moved to the bow, zipped up her coat, and sat facing the churning ocean. Her pulse beat in time with the pounding of the waves. She breathed in the thrill of living. She knew Smith wasn't perfect. There would be bumps. But after feeling the sparks, feeling wonder and optimism and companionship, she couldn't walk away, even if she got burned. She laughed. She was going to jump. And she couldn't be more excited.

Neon blue glowed where the waves crested, creating ripples of light.

"Look there!" a female voice yelled.

Claire popped to her feet and joined Smith and the group on the other side. She gasped. Dolphins.

The bioluminescence glowed where the dolphins agitated the water. They glided along with the boat as if making friends. They created the most beautiful bright lines and curves. Claire tried to memorize the shapes so she could recreate the paths with her brush on canvas.

"It's magical."

"Yeah," Smith said at her side.

She looked up at him, the beauty of the moment and abundance of fresh air making her heady. "Just put your arm around me, you big weenie."

He choked on a chuckle and then coughed. He put his arm around her shoulders and tugged her against his ribs. He pressed his face into her hair, his lips finding her ear. "Why are you thinking about my big weenie?"

She was glad the air was cold and the night dark as she tilted her face down and pressed deeper against his side. She was thinking about it now.

He laughed, but at least he didn't let her go. Thank Sung-ho's weird plant for that.

"Licorice?" Chris appeared with a massive tub of the red stuff.

"You can't go boating without it," Smith said.

"Law of the Chris-verse."

Claire allowed herself to take the candy. She allowed herself to relax and fully enjoy the strong arm around her back, the pleasant company, and the majestic ocean.

When they docked the boat, it was too soon.

"Thanks for coming," Chris said.

The entire group said nice things to her. They treated her like she wasn't from an older generation. She liked Smith's friends. They were cool, which made him cooler. She wanted to hang out with them again.

Back in Smith's car and driving home, Claire said, "Thank you for inviting me tonight. That was way more incredible to see from a boat than on shore."

"You're welcome." He made a left turn, looking away from her.

Too soon he was pulling up to her house. She didn't want to go in there and be alone again. She wasn't done with this feeling in her belly. She wasn't done with him.

Smith put the car in park but didn't turn it off. "Thanks for coming with me."

He was saying goodbye. It was the prudent thing to do. Maybe she should try to shift to a lower gear, slow it down, but instead she said, "I finished a painting today. Want to tell me what you think before you go?"

He eyed her suspiciously, but she saw the tiny spark of hope there, too; it sent a shot of dopamine through her system. He turned off the engine and climbed out, leaving his coat behind. Good, the better for viewing that torso.

They glided up her walkway, not touching. Inside, she dropped her jacket and keys on the end table. Heart hammering, she led him down the dark hall. Her bed seemed to wink at her through the opened door. She strode into the garage and turned on the light.

She stepped aside, suddenly embarrassed. What if he thought it wasn't good? What was she doing showing him her painting as if she needed flattery? He stepped up to the canvas, studying.

Her phone buzzed. She peeked at it. A text from Mona. Millie has thrown up twice tonight. I'm starting to freak.

Claire sighed. This was her real life, not this dream evening.

"It's amazing," Smith said, voice low with sincerity.

"That's nice of you to say. Thanks." She didn't look at the painting. Embarrassed and feeling untethered, she retreated into the house. She heard his footsteps and turned. Dim light from an outside halogen filtered through the hall window and sharpened the angles of his face.

"What's wrong?" He was looking at her, caring, listening. It was intoxicating.

"I'm ten years older than you. That's a decade."

"It doesn't matter to me."

"I have three kids. A grandchild. A dead husband. So much baggage. You need a young, fresh, elastic woman."

He looked as if she'd slapped him. "You don't get to tell me what I need."

She flinched at his tone.

"You don't think I've been with younger women? I've tried plenty of this so-called elasticity."

Unpleasantness slashed through her. "All right. I get the idea."

His face transformed as he grinned. "All I'm saying is I'm not a kid either. And I'm not interested in dating one."

Hope collided with fear, sending shock waves through her chest. "But I'm damaged goods." Claire knew it. She needed to make sure Smith knew it. Knew exactly what he was getting into. She'd give him every opportunity to run far away from her mess. She was afraid of being stuck, of powerlessness, of more heartbreak.

But she was more afraid of the regret she'd feel if she didn't give love another chance.

She was done letting Stevie control her from the grave. She blinked with sudden sharp clarity. No more. *No fucking more, Stevie.* She would be free of him. She would soar.

"You're not *damaged*." Smith's voice pulled her back to the romantic reality of her dim hallway. "You're interesting and wise. You're funny and clever and kind. You think about things and people and listen with compassion. You have a big heart, and you're generous with it, taking care of everyone. You're a creative genius."

Was he serious? He couldn't be serious. But he was looking at her with so much earnest interest her legs melted.

His voice softened to a velvet caress. "And you're beautiful. That face is perfection."

She was stunned silent. Any moment she would wake up and find she was alone in her cold bed. Or worse, next to a passed-out Stevie.

"How can you be so many sexy things all at once? It's not fair to all the other women."

His words were like molten pleasure through her body. "I want to believe you." She'd been with Stevie for seventeen years, and he'd never described her as clever or wise or interesting. Sometimes he'd tell her she was beautiful, but more often he'd said she was nuts.

"Why wouldn't you believe me?"

She blanked on a reply. She'd finally come to a place where she thought very well of herself. "Because I'm afraid."

"You're afraid?" His voice was incredulous. "I'm the one who accidentally fell in love with you."

All the air whooshed out of her lungs at the same time fire raced through. *Love.*

The phone in her hand rang. She looked down, away from his scorching gaze. Mona. Her daughter needed her. Smith had just handed her his heart. She couldn't compute.

"Will you wait one second?"

"Yes, Claire. I will wait."

Those words, in that earthy bass. They did something to her insides. Her voice came out raspy when she answered the phone. "Hi, honey, you okay?"

"Why didn't you answer my text?"

"I—"

"What are you doing?"

As if Claire wasn't allowed to be doing anything on a Saturday evening but be on call for Mona. "How's Millie?"

"She's throwing up." Claire held the phone farther from her ear as Mona's worried voice blasted through.

"Does she have a fever or other symptoms?"

"No fever. She's asleep now."

"Is she breathing without trouble?"

"Yes."

Claire had switched into her motherly calming voice. "I think you should let her sleep. And get some rest yourself."

"What if she wakes up and barfs again?"

"Then you'll clean it up. You are there with her. She'll be fine. I'll call to check on you both in the morning."

"Wait. You're hanging up?"

"I have to go." Claire was conscious of Smith's bulk at her side and the bubbling heat in her belly.

"Where?"

"Mona, I love you. Get some rest. Millie will be okay."

"Fine." Mona's voice was sulky. "I guess you have better things to do." She clicked off.

Claire lowered her phone, conscious that her hands were beginning to tremble. "I do have better things to do. She doesn't need to be so shocked."

Smith didn't reply.

She strode to the kitchen and set her phone down before returning to the dark hallway where he still waited, just as she'd asked him to. "I'm sorry."

He leaned his bulk against the wall. "For what?"

"For the phone call."

"Is that all?"

She stepped closer. "Do you want me to be sorry you *accidentally* like me?" She put her fingers on his chest and started sliding them up the heavy planes of muscle. He felt so good she could barely breathe. His hands wrapped her wrist, stopping her. She looked up at ocean eyes.

"I'm far past merely liking you. And just because it was a surprise doesn't mean it isn't welcome."

How unlike her first pregnancy. But now she couldn't imagine a world without Mona or any of her girls. Smith knew about her past. He knew her, and he was still here.

"Stop being so stubborn and tell me," Smith said.

Was she ready to say the L-word? Did she love him? She knew she did, but the words clogged and then dissolved in her throat.

"Tell me you want me to kiss you for real this time."

He'd let her off the hook, no pressure. She looked at his full lips just inches from hers. No more Stevie. No more clipped wings. Tonight she would finally break free and either fly or die. "I didn't think I could love again, but I was wrong. And I love you with a part of my heart that has never been touched before."

Smith slid his hands up her arms and over her back. "That was not what I expected you to say." Warm fingers on her waist, he drew her against his front. "But it was the sexiest thing I've ever heard." Her veins crackled as his body responded to her. His breath shortened. He seemed to glow in the darkness, waiting.

She chewed her lip. "Am I going to have to ask you to kiss me every time?"

"I do enjoy the petition."

"Dammit, Smith."

He was still chuckling when his mouth met hers, and her world filled with color. A riot she might spend the rest of her life trying to paint and never be able to truly capture. Behind her closed lids she saw golds and pinks and lacy blacks. He tasted of licorice and fire and sea breezes. A delicious dream yet she'd never felt so human, so grounded and real and alive. The heaviness in her core anchored her to the man who held her. Her man.

She sucked his bottom lip before opening up to him. He groaned, his tongue eager. She leaned into him, into this. To adventure and emotion and the delightful unknown. She flung her whole soul into love.

Her thoughts took a sultry turn as he drew her against his body, his hands hot on her skin. His thumb traced her ribs as he lowered his lips to her neck.

"It's been so long," she whispered, the words riding out on a heaving breath.

He lifted his head. "Then I'd better make it good."

He wrapped his big hands around her ass and lifted her up. She giggled as pure pleasure shot up and down her core. Pressed against his hard body, she nibbled on his ear as he carried her into her bedroom, where he proved that *good* was a hulking understatement.

Chapter 40
SMITH

Smith woke up in Claire's bed with a ginormous smile on his face. Sunlight streamed through the open window, cascading over the sleeping angel in his arms. Her head lay on his chest, her breath tickling his nipple. He ran his fingers over her silky hair, exploring the smooth planes of her back. She shifted, her hand trailing down his torso and coming to rest just below his belly button. *No, don't stop there!*

Last night. Oh ho ho. Last night. He'd never fallen in love *first* before. Or maybe it was just Claire was that glorious, but he would never ever get over this woman now. He was a goner. Done. Toast. Flayed.

She sighed and stretched like a cat. The sheet slipped lower as she arched, pressing her breasts into his ribs. Good thing they didn't have anywhere to be this morning.

Her eyes fluttered open. She glanced up at him, and an adorable sheepish grin took over her face. "Hi," she whispered.

"Hi."

"You're in my bed."

How could a forty-year-old manage to look so tender? "I like it here."

She smiled with a portion of her bottom lip curled between her teeth. "I really like you here."

Soft, sweet pleasure rolled through him. "Then I think I'll stay a little longer." His hand found her hip, drawing her closer, but she resisted, rolling back.

"A little?" Her tone was teasing, but the look in her eyes told of her true concern.

She still couldn't believe that he truly loved her. A fierce need to protect her flamed through his body. He was determined to heal every wounded bit of her, one kiss at a time, for as long as it took. With one hand around her back, he drew her up. He kissed the curve of her neck. "How long do you want me to stay?"

"Forever." She whispered the word into his ear, but it shot through his system with burning urgency.

He groaned and chuckled at the total blinding bliss. Her body was warm and satiny against his. He just needed to do one thing before he let her know just how happy he was to oblige. "Am I allowed pee breaks?"

She laughed—his favorite sound in the world—then rolled away and peeled off the bed. She walked across the room without a flicker of hesitation or embarrassment. He watched, enthralled, unable to find the words to describe what he felt for her.

"Mom?"

They both jolted at the voice coming from down the hall. Claire ran to her bedroom door, slammed it shut, and snapped the lock. She looked over at Smith, her chest rising and falling in rapid heaves. Smith stifled laughter.

"Mom?" Mona's voice was closer. The door handle jiggled.

Claire jumped, letting out a squeal as she tried to cover herself with her hands.

"Mom? What are you doing in there? Why is this door locked?"

"Um," Claire said. "Just one second, honey."

Smith couldn't hold back his low chuckle. He hadn't moved from his new throne of soft pillows and Claire-scented sheets.

"Is there a *man* in there with you?" Mona's voice was so shocked and insulted that Smith lost it.

He rolled onto his side, laughing so hard he nearly peed.

Claire glared at him, but that only made it worse. She threw his shirt at him. It hit his shaking shoulders.

"Open this door," Mona said, wiggling the door handle again.

"I don't think you want me to do that," Claire said, her own voice now betraying humor.

"Mom!" So offended was the daughter.

Claire laughed. "Give me a second." She stumbled toward her closet as she hissed at Smith, "Get up. Get dressed."

He stood, gratified to see Claire hesitate when her gaze tracked down his body. He stalked toward her bathroom and took a piss. When he emerged, Claire was dressed in joggers and a baggy T-shirt, as if she could hide her glory under sweats. She was frantically trying to make the bed not look so tousled. Not sure what the point was now, but after he washed his hands and tugged on yesterday's clothes, he helped her make it up nice.

Claire walked to the door, took a deep breath, and opened it with a smile. "Good morning, Mona."

Mona's focus darted past her mother and straight to where he stood back and off to the side, as if he could hide by not standing right next to Claire. *"Smith?"* Mona's eyes, dark from exhaustion, bugged out.

He gave her a friendly little wave. He shouldn't enjoy feeling a tad like the conquering hero at the moment, but he was a human male; he couldn't help the swell of hubris.

Claire frowned at her daughter. "I think I should be offended by that tone. You don't think I could get someone like Smith? Well, I did. So you can take your shock and insulting judgments and shove it."

Mona blinked at her mother. Smith grinned at his badass woman.

Claire's face softened. "Now. I'm sorry Millie's been sick. Come to the kitchen, and I'll make you breakfast while you tell me about it. I think we could both use a cup of tea."

Mona gave Smith one last defeated glance before nodding to her mother and retreating back down the hall.

Claire faced Smith.

"Do you want me to go?" he asked.

She nodded, her eyes sorry. "Only if you promise to come back tonight."

He strode over and dropped a featherlight kiss on her lips. She leaned in for more as he pulled away. "Tonight and every night."

Chapter 41
BANKS

Banks held Margo's hand as they walked the Crystal Cove path, watching the sun set over the Pacific Ocean.

"This never gets old," Margo said, inhaling sea breeze and sighing at the impressionist sky.

"It never does." He made sure to look at Margo as he said it.

She returned his gaze with a flattered smile. It had been almost four weeks, and he was feeling good about this. Margo was smart and interesting. She could talk about any subject with confidence.

"Smith is planning on coming over tomorrow afternoon to swim with Tommy. Would you join us?"

Margo stopped walking. The wrinkles between her brows deepened. "Meet your sons?"

He faced her, still holding her hand. "Yes."

"Doesn't that seem a little soon?"

Frustration filtered in. "I thought things were going well."

She sent him a seductive grin, but he was too stressed to enjoy it. "Things are going well, so I don't see why you want to complicate it."

"You think of my children as a complication." He didn't pose it as a question. It was a statement of fact, so obvious now. She didn't have children. She didn't want children. Wasn't even willing to acknowledge Banks had a young child at home. She wasn't interested in being a stepmother to Tommy. Which meant she probably wouldn't want to get rid of Claire, as he'd feared. That was good news. But no. He didn't have a future with someone who refused to even meet his boys. All the grief he'd held at bay these last couple of weeks by the distraction of Margo flooded in. The pain threatened to topple him. He wanted Helen back. Dammit, he wanted her back.

"I don't think of them as a complication," Margo said as he took his hand out of hers. "But I'm not their mother, and I'm here for you. I'm falling for *you*."

His ribs tightened painfully. "They are part of me. It's not an à la carte menu."

"I'm sorry. I didn't realize it was so important to you that I meet them."

He huffed out an incredulous breath. Didn't realize his sons were important? Seriously? How could someone so intelligent be so blind and coldhearted?

"I will stay tomorrow and meet them. It will be great."

Stay. Like she thought she'd still be going home with him tonight. At least he hadn't introduced her to Tommy yet. Banks turned and started back toward where he'd parked his car. Margo hurried to catch up.

"Banks."

"I'm sorry. You're a wonderful woman, but I can see that we aren't a great fit."

"You prioritize your sons above me."

"Yes." No hesitation in that answer. Upsetting that she'd even think otherwise. *Oh, Helen, I need you.*

Margo's face set in battle lines. "The woman should come first."

His temper flared over his hurt. "You haven't earned that right. My Helen was the queen. She was number one in every way, but you expect that when you don't realize she gained her respect through selflessness and kindness and by loving *all* of us."

Margo blinked at him.

He deflated, regretting he'd spoken. It wasn't even worth arguing about. He couldn't change her. He couldn't mold her into Helen. Grief pulsed and throbbed like a bruise that was being poked.

"I'll take you home." They walked the meandering path in silence. The darkness was a welcome blanket, hiding their stony faces. When he pulled up to the front of her house, he didn't get out of the car. "I wish you all the best, Margo."

"Goodbye, Banks. I'm sorry it didn't work out."

He was sorry she wasn't completely different. He was sorry she wasn't Helen. His wife was gone.

Instead of the fancy steak dinner he'd planned with Margo, he got cheap tacos at a drive-through. They tasted better than any porterhouse could have at that moment. He watched people come and go from the fast-food restaurant as he sat in the parking lot eating. Clearly he hadn't been that into Margo because he could already feel her fading from his thoughts. He would miss the sex, but the rest was a relief. He hadn't realized how exhausting she'd been until now.

Banks crumpled up the wrappers, opened his window, and tossed them into the trash. "He shoots. He scores." It had to be a good omen.

He headed toward home but flipped a U-turn at the Emerald Bay gate. He didn't want to return to an empty house. He wanted his sons. He wanted to know that Tommy was home safe in his bed, back in his father's care. Banks drove north to Smith's house, where Tommy was sleeping over so Banks and Margo could have the house to themselves again.

He parked in front of Smith's. It was 9:00 p.m. Tommy would probably be asleep, but Banks still wanted to take him home. He'd make him eggs in a hole for breakfast.

He strode up to the front door and knocked. He heard voices. Smith must be watching TV. Poor guy couldn't go out tonight because he was babysitting.

Smith opened the door. He wore gym shorts. No shirt. His blond hair was an unruly mass. "Dad. What are you doing here?"

"Ended it with Margo." Banks strode into the front room and stopped.

A wide-eyed Claire sat on Smith's couch. She held a blanket to her chest, partially covering the *tiny* camisole she wore.

Betrayal, jealousy, and resentment hit like missiles. He whirled on Smith. "You and Claire." He hated that his voice trembled. He hated that he was reacting with anything less than immediate happiness for them.

Smith didn't answer.

Was that pity on his disgustingly fresh face? His arrogant abs seemed to mock the old man. Banks's teeth ground together. "When were you going to tell me?"

"Soon," Claire said.

"This seems like as good of a way for you to find out as any." Smith's light tone was infuriating.

Banks inhaled, trying to control his temper but feeling the reins slip from his control. He was hurting so bad. He wanted to be happy for them, but he was so broken and angry and sad. Helen had been ripped from him, yet the world kept turning. It wasn't fair. The pain overwhelmed him. "You're fucking my nanny while Tommy is in the other room!"

To his left, Claire jerked as if slapped. Smith's face turned to granite, but his voice came out soft and low. "Tommy is asleep behind a closed door. He is safe and happy. He was thrilled to have Claire join us for dinner. And we're not doing anything but watching a movie." Smith pointed to the paused TV screen.

Smith's calmness really pissed him off, but Banks forced his own voice to level. "You're both half-naked. It's irresponsible."

The damn punk rolled his eyes. "Please, Dad. Do you know how many times I walked in on you and Mom? You two were the worst!"

Claire chewed on her lips. Was she trying not to laugh?

Dammit.

Banks put his palm to his eye as if he could rub away the last five minutes. He was being out matured by his own son and babysitter. The two lovebirds waited patiently for him to take several slow breaths. Inhale. Exhale. Shit. He'd been the one to really screw up tonight. Not them. He turned to the lovely woman on the couch. The woman who was making his sons so very happy. She was never right for him. He had no romantic feelings for her. As his personal sorrow settled, he felt happiness for them trickle in. "So." His voice was blessedly calm now. "You're my son's nanny, and now you're dating my other son?"

Below compassionate eyes, her mouth opened.

"They should make a movie about us," Smith said, sparing her from having to answer, protecting her from Banks. She didn't need protection from him. Banks was a good guy.

"I'm sorry if I hurt you, Banks," Claire said, drawing his attention back to her angelic form. She looked so vulnerable and distressed. She glanced up at Smith, and Banks saw it there, in the shining look they shared.

Love.

Time stopped as the moment crystalized, and his vision expanded. Banks had looked at Helen with the same adoration that glossed his son's gaze. Banks's great love was gone, but he'd had her for twenty-seven years. Glorious years. Inexpressible sadness washed over him in another heavy wave. He wasn't close to being done missing her. He didn't want to give up his grief yet. He'd thought he needed to replace Helen quickly, plug up the bleeding artery, but he'd been wrong. He needed more time.

He was getting better at taking over the parenting roles that Helen had mastered. Turned out it only took effort and practice. He enjoyed doing the laundry now on Sunday evenings. It was calming work, so different from the office. He'd expanded his breakfast repertoire. He was especially good at french toast. He now kept bandages in his briefcase. And for all the tricky bits that still daunted him, he had Smith and Claire to help him. He had all he needed right here. Claire wasn't leaving him because she loved his son—his sons. No. This meant she was staying.

He was a problem solver, prided himself on fixing things at work that others couldn't. But he couldn't snap his fingers and make the hole in his heart disappear or bring Helen back. He'd felt so alone at first.

But he wasn't alone.

He had love and support in spades, gathered in this very house tonight with him. The warm light of the lamps felt like embracing arms, the walls like steel shields against the darkness and danger.

Helen would be nothing but overjoyed that Smith had found such a wonderful woman to love. Banks would be selfish and cruel to be anything less.

He slumped to sit on the edge of the coffee table. "I'm so sorry about my outburst. It wasn't about you. Tonight was hard for me. I came in here sorrowing, and when I saw you together so happy, I was petty. I'm ashamed of myself. The truth is I'm grateful that you found each other. I can see how you are a good fit. I approve wholeheartedly." He meant it.

They both smiled at him with warm eyes.

"I'm so sorry. For all the times I've been a bugger."

Smith put a hand on his shoulder. "Of course, it's okay, Dad."

Claire nodded, voice gentle. "You're in pain. This is a really hard time for you."

His eyes watered, and he blinked rapidly. He thought of Helen again. She seemed particularly crisp in his mind tonight. Beautiful and patient. His chest pinched. It was going to be okay. Two steps forward and one step back. He forced a smile. "Please tell me you're not giving up nannying Tommy."

Claire shook her head, foresty eyes emphatic. "Of course not."

"He loves you. He needs you. Tommy and I can't lose you." Anxiety tightened his voice. What if this love affair didn't work out?

Smith sat down at Claire's side. "Dad, we're not just messing around here. It's serious."

"Serious?"

Claire chuckled. "Serious."

Banks straightened his spine. "I know that Helen would approve, and obviously I think you're both aces."

"Thank you." Claire smiled, and it loosened something deep inside.

A gentle peace—of a kind he hadn't felt since before Helen's first heart attack—wrapped him in warmth. *I'm not ready to say goodbye to you, Helen, but we're going to be okay.*

"So what happened with Margo?" Smith asked.

"Total bust. She didn't want to meet my sons."

"What an idiot." Claire frowned. "Drop her like a moldy grape."

Banks's lips curved up. "Just what I did."

"Well done, Dad."

He looked at his oldest son, his beautiful grown-up boy. He loved him so much. Smith deserved every good thing. And Claire was just that. He held out his hand. "I'm proud of you for turning a staunch spinster from her declared course."

Claire laughed, bright and tinkling. Banks had never heard her make such a happy sound.

Yes, this was good.

Smith took his dad's hand, muscles rippling. "However could you doubt?" His mouth twisted into the picture of amused arrogance.

Banks chuckled. "Where did you get your giant ego?"

"I got it from you."

He pulled a face. "I suppose you did."

"Because you have to have iron balls to propose to a woman before even taking her out on a date. That's second-level cockiness I'll never attain."

"Very funny," Banks said, tone flat. But it was a good sign if Smith was making jokes about it.

Smith grinned.

Banks smiled back as he stood. "Well, I guess that's my cue to bow out."

"I'll carry Tommy to the car," Smith said.

"Cool it, muscles. I can handle it."

Smith leaned back, putting his arm around Claire and drawing her against his side. "Close the door on your way out."

"Unbelievable," Banks muttered as he walked away. But there was a new lightness in his step.

He drove home slowly, listening to his son's soft breathing from the back seat and letting his newly found peace fill every tired cell of his body. He carried Tommy to bed—the boy was heavy as a sack of rocks—and kissed his smooth brow.

He spent a long time gazing at the picture of Helen and Tommy on the wall. "Your sons are doing well," Banks whispered. His eyes watered, and his heart was a giant ache. "We haven't stopped loving you. Never will." He dragged up the stairs and into his big lonely bed. "Good night, my love. I'll meet you in my dreams tonight."

Epilogue
SMITH

Smith held his newborn son while his wife napped in the hospital bed at his side. She was pale with exhaustion and swathed in weirdly patterned labor-and-delivery sheets, but she'd never looked more beautiful. What she'd done this morning was a wonder. He'd been floored by her bravery and strength. He'd watched her hours of suffering in complete helplessness.

He leaned down and kissed the tiny head, inhaling the intoxicating scent of fresh human. *His* son. The expanding of his heart was a tangible thing, painful and euphoric at the same time. Another soul he wouldn't hesitate to give his life for. He would work the rest of his days trying to repay Claire for all she had given him, and he wouldn't come close.

He looked down at his baby lying on his chest, skin to skin, like he'd read about in the parenting books. Babies needed to be touched and held.

Everyone needed that.

He thought of Claire, how she'd grown in confidence and radiance over their two years together. She laughed all the time now and had started making lists of things she wanted to do and places she wanted to go with Smith—her very willing partner in crime. He liked to think her bubbling happiness was from all his skin-to-skin time with her. He took that job seriously. He chuckled at his ridiculous thoughts. She was the one who'd brought color to his world and a dance to his step. He adored her with everything he was. He reached out and took her limp hand.

"Thank you," he whispered.

Not a flicker of life from the bed except the sound of low breathing.

His son blinked enormous unfocused blue eyes.

Smith's hand was larger than the baby's velvety back. He kissed the small head again. "I think you wore your old lady out."

"I might be old, but I'm not deaf."

Smith turned a smile of pure delight at Claire. Her hazel eyes went dewy with love as she looked over her boys.

A soft knock sounded at the door.

Claire pulled the sheet up over her swollen breasts as Smith said, "Come in."

Dad, Tommy, Mona, and Millie burst into the room.

"He's here!" Smith said, his voice oozing with pride.

Mona went to her mother first, kissing Claire's salty brow. "Indi and Edith are on their way."

Tommy and Dad made beelines for the baby.

"You still can't put on a shirt." Dad's voice was teasing, but his eyes misted as he looked over Smith and the infant snuggled together.

"You want to hold your grandson?"

Dad swallowed and nodded. A tear trickled down. Smith wrapped the tiny human in a blanket and passed him to his grandfather. He put his shirt on. Tommy started climbing onto Claire's bed. He was turning eight next week—not a small child anymore.

Smith reached out to pull his brother off. "No, Tom, you can't—"

"It's all right," Claire said, sliding over to the edge of the cot and guiding Tommy up to lie at her side. "Just be gentle." She still watched Tommy three afternoons a week. Dad came home early from the office the other two days. Smith wasn't sure how it was going to pan out with a new baby, but Claire wasn't willing to give up her Tommy time. She insisted that she always found a way to make it work for the people she loved. Smith couldn't argue that.

Dad had continued to work through his growing stack of women's phone numbers. Tommy was getting used to Friday-night sleepovers at Smith and Claire's house. Tommy and Smith still hadn't met a single one of Dad's dates. Dad was looking for someone in the same league as Mom and Claire. It might take a while. Although Dad insisted that his latest find was the most promising yet. He'd admitted that he was considering bringing the new girlfriend to Hawaii this year. Smith wasn't sure that was good karma.

Smith had sold both his and Claire's homes, and together they'd bought something fresh and new in Crystal Cove a year and a half ago when they'd married. They'd eagerly started trying for a baby on their wedding night. Claire had been worried about her advanced maternal age, but the doctors had assured her she was healthy and her body knew what to do.

Yes, it did. Smith kissed his son. Made a perfect baby was what Claire's body had accomplished.

An unfamiliar nurse walked into their hospital room and blinked at the large group. "Well, I found the party."

"It's a birthday party," Tommy said.

She smiled at him. "Congratulations on a new baby brother."

"I'm not the brother," Tommy said. "I'm the uncle." He patted Claire's arm. "This is my big sister."

Dad coughed, and the confused nurse looked at him holding the baby. "You're the husband," she said.

"I'm the father." Dad paused. "Of the father."

"I'm the father," Smith said, his lips curving up.

The nurse's jaw dropped.

Claire grinned.

"And if I'm baby's big sister," Mona said. "What does that make Millie? His niece?"

The nurse's brow furrowed. "You'd think after all these years I would have learned to never guess." She backpedaled toward the exit. "If you're all good here, I'll check in later." The door had barely closed behind her when the room burst into laughter.

Claire hissed and clutched her abdomen. "Nope. Nothing funny for me for a while."

Smith was at her side, a tender hand on her hip. "Are you okay?"

She tugged down on his forearm, drawing him in for a soft kiss. "I have never been better."

ACKNOWLEDGMENTS

I'm grateful to my delightful editor, Maria Gomez, and her entire team at Montlake for championing me and putting their expertise into making this book the best it could be. Thank you to my brilliant agent, Shannon Snow, for believing in me and working hard to bring my story into the light. And to everyone at Creative Media Agency. Thank you to Angela James for fantastic editing. Thanks to my critique partners and supportive friends and family. Thanks to Katherine Decker for reading so many early drafts and saying nice things about them. Thanks to Summer Andrus for being my writing buddy through endless editing hours. Thanks to Doug, Luke, Rachel, Henry, and Hazel for being proud of me and cheering me on. Thanks to God for giving me stories, and thanks to you for reading them.

ABOUT THE AUTHOR

Mary Beesley has received a Crowned Heart of Excellence Review and a five-star Readers' Favorite Award. She's been a daydreamer since childhood, but after having profound difficulty learning to read, she couldn't be more surprised to have fallen in love with books. She writes stories that find hope in hardship and shine light on the goodness and strength of the human spirit. Mary loves traveling, cooking, painting, hiking, and pretending to play the piano. If she's not in her writing chair, you'll probably find her on her yoga mat or enjoying her local Southern California beach with her husband and four children.

Join Mary's *Tuesday Tea* newsletter on her website, www.marybeesley.com, or connect with her on Instagram @marybeesleywriter or Twitter @BeesleyAuthor.